PRAISE FOR JEN LANCASTER

"Scathingly witty."

—*The Boston Herald*

"Witty and hilarious . . . Jen Lancaster is like that friend who always says what you're thinking—just 1,000 times funnier."

—*People*

"No matter what she's writing, it's scathingly witty and lots of fun."

—*Publishers Weekly*

"Hilarious."

—*InStyle*

"Witty, bitingly funny, and even thought-provoking."

—*The Book Chick*

"Jen Lancaster is like a modern-day, bawdy Erma Bombeck."

—Lisa Lampanelli, *New York Post*

HOUSE MOMS

OTHER TITLES BY JEN LANCASTER

Nonfiction

Bitter Is the New Black
Bright Lights, Big Ass
Such a Pretty Fat
Pretty in Plaid
My Fair Lazy
Jeneration X
The Tao of Martha
I Regret Nothing
Stories I'd Tell in Bars
Welcome to the United States of Anxiety

Fiction

If You Were Here
Here I Go Again
Twisted Sisters
The Best of Enemies
By the Numbers
The Gatekeepers

HOUSE MOMS

A NOVEL

Jen Lancaster

Little
a

Text copyright © 2023 by Jen Lancaster

Published by Little A, New York

www.apub.com

Amazon, the Amazon logo, and Little A are trademarks of Amazon.com, Inc., or its affiliates.

ISBN-13: 9781662512001 (hardcover)
ISBN-13: 9781662512018 (paperback)
ISBN-13: 9781662510168 (digital)

Cover design by Tree Abraham
Cover illustration by Kaja Merle

Printed in the United States of America
First edition

For Liz, because she knows how to turn dreams into reality

house•moth•er / *noun*

1: a woman who serves as a hostess, chaperone, property manager, caretaker, counselor, and often a housekeeper in a ladies' boarding school or collegiate Greek fraternal organization's residence (see: *Garrett, Edna*)

2: a female dressing-room attendant, tasked with providing meals, toiletries, and costume repair for exotic dancers in a strip club

Prologue

"They hate me."

"They don't hate you; they just don't know you," my husband said, rubbing his soft palm against my bare shoulder blades in an attempt to soothe me. "They will love you just as much as I do; I promise."

But I didn't need Chip's comforting hand; what I needed was a wrap, a layer of protection, something to cover me up so I wasn't so exposed. The pastel strapless dress was a mistake. I should have gone with a more conservative gown, something black, loose, and plain, with a higher neckline. Matronly. Chip had assured me I was a knock-out in this pink taffeta Ralph Lauren confection, with its princess A-line silhouette. Yet the moment we walked into that banquet hall at the Hilton Chicago O'Hare, my greatest fear was confirmed. Those in the crowd looked more like they were attending a funeral than a fundraiser.

Awaiting our cue, I peeked through the porthole window that led to the service bar. It was my first time speaking at an event as Mrs. Charles "Chip" Barclay III. I felt passionate about the cause—this specific type of breast cancer had claimed my beloved mother only weeks after Chip and I had returned from our abbreviated honeymoon. In fact, I had begged the director to allow me to say a few words. (Only upon my father-in-law's intervention did the director grant that request.)

Chip placed a brief kiss on my forehead so he wouldn't smear my lipstick and guided me to the dais. The applause when he greeted the crowd was deafening . . . and then he introduced me.

Their response was tepid at best.

They hated me because I had stolen their Prince Charming. I was just some usurper from the East, who'd swooped in and snagged the city's Golden Boy. He had been on every social-climbing mother's radar for almost thirty-three years. Not to mention the universal love for Bitsy, his hometown ex-flame and my ex-friend, a woman whose connections far surpassed her beauty or repartee. This crowd would have been willing to let him go if he'd ended up with one of their own.

It was the advent of the dot-com era. Brand-new to the City of Broad Shoulders, I was only twenty-three years old, with a shiny new wedding ring and an even shinier new husband. Chicago, I quickly learned, was an insular town, a sorority that I was not invited to pledge, with a population as icy as its winters.

Behind the podium, I stumbled over every other word of my speech and even briefly, unforgivably, cried when I talked about my beautiful mother. I was mortified.

Sometimes my hometown is called the City of Brotherly *Shove*, but that's an unfair characterization. If a Philadelphian doesn't care for you, they have no qualms about telling you why, no matter what their social status. Their contempt is right out in the open, not festering behind that "Midwest nice" that I found so disconcerting in Chicago.

The truth was, Chip had pursued *me* to a point that could be called "problematic" years later when we all figured out exactly what stalking meant. He was the one who'd wait for me outside the Canaday Library with flowers and notes, but that didn't matter to Chicago society. He'd never pursued Bitsy, my roommate, like that when they'd dated. No one ever cared to learn that it was *she* who dumped *him*, and not vice versa. And she was the one who eventually gave me her blessing to go out with him . . . until she realized we were serious, and she changed her tune. Instead, it was more fun for them to smile to my face and call me a gold digger behind my back.

As though *I* needed to dig for gold!

I brought more assets to the marriage than he did. I was the only child of the Foldable Map King of Philadelphia. My father's company made those large paper atlases—you know, the detailed ones that would origami themselves into the size of a dinner napkin. The ones that were in every glove compartment of every vehicle before the advent of the smartphone. I had my own wealth, my own pedigree; I was legitimately an heiress. But who cared for the truth when the opportunist narrative was far more scandalous?

At my Chicago charity circuit debut, I gripped the podium and channeled all the confidence I could muster, buoyed by the adoration of my new husband, who I still thought was a good man.

Even now I recall how my emerald-cut engagement ring caught the spotlight that night, a spray of prisms illuminating the walls of that frigid banquet room. I couldn't have shown off more if I'd tried. I turned my ring around as soon as I noticed, but it was too little too late.

I tried so desperately to fit in when I first moved here, fresh from a successful academic career at Bryn Mawr, where I was terribly popular among the Mawrters. There, I had thrown myself into every activity and tradition in what was a nurturing and supportive environment, a true sisterhood. I also had scads of friends at Haverford, our brother college, plus pals from the art history classes I'd taken at Swarthmore and Penn. So accustomed to being part of a vibrant social network, I found it very difficult to be suddenly friendless and shunned by Chicago's elite.

I'd grown up learning social graces from one of the Main Line's great hostesses—my mother. Through years of cotillion classes, I'd become an etiquette expert. I can speak with anyone about anything, drawing out their interests and making them feel like the most fascinating and important person in the room. I can fox-trot with the minister at a wedding reception as easily as I can charm a team of weary

3

hospice nurses. I can set a formal table for a twelve-course meal with nary an oyster fork out of place. I always know exactly whom to tip, when, and how much—for example, never hand cash to an employee at the Colony Club in New York; it's simply not done and insults all persons involved. I am a social butterfly everywhere else in the world, save for Chicago. In Chicago, I was considered a social pariah, treated like a person who'd tried to put ketchup on a hot dog. They mistook my poise and patrician nature for dispassion. My luncheon invitations were frequently rejected and my parties sparsely attended.

Bitsy, said former roommate and now ex–best friend, made sure of that.

It hurt.

The harder I tried, the less amenable everyone was. I was a striver. Exclusions came hard and fast. Even volunteering—something I loved to do—became difficult. On the rare chance a nonprofit organizer found a spot for me, it was inevitably handing out name tags (the lowliest job) at third-tier events, shivering at a drafty card table outside the main doors, all because I'd had the nerve to marry Chicago's favorite scion, the Windy City's version of JFK Jr.

Also, no one from Chicago calls it "the Windy City" or "Chi-town," a fact that Helga Rathbone informed me of in front of an entire benefit table of other women. I wished then that the Midwest were in an earthquake zone so the ground would open and swallow me whole.

Eventually, I stopped trying. I couldn't bear feeling so drained and disheartened. Mostly, I withdrew. Then one day, I snapped.

Hayden, my only child, was going through a phase of sporadic sleep, like a heavy metal musician on a coke bender, and I hadn't yet given in and hired a nanny. Until then, I hadn't needed to, because she was the embodiment of sunshine and light. I was perpetually exhausted and doubting my worth as both a mother and wife. On top of that, I was grieving. I'd been traveling back and forth to Pennsylvania to settle my father's estate after his untimely passing. I was heartsick, and that was when I discovered explicit texts between Chip and his "secretary."

Two things to note here: one, we still called them secretaries back then, and two, texting was far more difficult on a flip phone. For her to discuss the "intercourse" she hoped to have with my husband entailed significant effort via alphanumeric keyboard.

Of course, Chip denied everything. I was too tired and too overwhelmed to take any real declarative action, instead tabling the problem until I regained some equilibrium, a task made more complex by how diligently he parented our child.

I should have seen it coming. Bitsy had told me he'd dumped his previous girlfriend to pursue her. How did I not think he'd do it again? My *grand-mère* always warned me, *"Un chien qui donne un os prendra un os."* (A dog that gives a bone will take a bone.)

I was hanging on by a spider's thread at that time, so when Poppy Pierce told me my floral arrangements were too small for the tables at a planning committee meeting for a community garden at Cabrini-Green, I . . . I am not proud of what flew out of my mouth next.

I smiled sweetly and then said, "Poppy, darling, why don't you bend over? I'm sure I could find a place where my small arrangements would fit perfectly."

I regretted these words immediately. *That's it,* I thought. *I may as well pack it all up because Chicago is clearly never going to be my kind of town.* I was shocked when everyone laughed. Years of ice had finally broken.

It was odd.

The more distant I was, the colder I acted, and the fewer cares I had to give, the more the same women who'd summarily rejected me sought me out, especially after Bitsy moved to San Francisco with an even wealthier suitor. The women started peppering me with questions, like *"Oh, CeCe, which caterer should I use?"* and *"Please, CeCe, can you recommend a good decorator?"*

Everyone ate up my saucy new attitude, one that I'm sure had my mother rolling in her grave at Laurel Hill Cemetery.

Suddenly, I found myself at the top of every invitation list, the member everyone wanted in her club. Chip always said that women seek out whatever it is they can't have, a trait I'd come to find he shared. The more inaccessible I made myself, the more calculating and self-congratulating I came across. The more casual I was in my cutting cruelty, the more my star rose.

There was something profoundly wrong about the whole enterprise, but I saw few other choices.

I believe this is what supervillains call "an origin story."

Chapter One

Cecelia "CeCe" Elspeth Bondurant Barclay

Two months before sorority rush

"You'll never know how much of a difference you can make until you try," I tell the crowd. I pause.

To milk the gravitas of the moment, I lift the heavy crystal tumbler and take a quick sip of Johnnie Blue scotch and soda. The smoky, peaty spirits are a much-needed balm for my nerves. I'm not usually one for brown liquor, but Chip left his cocktail when he stepped away to take a call, and this is all so overwhelming that I need something stronger than my usual Aperol spritz. I can feel the alcohol coursing through my system, smoothing over all the jagged edges and laying everything to rights. Dr. J. Walker, MD, to the rescue.

I survey the Aon Grand Ballroom, appreciating how far I've come from that disastrous benefit at the Hilton by the airport. This night is positively glorious in comparison! The two-story glass walls overlook Lake Michigan, still full of boats merrily bobbing outside on this balmy June evening. On either side of Navy Pier, the dinner cruise ships line the docks, waiting to take out scores of tourists who don't know any better. Twinkling lights run up each rib of the high domed ceiling, casting a soft glow down on everyone, including Helga Rathbone. She looks better for the ambience, largely because we can't see her enormous new veneers in the dim lighting. One day at the club, after she'd consumed too many G&Ts, she demanded I be honest and tell her if she'd gone a tad too big with her cosmetic dentistry.

I told her the truth.

"Both Rose and Jack could have floated to safety on one of them at the end of *Titanic*." Not long after that, she found a new doubles partner. I'm sure I should have felt bad, but she just doesn't hustle to the net like a competitor, so I was delighted to be rid of her.

I've outdone myself again with this spectacular event. The atmosphere I created is *everything*. I had my designers suspend enormous floral sprays from the ceiling that look like fluffy clouds. They evoke the feeling of being both outdoors and indoors, enveloping partygoers in a heady perfume of jasmine and plumeria. This is simply perfection, or it *would* be perfection if Stefanie Armor would stop her infernal sneezing. If you're triggered by flower pollen, take a Benadryl or avoid my galas. My floral work is legendary, and I will not cede that crown to compensate for any rhinitis.

I bask in the admiration of the surrounding glitterati before I continue my welcome speech. So many beautiful people gathered for such a beautiful cause (save for Helga and her mouthful of subway tiles). One could go blind from the jewels glinting off all the ladies.

Every monied and important family from the city is at my annual event, from the Blums to the Zells. There's a contingent of Daleys, of course, as they're the closest we have to Chicago royalty. We have an entire table of Walgreens, and another of Pritzkers, although the governor couldn't make it this evening—a shame because I added an extra wing onto the dessert bar, just for him. I'm told he sends his kind regards, which won't matter if his regards don't include a check with an adequate number of zeroes.

Tickets for this benefit have been the hottest, well, *tickets* in all of Chicagoland, with whole tables selling for a minimum donation of a quarter million dollars. Even the terrible individual seats by the powder rooms start at fifteen thousand. A bargain, really.

Granted, a portion of the proceeds will funnel back in to pay for the event, but every fundraiser knows that is a necessary evil. Chip always says we must spend money to make money. I mean, he did insist we buy *actual* glacier ice for the ice sculptures, as it's all the rage, so I had to arrange for shipment in specially refrigerated vessels. Plus, it's not like I could use anything lesser than Royal Ossetra caviar for the blinis; I'd never hear the end of it! I'm told the Mayers were dinged for membership at Cherokee Hill for a similar offense at their last gala. How mortifying!

I pat myself on the back for my attention to the décor. The platinum-level tables required extra-special centerpieces, something that would truly pop. Their form was inspired by the Star of Africa diamond, each towering arrangement almost fifteen feet atop its pedestal to allow for face-to-face conversation. I had the flowers flown in privately this morning from Endura Roses, the UK florist who designed them. Nestled between the heart-shaped scarlet roses shimmering with diamond dust are the towering cherry-blossom branches and the fragrant Tahitian double-blossom gardenias. Some of the petals have been preserved in 24-karat gold, so it feels less like a floral display and more like an art installation. At fifty thousand dollars each, I practically stole them!

How was I *supposed* to have the tables decorated tonight? Slap together a bunch of wilted daisies in a jelly jar like Genevieve Kingman when she tried to portray herself as a free spirit at her ill-conceived event? People should be *inspired* to open their wallets, and a fistful of weeds does quite the opposite, I'm sure.

We're on track to surpass what we collected at the New York gala last week, where Matthew Broderick and Nathan Lane reunited for a

Producers performance. Oh, that Ferris Bueller is a charmer—people were throwing their checkbooks at him (and in Sascha Gersh's case, her undergarments)! That wasn't even the biggest surprise, which I delivered, in the form of a sing-along from Sir Paul *and* Ringo, accompanied on the piano by Billy Joel. "Come Together," thanks to me.

Everyone walked away happy, and slightly less wealthy. Rumor has it that Meghan and Harry RSVP'd yes to our upcoming Montecito event. Fingers crossed!

While it's terribly gauche to discuss money, there's an exception when it comes to charity, and tonight should rake in scads and scads for my foundation. I'm curious how Chip plans to grow tonight's receipts. He took my initial funding donation from my inheritance and turned it into $50 million through tech investing.

I was reticent about his strategy—my father invested in staid, stodgy bonds with predictable returns. I wondered if we shouldn't just hold on to some of that cash for liquidity purposes, or perhaps convert it to something more secure like gold. I was also hesitant because of, well, the "unpleasantness" caused by his roving eye (read: hands). Yet I pushed past my reluctance because of the optics—how would it look if I *hadn't* let him invest? I decided to focus on the good we've done instead of the financial details. I'm eager to see how much more we'll be able to do for the local homeless community after tonight.

I'm positively abuzz over the plans to expand our programming with Alexis, the foundation's director. When I first met her, she barely seemed old enough to run a social media account, let alone a foundation as grand as mine. But Chip swayed the board to hire her, so she must have had more credentials than what I'd seen. Thus far, everyone confirms she's been a superstar, and I do appreciate her enthusiasm.

I swallow my sip of scotch and smooth down the front of my seafoam-green Armani Privé gown. The bodice is a trim bateau-neck column with a plunging back (never a plunging neckline!), with a three-dimensional chiffon floral appliqué. The train is a soft, voluminous, billowing dream, and lengthy enough to force people aside when I pass. Poppy Pierce trod on the edge of it with one of her hooves, which is so ironic considering I *already* petitioned for her removal from the board of directors.

I've paired this breathtaking frock with a Cartier Panthère Flâneuse necklace, comprising round emerald and rubellite spheres nestled around the Maison's iconic diamond-studded panther who sits at the hollow of my throat.

Instead of my trademark chignon, I had my pearl-blond bobbed hair styled in gentle, old-Hollywood finger waves to frame my face. We kept my makeup simple, but classic, focusing on a modified boy brow and a red lip. Anyone devoted to all the contouring nonsense should simply find themselves a better plastic surgeon. I'm a fan of Dr. Conseco, as his motto is that one's face should *belie* one's true emotions, not *convey* them.

I lean toward the microphone, poised to funnel my audience into the kill zone. "Cherished friends and esteemed guests, while I'm loath to be *that person*, I must first recognize my beloved, Chip Barclay. Of course, you all know him; he's the one who's been padding your portfolios so proficiently!"

The crowd hoots and cheers. The Barclay Group, the venerable asset management firm Chip's great-grandfather founded, had consistently returned 10 percent per year, practically since the beginning of time. Since Chip's father passed last year, Chip's returns have been higher than almost any other competitor. With his recent venture into cryptocurrency, the sky's been the limit. Chip says investing in any blockchain protocol is like having a license to mint money. I don't really understand the whole thing, but Chip tells me it's bleeding edge. And Elon promises it's what's next in the world of finance. Call me old-fashioned, but like my father, I prefer that which is FDIC-insured; everything else feels like legalized gambling.

"CeCe, you're the best!" someone yells from the audience. I blow a kiss in response. The lights up here are so bright, I can't quite make out who said it, but it doesn't matter. The crowd simply cheers louder.

I thought about starting a foundation for years, but I wasn't sure how to proceed. I told Chip, "What do I know about running a foundation? I've never even held a real job!" He pointed to the charitable work that's defined my adult life, promising he'd guide me the whole way. And now I finally have some help, by way of Alexis. Still, I'm glad she's not a blonde. Chip has . . . proclivities. Fortunately, he keeps his dalliances quiet, and they never last long, so it's easy to look away. Our life together is far too complicated to unravel.

I started the foundation when I realized I needed something to occupy my time and talent after Hayden left for college. I was at loose ends after renovating the kitchens in our Aspen and West Palm homes. Chip said I needed a new project, and he was, pun intended, *on the money*. A few short years later, the foundation has become my life, my purpose, my North Star. Plus, it feels so satisfying to give to those who haven't been as fortunate as us.

I tell the audience, "Tonight, keep in mind what Chip has done for you. I humbly request that you donate *exactly* what you feel we deserve!" The cacophony of clapping and whistling is practically deafening, as it's been a banner year. Chip recently appeared on that stock market show, where the sweaty little man with the shirtsleeves and sound effects practically sat in his lap. I found it unseemly, but Chip watches the segment on repeat.

I take another sip and sigh with content. I feel totally at peace, doing exactly what I was born to do.

"Chip, we'd love for you to come up and say a word." I clap, and the audience follows suit, the noise ratcheting up until I finally signal everyone to stop when he doesn't appear after a few moments.

I peer at the head table again. The seat next to mine is empty.

"Chip, darling, are you hiding?"

Honestly, isn't it just like him to slip away from the spotlight when I actually need him? I wonder if that phone call wasn't just a ruse, especially as it looks like he dragged poor Alexis along to keep up the façade that he's so very busy working.

I don't *do* awkward, so I laugh and tell the crowd, "Oh, you all know Chip! I'm sure he's chasing a hot tip. But time is money, and I can't collect yours until we get this party started. Raise your glasses, and join me in a toast." Everyone laughs again as they lift their champagne coupes to the sky. My goodness, I'm fantastic in front of a crowd!

I raise my tumbler and say, "To you, and to the Barclay family's foundation, better known as Homeless, Not Homely. Salut!"

The clink of crystal reverberates through the room for a solid thirty seconds, and I bask in the sights and sounds and smells and . . .

Wait.

Who are all those plain people in windbreakers rushing the doors?

Chapter Two

Gina Marie Ferragamo

One month before sorority rush

Gina's Daily Do-List

- *Bring trainee up to speed*
- *Inquire about availability of gluten-free dinner rolls*
- *Finish reading Putting the "I" in Winning*
- *Less coffee/more water*

"Do you know what's more satisfying than crossing off a completed task?" I ask, trailing off so my trainee fills in the blank.

Full disclosure: I live for lists, any kind of list. There's something so motivating about putting pen to paper. Lists are a call to action. Did you know that if you write down your goals, you're almost 35 percent more likely to accomplish them? I read that recently in *Goal Tending for Go-Getters*, a new business book my favorite librarian recommended. That's why the surest way to my heart is through a bullet journal.

Becky, the trainee, stops in her tracks. "I wasn't told there'd be a quiz."

Damn, Gina, I say to myself. *Are you going about her training wrong?* I was feeling so confident about my ability to develop this new assistant. I wrote up a ten-step plan and put together a three-ring binder that I'm calling *The Housemother's Bible* so she'll always have a point of reference. It's lists upon lists upon lists—a thing of beauty.

Putting in this effort isn't part of my job description, but I thought the documentation would make it easier for Becky to slide into her role. I must be training her wrong if she doesn't immediately grasp that nothing is more important than completing tasks and crossing them off. I saw a quote that says, "There are no bad employees, only bad managers." What if that means me?

I probably need to encourage Becky more. Okay, new plan. First, I'm going to square my shoulders to project more confidence. The book *Management for Morons* says that if I'm a better leader, she'll be a better follower. I will simply try harder—and maintain a positive attitude, of course!

I explain, "No, no, see, it's a trick question because the answer is *nothing.* Get it? Because we've been talking about checklists exclusively since you got here? Like, nothing feels better than checking an item off our list?"

I slash my Sharpie through the task we just completed, which gives me a tiny rush. My love of lists is a running joke around here. The Omega girls haze me mercilessly, but deep down, they appreciate my goal-setting and organizational skills. For Christmas, they gave me a stack of ruled journals and a top-of-the-line Cricut machine, and now there's nothing without a label here. (I labeled the cabinet where I keep the label maker, to their squeals of delight.)

Becky gives me a blank look.

"That was a joke," I add, even though the best jokes require no explanation.

Becky stands in the middle of the girls' lounge, completely motion-less, as though frozen in carbonite, just a person-sized statue. Her extra-large, unblinking eyes stare right through me, less like a deer in the headlights and more like . . . a department store mannequin.

From her spot on the couch, Desiree looks up from her phone and whispers, "I think you may have to reboot her, Gina."

I try to engage Becky again, gesturing to some of my charges hanging out in the lounge area. "Obviously that was a *bad* joke. Des over here always tells me I'm too sincere to be funny."

Desiree waves. Becky does not wave back. What if she *is* broken? Then what? From the corner, Ariel chimes in with her opinion. "Gina, you're good at a lot of things, but comedic timing isn't on that list." During Mass a few years ago, the priest said that when we encounter difficult people, we need to serve them until we love them. I feel like I serve Ariel *a lot*. I clear my throat and try to gather my wits.

"Being goal-oriented and being organized are the best ways to be successful on the job. We have a lot of tiny details to manage," I say.

No response. Becky just stares. Perhaps I'll be serving Becky frequently too.

"You sure she doesn't have an on/off switch?" Des asks.

Becky finally blinks. Then she blinks some more—maybe she needed a moment to collect her thoughts. After a pregnant pause, Becky asks, "Should I write down that you're not funny?"

Des stifles a snort, and I give her a pleading look—I can't afford to lose this new hire. Des throws up her hands and goes back to texting.

"Um . . . moving on. Now, our job is to take care of the facility and the women," I say. I outline her assistant housemother duties and point out where I've neatly categorized each of them in the tabbed, color-coded *Housemother's Bible*, broken out first by task type, then by the times the tasks must be completed, each with a box to check when finished. The thrill I get when I mark off those boxes—it's better than sex (at least that I can recall—clearly, it's been a while)!

My girls laugh at how old-school I am with my love of paper files and clipboards. Ariel tells me I'm an anachronism, saying, "Gina, I promise you there's an app for that," but there's something so comforting about a page full of checkmarks, clear evidence of a job well done. Plus, I'm on TikTok; I'm not a dinosaur, or per Ariel, a "Ginasaur." I mostly follow cat accounts, so I worry that she's right sometimes. Also, I did have to google "anachronism." Ariel's been throwing around the big words since she applied to law school. I won't miss serving her when she leaves this fall.

Becky follows a few steps behind me. The management book *Be the Ball* says that the best way for a manager to solicit desired behavior is to model it, so I pick up the pace, hoping to demonstrate a sense of urgency.

We cross through the lounge. The girls are sprawled on the ancient couches that line the periphery of the pink cinder-block basement walls. A giant black Omega symbol is painted in the center, keeping watch over the decades of young women who have cycled through this place. The stories it could tell! A couple of cardio machines sit neglected in a corner, covered in discarded athleisure jackets. The girls keep reminding me that StairMasters are *so* 2006, but I splurged on the expensive bike, so I won't have a budget to replace anything else for a while. Also, I keep reminding *them* that their actual mom doesn't work here and to pick up after themselves. (It's a losing battle.)

Sofia, a stunning Colombian with glossy black hair, pedals furiously on the new Peloton, while Ariel paces in her cycle shoes. Her cleats click impatiently as she shoots Sofia murderous looks.

"Slow down! You're going to lose all the Kardashian in your ass," Ariel tells Sofia. "You're burning way too much fat."

"You wish," Sofia responds, flashing her the bird, then pedaling harder.

I tell Becky, "In a situation like this, I intervene before it gets snippy." I point at the clipboard hanging by the bike and I say, "Ariel, Sofia reserved her time for Cody's '80s ride and you didn't. If you don't respect the clipboard, the clipboard won't respect you. Use the StairMaster if you need some cardio."

Ariel grumbles. "I'd live in a fifth-floor walk-up if I wanted to climb stairs." Still, she dutifully removes the Lululemon hoodie draped over the unpopular machine's screen and climbs on, swiping at nonexistent dust (I run a tight ship). Ariel shoots a look of disgust in Sofia's direction each time she stomps, still in her cycle shoes, but Sofia's in the zone and doesn't react.

Des is now fully reclined on the old plaid couch closest to the television. She's fighting for the remote with Carina, who's sprawled on the floral love seat. Des insists on watching *Love Island* for the hundredth time while Carina demands they switch to CNN. Carina has a thing for Anderson Cooper. Who doesn't? AC is smart and handsome and compassionate. He seems like a wonderful father. I bet his manners are perfect and he always knows which fork to use, so *of course* he's gay. For a while, I thought maybe I'd meet a better class of guy on CatholicConnect.com, but when my most recent date said, "Do I have to feed you, or can we just bang it out in my car?" I deleted my profile. I sense a cat adoption in my future.

Des holds up her French-manicured hand, and we fist-bump as I pass. I try not to play favorites, but Des is totally my favorite.

"Gina, back me up," Des pleads. "It's my turn to pick the show."

"But it's infrastructure week!" Carina counters.

"Desiree, Carina, you know I'm Switzerland here. Work it out," I say.

"I would like to formally rescind my fist bump."

I clasp my fist to my chest. "Too late."

Des exhales loudly, then challenges Carina to a game of rock, paper, scissors for control of the remote. "See? They've got this," I tell Becky. "If we do too much for them, they'll rely on us to solve their problems instead of figuring it out for themselves." I learned that in *Your Mom Doesn't Work Here.*

"I wasn't told there'd be problem-solving."

Dealing with Deadweight says to identify your problem employee's core strengths and then play to those. Unfortunately, the books offer no guidance on what to do if your problem employee has no clear strengths. I'm one to look on the bright side, but I'm struggling to see the benefit of having Becky on board. She wasn't my last choice; she was my *only* choice.

"Well, it's more like we help them find a way to compromise. We don't just do it for them," I say.

Becky nods and scrawls *Don't do it for them* in the margin of her *Housemother's Bible*. I try hard not to point out the "notes" tab I've added for this exact purpose. I keep quiet, but I can feel my right eye twitch.

I swoop down to retrieve an empty limoncello-flavored LaCroix can from the floor next to the recycling bin. The trace of bold red MAC Werk Werk Werk lipstick clinging to the lip of the can calls out the culprit. "Marisol, looks like your jump shot could use a little practice."

"Sorry, Mama Gina!" Marisol offers sheepishly, her eyes trained on the *New York Times* crossword.

"Don't be sorry," I say. "Be better."

Marisol replies, "I'll be *exceptional*, the eleven-letter word for better than better." Becky writes *be eggsepshenal*, and I die a little inside. I may not have much formal education, but at least I know how to spell.

I continue with the orientation. "Omega leadership says our priority is to maintain order. We do that by helping and facilitating. Housemothers are all things to the girls—we're therapists; we're friends; we're nurses; we're short-order cooks; we're tailors. Sometimes, we're even plumbers."

Becky frowns. "I wasn't told there'd be plumbing."

"I promise it's not usually an issue."

Des, feeling frosty because she threw *scissors* to Carina's *rock*, says, "Unless it's burrito night, *Carina*." She emphasizes this point by making moist fart noises into her flattened palm.

"What are you, twelve?" Carina replies. She flips Des off, then continues scrolling through the channel guide, as though there was a chance she wouldn't settle on everyone's favorite silver fox. Des half-heartedly kicks her with the tip of her sneaker, but there's no anger behind it. They're all friends here. No, they're more than friends; they're a sisterhood.

"Uh-oh, are they going to fight? Do we call someone? Are we safe?" Becky asks, with real concern.

Ugh, this labor market. There's no one decent left to hire, just Becky, fresh from a drive-through window. *Last-Choice Leadership* says in a tight labor market, an effective manager makes do, so it's on me to make do. I arrange my face into a smile. "Here's a piece of advice—if we acknowledge the disagreement, that makes it a *thing*. Trust me, we do not want to make it a thing."

Becky's eyes widen, and she pens *not a thing* as she nods. I cover my sigh with a cough. I haven't had a full day off since I lost my last assistant months ago. I *will* make this work. I glance down at the checklist on my clipboard. "That reminds me; let's talk dinner."

Becky comes from food service. Maybe this is where she'll shine. I hustle her into the kitchenette. Empty steam trays line the counters, and there's a long farm table with a couple of dirty plates containing the remains of kale salad, couscous, and grilled chicken stacked on the end. Ten bucks says Ariel left them. I sweep everything into a bus tub in one deft motion; then I wash and dry my hands. I notice Becky writing *wash hands—use soap???* I hope she never touched the chicken at Kentucky Fried.

"Dinner's served at 6:00 p.m. sharp. God help you if the food's late. Oh, shoot."

I cross myself and then tap the gold crucifix at my neck, like I do every time I accidentally take the Lord's name in vain. I've worn this pendant religiously—pun not intended—since my First Communion. It's my touchstone. It's what grounds me when I'm feeling stressed. I joke that giving me this necklace is the one good thing my father ever did, except that part's kind of true.

Becky remarks, "Did you go to Catholic school or something?"

"Eleven and a half years." *Not twelve,* I think, but I don't say it out loud. Regardless, Becky doesn't (can't?) do the math.

"If you turn to section three of your *Housemother's Bible,* you'll find a grid of everyone's dietary preferences and allergies. You'll learn whose preferences to take seriously. I mean, Ariel claims she's gluten-free, but those Double Stuf Oreos didn't inhale themselves." All twelve of my gray hairs come from Ariel. Fact. Do not even get me started on how that girl tortured us when she was taking a Mandarin class last semester. I still hear *Ni hao!* in my dreams.

"And here," I continue, "is the housemother's little helper." I pause in front of the Nespresso machine and show Becky how to make an iced Americano. I fill a to-go cup with ice, then quickly brew four pods of the espresso. Then I add a couple pumps of sugar-free vanilla syrup, and I'm set for the night.

"Why are you leaving the Omega?" Becky asks.

"I'm not leaving. I'm just going to be unavailable a few times a week, and I need someone to fill in for me," I explain.

Becky places a comforting hand on my shoulder. "Community service. Been there."

I'm so relieved she assumes I'm on probation that it doesn't even occur to me to be concerned about her familiarity with the legal system. And my truth feels more shameful, anyway.

The lights blink twice, so I move Becky back into the lounge.

"Ladies? Twenty-minute warning!"

Almost all the girls leap into action, whipping off boots and cycle shoes. They slip out of their tie-dyed sweats and lounge attire, replacing them with G-strings, flossy sequined bras, and in Ariel's case, a laser-cut, high-gloss PVC, BDSM-style catsuit. It takes two girls and a half bottle of talcum powder to stuff her into it, but the audience goes wild for the look.

"Welcome to showtime at the Omega Lounge," I tell Becky.

"Newark's top-rated gentlemen's club," Des, Marisol, and Sofia say in unison, just like they do in our promotional video.

Becky looks unimpressed. I'm sick of people making assumptions about what really goes on here. "Listen. The girls worked hard for that rating, and so did I."

Des, as always, has my back. "When we started here, things were way different. The Omega was every negative strip club stereotype you can imagine, and a few you couldn't. I'm talking Sodom and Gomorrah up in here. Chris Rock was wrong; there was *absolutely* sex in the champagne room. Plus, drugs and gambling and a shit-ton of other illegal activities. Remember that day there were feathers and blood in the back room?"

I shudder. We assumed a cock fight or someone practicing Santería, but there was no place for either of those things if the club was going to become a positive work environment.

Des continues. "Well, your girl here helped change everything. She got people into treatment. She figured out childcare for the women with kids. She even lobbied for health care and profit sharing. The Omega went from having the worst reputation to the best. Mama Gina is good people; take notes."

I feel embarrassed when she lists my accomplishments, so I add, "And after all the changes, the girls started making more money than ever."

"Gotta stop calling us girls, Gina," Ariel admonishes as she applies a double set of mink lashes at a lighted makeup table. "It minimizes and infantilizes us."

"Sorry, Ariel. I meant women." I explain to Becky, "Ariel's a feminist, and she's constantly on me about my language. She's right; I need to do better. You should catch Ariel's set. She's trained in ballet, and her moves will take your breath away. She does this thing where she's upside-down at the top of the pole, holding on with her ankles. Then she flaps her arms like wings and plunges ten feet face-first and—well, you've got to see it. I can't do it justice."

"My dying swan drop has more than seven million views," Ariel adds. "YouTube even sent me a congratulations cake." Which she ate, despite the gluten.

Becky leans in to my ear and says, "Don't you find this whole business, like, kind of yuck?"

The Omega has been as much a home for me as my childhood home was for the first eighteen years of my life. My mom was always working because my dad was so useless. Then, after she got sick, it was . . . not ideal.

"Becky, if you're going to be a successful housemom, we need to clear up some things. These girls—no, these *women*—sorry, Ariel, aren't addicts. They're not prostitutes. They're athletes; they're entertainers. They take pride in being very good at what they do."

"Preach, baby girl," Des interjects while using the edge of her dressing table to stretch out her hamstrings.

"The diet, the exercise, the classes—they're committed to putting on a show, and they earn a lot for it. If any one of them walks out of here with less than two grand tonight, something went wrong. These women have goals and ambitions. Des is going to open her own pole-dancing fitness center."

"Less than ten bills away," Des adds.

"Sofia speaks six languages. Marisol is an artist, and her watercolors are beautiful. Carina's little boy has an IQ that's off the charts. And Ariel just graduated from NYU without a penny of student loan debt, thanks to what she makes here a couple nights a week."

"Trust me. The Omega is the *only* reason I'd come to New Jersey," Ariel adds as she yanks her hair back into a severe bun. She really works the whole bondage/ballerina thing.

"The number one rule is, we don't judge. Any kind of sex work is *work*." I get so mad when people put down the dancers. Most of my friends from high school turned up their noses when they found out about my job, yet they're the ones who fill their Instagram feeds with half-naked shots of themselves at the shore. Such hypocrites.

Becky narrows her eyes at me, and I can feel the heat of her judgment. "Did *you* ever dance here?"

I pause for a beat, remembering my audition eight years ago, standing, terrified, on that stage, blinded by the lighting and hesitant in every move. I didn't own any sexy clothes, and I didn't yet realize my school uniform was a fetish, so I performed in the one-piece swimsuit I used to wear for gym class. It was a hot mess, except not *hot* in any way, shape, or form.

Fortunately, Sal, the night manager, recognized my desperation. He took pity and hired me as housemother. I'm the same age as many of the dancers, but sometimes I feel decades older. This isn't the life I anticipated, yet here I am, so I make the best of it. Des tells me I trend toward toxic positivity, but how is focusing on the good a negative?

To Becky, I simply reply, "Nope."

Carina is still prone on the couch, her eyes glued to CNN. "Carina, shake a leg; you're on the main stage in thirty. Please get ready. No one wants to stuff a Benjamin into the waistband of your sweatpants."

Anderson Cooper's reassuring voice overlays a montage of photos of an impeccably clad, sun-kissed, middle-aged man posing on a yacht. "I legit cannot look away from this story," Carina says.

Anderson continues. *"Authorities are still looking for financier Chip Barclay. He disappeared last month after bilking investors out of billions. Whether the fraud was intentional has yet to be determined by a court of law. What's so troubling is that right before he disappeared, he liquidated almost fifty million dollars from the charity founded by his wife."*

Barclay looks like a lot of the Wall Street–type guys we get in here, all buttoned up and impeccable on the outside, but no moral core whatsoever. Don't get me wrong; the ladies love it when the brokers and traders come in. It's not because they're such big spenders, all trying to out-alpha-dog the other. (That part doesn't hurt.) It's really that these finance bros have no clue anyone's listening to their insider-trading conversations. They assume the employees aren't capable of understanding. Big mistake. A few years ago, Daphne shorted a meme stock based on what she overheard, and now she owns a six-bedroom home in a gated community. She comes in occasionally and overtips everyone.

"Tell me the story while you put on your costume," I reply, but Carina doesn't budge.

"This Barclay guy? They're calling him the next Madoff. He ripped off everyone and then ran away. He's just like my uncle Pauly. Except he stole millions, not just my aunt's Hyundai."

Becky sits down to watch with Carina but jumps back up when I give her a curt headshake.

"Cool, cool, cool. So, do you think he's bringing his millions here tonight? And that he'll buy enough private dances to cover your son's tuition at the gifted and talented school I keep telling you about?" I ask.

"Well, no," Carina says. "Why would he? He's from Chicago, and he's missing. Anderson speculates he's left the country."

I shoo Carina to her dressing table. "However, Mr. Cavalcante *will* be here tonight," I explain. "He's your best customer, and he definitely *will* request a private dance." I place a tub of glittering body lotion into her hand. The spotlight really picks up the sparkle, plus it smells like coconut and lemongrass. The girls nicknamed it Rack Spackle.

Des chimes in, "Cavalcante sucks. Dude's in the Mafia."

"No, he's not; he's a grandpa!" Carina argues.

"You can be in the Mafia *and* be a grandfather," Des replies. "Marlon Brando much?"

I hold up a finger. "Both of you, stop. Mr. Cavalcante has never been anything but a gentleman to everyone, and that mob nonsense is all rumor. You know what's not a rumor, Carina? Your son Henry's limitless future if you get him into Abernathy Day."

I'm embarrassed to admit how many times I've looked at Abernathy's website, imagining where I might be if I'd had that kind of education, those opportunities. I picture myself as a little kid, sitting in front of the ivy-covered walls, reading smart stuff like *War and Peace*, solving equations on whiteboards. Maybe eating sushi with chopsticks in the cafeteria. Speaking Mandarin to my friends. *Ni hao!*

When I think about my schooling, mostly I remember the nuns rapping my knuckles with a ruler when I'd show up with wrinkles in my oxford shirt, as though it were my fault that my dad didn't pay our electric bill and I couldn't iron my uniform.

My hand finds its way up to my crucifix again. I've touched this thing so many times, Jesus's face is worn smooth.

The lights blink again.

"Okay, everyone," I say. "It's showtime!"

I gather my things so that I can dash out, grabbing my notebooks and topping off my coffee. I'm leaving the women in Becky's incapable hands. She only has to help them with their costumes for the next few hours; we've completed all the other tasks. Surely, she can handle tightening a strap, maybe steaming a garment, possibly flat ironing hair extensions. That can't be so hard, right? (I cringe a little, thinking of her with a hot iron.)

Before I go, I remember the one thing I wanted to ask Becky. "You never did give me the reason why you left KFC. I have to put it on your new-hire paperwork."

Becky explains, "They said I got in too many fights."

I touch my cross and think, *Jesus, take the wheel.*

Lately, I've had trouble getting my car to start. My ritual involves prayer, followed by pounding on the steering wheel. Tonight, the engine only sputters and coughs briefly before it turns over. The mechanic's exact quote was "You don't need an alternator so much as you need an alternate vehicle." His estimate contained a comma in it, and now I get to decide which I'd rather have—transportation or shelter. Adulting, zero stars. Do not recommend.

It took me almost three years after my mother's passing to pay off her hospital bills. My dad wasn't in the picture then. The administrators worked with me on a payment plan, and I was proud once I cleared that debt. I even managed to start a savings account. I had some money, and we'd overheard a tip, so I was going to put it toward Tesla stock at twenty dollars per share. That five thousand dollars would have been worth a life-changing hundred thousand dollars today (and it's why we lost half our dancers). The girls in the club capitalized, while my dad convinced me to use my savings to bail him out when he popped back up on my radar, needing help. I've been falling more and more behind ever since, waiting for him to pay me back. Of course, he's vanished again. Even if I could locate him, I'm sure he'd have more excuses.

When I was a kid, I convinced myself he was a superhero and that he was out solving crimes during the long stretches he was gone. Now I know he wasn't *solving* crimes, and there wasn't a super thing about him. But he's the only family I have, so . . . *Don't Dwell on Downers* recommends denial when negative thoughts come, so I try to push them away.

I hum to myself as I drive, since my radio stopped working last winter, and arrive at the community center just in time for my night school class. I'm making a positive step toward my future, but I despise not being early, so I'm a bit flustered. If all goes well, I should have my GED in three months.

You know how many doors are open to people without a diploma? Trick question, because the answer is *none*.

I settle into my desk and open my Algebra II book, pulling out my homework, a pad of graph paper, and a mechanical pencil. Mrs. Duncan is a stickler, so I silence my phone. It's blowing up with texts. My car is so loud, I must not have heard them. But I need to be here, to be present, to put myself first for once. I can't get sucked into anyone else's drama. That always knocks me off track. My phone vibrates, and then vibrates again. It shakes my desk, and Mrs. Duncan scowls at me.

"Is there an issue, Ms. Ferragamo?" She always pronounces my last name wrong, to the point that I wonder if it's intentional.

"I'm so sorry!" I reply, shoving my phone in my bag.

Mrs. Duncan is proof positive that you can't judge a book by its cover. At first glance, she seems all warm and sweet. For example, her sweater has a giant embroidered apple with a felt worm sticking out, holding his own apple with its own felt worm, and so on with the worms and apples. *Inception* for sweaters. You'd think someone who only wears novelty cardigans would be a little more whimsical.

My phone must have shifted next to my keys and the laundry quarters I keep in an old aspirin bottle, so when it vibrates again, my bag rattles violently, and twenty sets of eyes stare at me. I want to fall into a parallelogram and die.

"Why don't you take care of whatever the problem is and return when you're ready to stop wasting your classmates' time?" Mrs. Duncan suggests.

Humiliated, I rush into the hallway.

The texts have been flying in fast and furious, from dancers and management alike. I can tell it's serious because everyone's using punctuation.

Marisol: Becky with the bad hair has got to go! She broke the strap on my platform Mary Janes when she tried to stuff her giant foot into it!

Oh no, Marisol loves those shoes! She special-ordered them from the UK. I think a Spice Girl once wore them.

Des: What's the new girl's problem?! I asked her to help lace my corset and she was all, "I wasn't told there'd be lacing." WTF? That is some serial killer shit right there.

Ariel: Mrs. Potato Head just accused me of using drugs.

Des: She just laced me up so tight, she knocked the wind out of me. Again, serial killer shit! I couldn't get out and I had a panic attack.

Des is claustrophobic.

Des: I had to breathe into a bag to calm down! Then this heifer went around saying, "Who has drugs?" like that was supposed to help me.

Thanks to me, the hardest drug at the Omega is Sudafed for Marisol's seasonal allergies.

Ariel: Drugs! She accused me of having drugs! Me! You know I won't even do vaccines! My bod is a temple and I'm super triggered!

Marisol: She sat on my Chanel compact and crushed it into a fine powder! I'm going to look greasy onstage, not dewy!

Des: Carina had to cut me out of it because I was suffocating! And it was La Perla!!

Carina: Your trainee made Des cry. That is NOT OKAY.

Sofia: She burned off a chunk of my hair with the flat iron! En llamas! Marty had to dump his water on my head, but he forgot it was Sprite, and now everything down here is sticky!

Jesus Christ. My hand flies to my necklace.

Marty: Where do you keep the mop?

Ariel: Have you seen my Oreos?

And then . . .

Sal: Chaos here, canned the new girl. She started fighting with everyone! How is that even possible? Need u to come back and calm everyone down.

I enter the classroom again and quietly gather my things.
"Leaving us so soon, Miss Feh-RAH-gamo?" Mrs. Duncan asks.
"Sorry, I have an emergency at work," I reply.
She glowers at me. "Yes, well, if you ever decide to be serious about your education, perhaps you'll grace us with your presence again. For the rest of you who aspire to something more than your current circumstance, open your textbooks to page twenty-six."
I stuff my schoolwork back into my bag and skulk out. Back to the Omega.
Like always.

Chapter Three

HAYDEN ELSPETH BONDURANT (BARCLAY)

One year ago

"Oh my freaking God, I don't believe it! Hayden Barclay, is that *you* back there in that apron?"

I knew this was bound to happen; I just didn't realize it would be so soon. I steel myself and fake smile because I know that LaVonne, my new boss at Eli's House of Beans, is within earshot.

"Hi, Addie. What can I get you?" I gesture to the beverage menu above my head, hoping that I can just take her order, make her drink, and move her TF out of here.

"Um, first of all, an explanation," Addie says, holding up a finger tipped with a long, pastel nail that's been tapered to a sharp point and accented with tiny rhinestones. Addie's so *extra* that they could be tiny diamonds, who knows? "How are you not in Monaco? Or Gstaad? Or like, anywhere with cabana boys and a swim-up bar? I mean, *Chip Barclay's* daughter? In an apron? Is this for TikTok?" She sweeps the shop with her eyes, looking for a tripod and a ring light. "Is this real life? Are you doing a *thing*? I am literally dying to know, so you'd better spill that tea right now, girl!"

"I'm sorry, Hayden *Barclay*?" LaVonne says, turning from the espresso machine she was cleaning. Her eyes are round as saucers, and she raises an impeccably sculpted eyebrow. LaVonne is addicted to makeup tutorials, and every day I've been here, she's come to work in a new *lewk*. Today's includes three shades of winged purple shadow that extend to her temples, violet contact lenses, and iridescent lilac shimmer powder on every raised point of her face. She's got metallic purple strands of tinsel woven into her twists. On the spectrum of what I've seen so far, this look is sort of tame.

LaVonne continues. "Like, *Barclay* Barclay? Like the Eli Whitney University Barclay School of Finance and Barclay Hall and the Barclay Student Center? Why did I think your last name was Bondurant?"

Shit, shit, shit. I am not prepared for this. I should be, but I'm not.

"Absolutely!" Addie confirms. "The Barclays are, like, American royalty! I'm talking Kennedys and Vanderbilts and Astors and shit. Plus, they're the second most important name at this university after the Whitneys! Her whole family went to school here, and her great-grandfather donated all those buildings. Major donor. Like, *major* major. But you had to know that."

LaVonne glances back and forth from Addie to me. Until now, I thought I was pulling it off, like on *Undercover Boss*, just a privileged person working a regular job, except I'd do it indefinitely, not just for one episode's worth of content, and I actually need the money. LaVonne must have registered the naked panic on my face, so she's going along until Addie leaves. I appreciate her restraint.

LaVonne plays it off. "Of course, I did, girl, yeah, I just forgot. Too much caffeine negatively impacts the memory and all. So, Hayden Barclay, if you need me, I'll be right over here, just two steps away, refreshing the dusty old pastry-display case."

This is a task I completed no less than thirty minutes ago. LaVonne watched me swap out yesterday's dry palmiers for a fresh batch. She's silently telling me she's going to be cool, but that she plans to eavesdrop and grill me mercilessly, and I don't blame her.

"Ooh boy," LaVonne exclaims. "Are these pastries a mess. I'd best roll my sleeves up and dig in."

"I thought you graduated," Addie says, her eyes roving over me, memorizing each difference from then to now so she can go back and break the gossip.

"I did," I say. "Then I took a gap year, and now I'm about to start grad school."

Addie twirls a strand of her long, black hair between her fingertips, while staring at mine, probably because it looks so different now. Apparently not different enough, though. This is why changing your appearance never works on shows like *Undercover Boss* either. Your face is still your face. "Why did I think you were doing an MBA at Wharton?"

"That was the plan—until I changed my mind."

"And you changed your hair, and your jewelry, and, like, your whole vibe," she says, nodding toward my woven friendship bracelets where the Cartier stack used to rest. She surveyed my plain black leggings, batik tank, old sneakers (like, actually old, and not faux Golden Goose, buy-them-pre-dirtied old), and bandana holding my hair back. "Do you own this place?"

Ignoring her question, I ask, "Are you still a skim iced latte girl?" I'm desperate to move on. I never really liked or trusted her, but she was my best friend Smythe's little sister in the sorority, so I was sort of stuck with her.

"Oh no, I'm on keto, so how about a large cold brew with a splash of heavy cream," she says. She's as easily distracted as a baby shown a set of shiny keys. Same old Addie.

"Do you want a pastry to go with it?" I offer. "We have almond croissants to die for, and they're superfresh."

"Ugh, no, way too many calories. And not keto. I'm a flyer this year," she says, referring to her position on the college's cheerleading squad. This means she gets tossed in the air at football halftime shows, executing flips and twists. Whitney's football team is a perpetual disappointment, so the cheerleaders compensate. Flying was Addie's dream, and she'd been struggling to lose ten pounds for a couple of years to move up. I'm glad she's reached her goal. I'm not her biggest fan, but I don't actively root against her or anything.

"Have you talked to Smythe lately?" she asks.

"Not since we parted ways in Paris," I replied. Technically, this is the truth.

I set land-speed records for assembling her drink, pouring the strong, dark, nutty cold brew over a cup of crushed ice, and throw in a dash of cream. Before I can hand it to her, Addie asks, "Can you do more cream, please?" so I add another splash.

"Little more." She gestures for me to really dump it in. This time, I add a healthy glug of cream. It's so rich, it oozes rather than pours. If it were any more solid, it would be butter.

"Just a touch more." I pour out some of the beverage to make room. There must be a cup of heavy cream in that drink. From a fat/calorie standpoint, she'd be better off with one of our decadent fudge-iced custard éclairs. At least she could chew those.

"Some diet," LaVonne mutters, reaffirming why I already like her more than my old crowd.

LaVonne is a scholarship student from Flint, making her way through university with loans and side hustles—our paths never would have crossed in a meaningful way in undergrad. I was a different person then, spoiled and entitled, with little regard for anyone or anything but myself. Those days are over, and I'd like to think I'm better for it. I imagine it's going to be weird when my old life seeps in, like right now with Addie.

I ring up her order. "That's five dollars, please," I say.

Addie breaks into peals of laughter. "OMG, you're still so funny, Hayden. Since when does anyone pay for anything when they're with you? Remember when you took that huge group of us on your PJ to

Tulum for the weekend because you needed a tan? You were like, *'Your money's no good here, betches!'* Or that time you wanted a new dress, so we all came to Milan with you? How about that spring break at the family lodge in Aspen? Fun!"

I hear choking noises behind the pastry case. I need to get Addie out of here before LaVonne bursts a blood vessel.

"Right, so fun, and this is totally on me, of course," I say quickly. "Great to see you; come back soon!" I hand her the drink, and she scurries off, never once looking at the tip jar or saying thank you, just like always.

LaVonne wheels around. "You know, I wouldn't make poor ol' Hayden Bondurant the grad school student pay for shit. But Hayden Barclay with Daddy's private jet? Fork it over." She points at the till.

I pull a five-dollar bill out of my pocket and place it in the register to cover Addie's drink. LaVonne reaches for a napkin, writes *Back in 20 mins*, and tapes it to the front door and locks it. "You and me, we're going to have ourselves a conversation now."

"Can we just shut down the shop like that?" I ask.

"Depends," LaVonne says.

"On?"

"On whether you're filming some *Secret Millionaire* shit," she replies. "If that's the case, I want a red 1967 Ford Mustang convertible with a V8 engine, because they're always giving the sassy coworker something nice for their sad story, unless that worker gets caught fucking around on the job, doing stuff like closing midday for twenty minutes to chat. Do you or do you not secretly own this place, Hayden Bondurant Barclay?"

LaVonne knows damn well that Professor Oxnard owns this place, especially as he's the one who's given her free rein over it. "I don't."

"Then we'll take our chances."

LaVonne grabs two bottles of Pellegrino from the cooler and a couple of the almond croissants. She heads to the battered wooden table by the picture window, pulling out a heavy wrought iron chair and settling in.

"Come sit your rich ass down, Barclay."

I grudgingly oblige; I have no choice. LaVonne has been so good to me, and I owe her an explanation, even though I would legitimately rather clean the bathrooms than face her inquisition. My disinfecting method is quick and painless—the trick is to spray everything down with antibacterial spray and wipe from the top down in long swipes. If you use clean white bar towels, they can be bleached and reused. They don't produce waste like paper towels. A year ago, the idea of sanitizing a public washroom would have made me throw up, but after traveling to places where the bathroom is just a hole in the floor (if you're lucky), wiping off a porcelain toilet is no big deal.

My original plan for my gap year was drinking and beaching and shopping with Smythe all over the globe before coming back to get an MBA and eventually joining the family business. The fact that my travels popped the bubble of my whole charmed life was an unintentional side effect. I do feel like I've become a better person for it. But how do I explain this transformation to people like Addie, who only knew who I was in relation to what I could do for her, not who I could become?

I protest, "*I'm* not rich." This is 100 percent true.

LaVonne cups her chin in her hands. In the sunlight, I can see how flawless her skin is. How does she manage that with all the makeup she wears?

"Why is your skin so perfect, LaVonne? You don't have one pore," I say.

"Nope, you've had a month to talk to me about my seven-step cleansing regime. Now is not the day, and you are not the one. Girl, does your family have a private jet or not?"

"No. My dad's company does, so it isn't really *ours* ours."

"That's some Orwellian doublespeak right there." LaVonne is a lit major. "Just tell me—are you allowed to use it without paying for it, yes or no?"

"I mean, it's a gray area."

LaVonne isn't having it. She slaps the table with an open palm to punctuate each of her sentences. "Semantics. Spill. Start with the last name on your timecard."

I explain, "Before I get into it, let me point out your reaction when you found out I'm one of those Barclays. Multiply that by every person I've ever met. It gets old, having the world trying to count your money and figure out what they can get from you."

"Mmm hmm." She's not on my side yet, but it does seem like she's trying to understand me.

"After I graduated, I started going by my mom's maiden name when I was traveling. I was advised it would be safer in some countries where kidnapping isn't unusual, and the bonus was I got fewer questions that way. Anyway, I wasn't even planning on coming back here for school, but some stuff changed last year, and I readjusted my priorities, and this is where I ended up. I figured if I returned to campus with a new look and a different last name, I'd fly—"

She makes a noise somewhere between a snort and a laugh. "You'd fly private."

"No, I'd fly *under the radar*, especially as all my good friends have graduated. People like Addie aren't friends. They're just leftovers from a previous era."

"Cool, cool, cool . . . so tell me why the hell you're working here. Don't you have a trust fund? Don't all rich kids have trust funds, or did *Gossip Girl* lie to me?" LaVonne always gets right to the point, and I appreciate that about her. When she was training me, she flat-out laughed at my first attempt at making a cappuccino. She told me I'd have to figure it out quick or I wouldn't have the job long, which is just what I did. Sometimes tough love is the best love.

"Because I need the money."

"Why, you buying an island?"

Here's the thing about being rich: even when you aren't anymore, no one forgives you for what you once had, and no one forgets. "No. I had a *thing* with my family, a falling-out, and now I'm supporting myself. I'm paying my own way, so I took this job."

"And you're way too rich on paper to qualify for financial aid?"

"Probably, until I establish that I'm on my own."

"Can't you just sell some of your good shit on eBay and live like a queen? Could probably pay your whole tuition with one Birkin bag. Wait, do you have a Birkin?" She slaps the table again, and a couple almonds fall off our croissants. "Tell me you don't have one, because I will die."

"I didn't have one," I reply. Again, the truth. Technically, I had a whole bunch of them, in multiple colors and materials. "I ended up donating a lot of my stuff. I couldn't walk around with those stupid designer bags after I met kids who didn't have access to clean water."

"For a Birkin, I might be able to." The sunlight picks up the glitter tinsel in her hair and all the highlight powder on her face.

What I didn't give away, I left at my parents' various houses, and I don't have access to any of it now. I mean, I *could* go back and get some things to sell. For that matter, I could make one call to my dad, and all my problems would vanish. It would be so easy to ask for help, but what's the point of making a stand if you're not going to live by it? That call would indicate forgiveness, and I will not forgive him.

"I don't have any expensive stuff anymore."

LaVonne looks far more stricken than I feel. Here's what people don't understand—if you never earned any of your family's money, it's not so hard to walk away from it. None of it feels real. "Not even one Gucci? Not even a little teeny Louis V. pochette?"

"Nope."

"You really think you're going to afford to live on your own and pay your tuition with what you make at this shitty, no offense to myself, McJob?"

I shrug. I've been trying to think through what I'm going to do. Worst-case scenario, I could talk to the attorney in charge of my trust. Maybe there's some sort of early disbursement for education. I had some money left after my time abroad, but I need all of it for tuition, and even then, I might be short. I'm not sure how I'd feel about using more family money to get my degree. Would the ends—getting a sociology degree so I can do aid work—justify the means? There's a "white savior" vibe to the whole postgrad plan, and that is not my intention, but it's the best plan I've come up with. I just want to do right by people who haven't had my privileges, and I'm not entirely sure how to make that happen if I can't pay for school.

"I'm going to have to try."

Chapter Four

CeCe

One month before sorority rush

"I just can't decide which is worse, the stress or the mortification. Can it be both? I feel like it could be both. They're equally burdensome," I explain from my prone position on the sofa, staring up at the popcorn ceiling. A popcorn ceiling! In this day and age! Perhaps this is not the time to nitpick, but if you're going to offer a couch to recline upon while sharing feelings, I suggest buying a piece made with higher-quality insert material. I can feel the cheap Ikea feathers stabbing me in the back.

And I know a little something about being stabbed in the back.

Marcy nods as I unload. She offers little response in return. She does this thing where she doesn't talk, so I have to fill in all the blanks, as though she wants me to find the answers within myself. I guess it's not an ineffective strategy, but input would be useful from time to time.

"When I think about what Chip did, I'm so angry. Everyone's comparing him to Bernie Madoff, and that doesn't feel completely fair. First of all, the SEC knows damn well the Barclay Group was run legitimately since his great-grandfather's time! It was never a Ponzi scheme. Chip was the genuine article! I'd never have married him if he weren't; Daddy would have forbidden it."

My father never did warm to Chip. Daddy said he couldn't trust anyone who was so effortlessly handsome. Still, TBG grew exponentially after Chip Sr. died. Of course, I'd assumed all the growth was thanks to Chip, not just an unprecedented postpandemic bull market. I tell Marcy, "Chip didn't steal from his clients, per se. As my attorneys explained to me, his high-risk investments tanked when the market turned. Losing money isn't illegal; it's just bad business. He must have panicked, which is why he falsified all those statements with inflated numbers to keep them calm until he could replace their losses. That part? Highly illegal. But he didn't come under federal scrutiny until after one of his biggest investors tried to cash out and Chip couldn't cover the redemption. I'm realizing that Chip wasn't as smart as he led me to believe. I mean, I honestly believed he went to ASU—forgoing his legacy spot at Eli Whitney—so he could golf year-round."

Marcy makes a noise that's somewhere between a groan and a growl.

"The only entity he legitimately stole from was my foundation, and that's what gets me. Instead of being a man and facing the consequences, he treated my charity like a piggy bank, smashing it open and running off."

Chip made *me* look bad, and that is unforgivable. I feel the tears coming on. I gesture for Marcy to hand me a tissue, as they're all the way across the room. She brings me the box, setting it down rather unceremoniously beside me on the glass end table. Glass tables! I'm sorry; are we in a discotheque or something? I blot my eyes with this off-brand sandpaper.

"People are comparing me to Madoff's wife!" I add, my sadness morphing back into anger. "Chip and I never talked about business. I found those discussions so very tedious. But now people are looking at *me* as the mastermind! Me! I may be a lot of things, but dishonest is not one of them! I'm terrified that I'm going to end up like Ruth! Do you know what happened to her? They took everything, and she now lives in a small condo and drives a Prius. A Prius!"

Marcy's lips flatten into a straight line. "I drive a Prius."

"Anyhoo, my point was that Chip inherited a successful business. He didn't create a fake one so he could get money from the unwitting. The Barclay Group was legitimately a powerhouse asset management firm. His father got the best returns because he worked harder than anyone else, reading ten newspapers a day. If his father heard that a New Delhi company was about to go big with their use of hydroelectric power, he'd hop on a plane to India and see that damn dam for himself before he even slid so much as a rupee their way. *Trust, but verify.* That was his motto. I don't know how Chip strayed so far from that path."

I notice Marcy's just sitting there, picking at a hangnail. "Should you be writing any of this down?" I ask.

"I'm good," she replies.

"So, new funds started popping up, and Chip was losing market share to them. His father's returns were always ahead of the S&P, but when Chip saw these younger kids making an absolute killing, something switched. With his dad gone, he finally had the latitude to make changes. He said he wanted to be less Warren Buffett and more Sam Bankman-Fried, whatever that meant. Honestly, I think he started to get jealous when children in hoodies were suddenly driving around in tacky Lamborghinis. Why would you want something in such a lurid color? I guess I'm like Henry Ford in that respect—your car can be any color you want, as long as the color you want is black. That's why Chip dipped a toe into crypto, and it paid off. Then he dipped his foot and got a bigger payoff. Then he submerged his whole self, and he was just swimming in returns, Scrooge McDuck style."

Marcy exhales audibly. "I don't get the reference."

"Miserly duck, based on the Ebenezer Scrooge character? Anyway, McDuck was always diving into giant swimming pools of gold coins to demonstrate his wealth. He was partial to dressing in a waistcoat and a top hat, even wore spats on occasion, but he never could seem to locate a pair of pants. I found that part deeply disconcerting. Draw some trousers on him, for goodness' sake."

Marcy nods.

"Chip's clients were over the moon with his returns, so appreciative of how things had changed with Chip in charge. He'd always been successful, but this was next-level success. Wildest dreams success. Conservative old traders couldn't wrap their minds around the crypto market; it was like they were speaking Greek. When everyone else was zigging, Chip began zagging."

Forbes put Chip on the cover with the quote "I zagged." It became a *thing* with the cryptocurrency crowd for a while. I framed some copies and hung them in a few of his home offices. But no one gets something for nothing, at least not long term.

"Then Alexis entered our life to run the foundation, because Chip insisted I needed the help. Maybe I did; maybe I didn't; who can say. I thought I was growing it nicely on my own, but he said there were so many regulatory issues to deal with that I couldn't go it alone anymore."

"Were you angry about this?" Marcy asks.

"*En quelque sorte.* She just had these bold ideas for growth, once she saw how much money we had on the books, and she had Chip's ear." I am too genteel to mention which other body parts of his she must have had her hands on. "I wanted to put that money in bonds, or, if we were feeling saucy, an index fund like my father had always done, but I guess they weren't 'sexy' enough for her. She explained that the future was in NFTs."

Marcy looks puzzled.

"Right, they had to explain them to me too. They're what's called a nonfungible token. Of course, as we've since discovered, they're magic beans."

Marcy scrunches her forehead. Mental note: discuss the benefits of Botox with her.

"Anyway, NFTs are digital assets that exist solely in the digital universe. Alexis knew an artist who was introducing what was supposed to be the biggest launch of all time, the Smoking Snakes. Each would be some variety of a digital little cartoon snake, but every one would have a slightly different detail, like one snake would have a corncob pipe and another would have a cigar. Some traits would be more valuable than others, like if they had glasses or a gold fang. Everyone was anticipating the drop, from Bella Hadid to that Snoopy Dog gentleman. I petitioned the board to not let her do it. That damned Poppy Pierce was the deciding factor. I should have gotten rid of her sooner."

"The NFT market sounds risky to the point of stupid."

"*Exactly.* But Chip was fascinated. He and Alexis started to meet. That must be when their *extracurricular* relationship began. Chip got over his skis when the crypto market cooled so suddenly, and he needed to generate some quick gains."

I feel a tickle forming in my throat. "Marcy, would it be too much to ask for you to bring me a cup of tea? Pretty please?" I flash her a dazzling smile. Marcy complies. The smile is such a powerful weapon in the war of persuasion. She sets the pot on the stove and roots around in the cabinet for a mug.

"Chip went all in with his investors' money, and when the NFT market tanked, he lost so much, it triggered the whole chain of events. Apparently, the snake NFTs were encouraging children to smoke. There was some scuttlebutt about hidden messages, placed there by Big Tobacco. Apparently, they were behind the whole launch."

Marcy gasps. "That is truly despicable."

"On all counts. What got me was, how could anything be allowed to drop in value so quickly? I thought there were guardrails, or some sort of oversight by the Securities and Exchange Commission to prevent this sort of thing."

Marcy places a cheap tea bag in the mug, and the hot water sloshes over the side. I feel like her service could use a tweak, but I don't want to go off on that tangent when I'm so emotionally raw. She plonks the mug atop a coaster on the terrible glass table. At least she's using a coaster; perhaps there's hope.

"What's so upsetting is that Chip didn't come to me, not once. He didn't tell me anything. I could have helped; I could have made discreet inquiries, gotten us loans, something. But now our name is synonymous with theft and failure, and I'm not sure we can bounce back. It's just so devastating. I mean, I was asked to resign from the Cherokee Hill club! Me! Kicked out! I couldn't even clean out my locker—they sent my tennis gear via courier. And that person stood at my door with my bag full of racquets, as though I would tip him for the indignity! I mean, I did, but grudgingly." I wince as I take a sip of my tea. "Would you mind getting me a splash of milk? This is so strong; it steeped too long."

Marcy plucks the mug out of my hand. "Is two percent milk okay?"

"If you don't have oat," I reply.

She returns and plonks the mug down again. I take a sip; it's much improved.

"All the women in my circle, all these 'good friends' who never gave me any credit for what Chip achieved. With all my support. Just *blah blah blah*, and how feminists wouldn't paint the wife with the husband's brush of success since they are two separate entities. Well, suddenly, I was guilty by association! Every one of them turned their backs on me! Even horse-toothed Helga and sniffly Stefanie! It's like they were never really my friends at all. I swear, women are the worst. By the way, do you have any honey? Manuka, preferably? This could use a bit of zing."

Marcy grabs a plastic bear half-full of honey and sets it down next to my mug.

"Now, my social status has been obliterated, poof! Like so many pairs of McDuck's pants."

"That has to be difficult," Marcy offers.

"Yes, and now the conditions I'm forced to live in? They're just so far below anything I could have imagined. The thread count alone on those sheets! I'd simply remake the bed with my own linens, but the Feds were ruthless when they seized my property."

One of my attorneys said it's technically called a "civil asset forfeiture," and I could get back what I can prove was always mine. That process could take years, and the Feds walked out with almost everything I own. They left me with some clothes and toiletries and a single vehicle, but that's it. I had some money, but almost all of it went to my attorneys' retainers. Now, I'm like Blanche DuBois, relying on the kindness of strangers.

"Of course, nothing is finalized until Chip stands trial. If he's found guilty, they'll likely sell everything off to refund the investors with the proceeds, as well they should. But if we can't find him, he won't stand trial, and I'll never be able to prove what was mine, so I'll lose everything too."

Marcy raises an eyebrow. Again, so much motion in her forehead! "What you're telling me is *you're* the victim here?"

"In some respects, yes. It wasn't bad enough that Chip lost everyone's money. That's deplorable. What is *unforgivable* is how instead of facing the music, he ran off with all my foundation's cash. I guess that part was easy because Alexis was a signatory on the accounts. They're both missing, as is the money. It's just so scandalous, I can't believe it's not a podcast."

"I'm sure it will be. I keep wondering, How did he evade capture that night?"

I reflect on what was supposed to be my perfect evening. "Everyone was looking for him on land. Traffic stops, train stations, airports. No one guessed that he'd gotten on a boat, but it makes sense since we were on the water that night. He had to have known it was coming and staged his getaway. He could literally be anywhere in the world by now. They're speculating that he and Alexis sailed to Canada and then got out of there on false papers."

"You can sail to Canada from Chicago?" Marcy asked.

"Yes, you can definitely sail to Canada from Chicago. Remember, I grew up staring at maps, so I can tell you how to get almost anywhere. Anyway, I'm devastated about the foundation and furious how the press has been covering our story, treating what I created like a joke. Homeless, Not Homely did fantastic work. Yes, the name is silly; an intentional choice to catch people's attention. But what we did was no joke. We helped the housing-insecure prepare to reenter the job force, with quality-of-life help, like haircuts and medical care and interview-wardrobe assistance. Yet all the press can talk about is the woman whom we helped get implants. Fake news."

The truth was, we covered her implant surgery after her double mastectomy. The poor thing was uninsured, and the medical bills had bankrupted her. She'd been working as an exotic dancer, and she had no income with the loss of what she called her "moneymakers." She wanted to return to work, and we gave her the ability to earn a living again. Did the *New York Post* mention any of this in the story that accompanied the "Barclay's Boobs for Bums" front page headline? Of course not.

A timer chimes, and Marcy stands up. She tells me, "I'm sorry; we must stop. I need to get my kids from soccer practice now."

"I wasn't done with my story," I protest. "Shall I come with you?"

"No!" Marcy clears her throat. "I mean, no. You should just relax while I'm out."

I nod. "We can pick right up when you get back." The nice thing about staying with my cousin Marcy is it's like having a built-in therapist, twenty-four seven.

A funny expression crosses her features, which are a lot like the Before version of my own. "You're definitely going to be here when I get back?" she asks.

Marcy seemed a bit surprised when I showed up in Winnetka with all my things. But where else was I supposed to go after the asset forfeiture? The Feds padlocked the iron gates at the Lake Forest compound! My entire social circle blackballed me! You'd have thought all my friends were just waiting to slam their doors in my face or something. "Of course! Where else would I be? Now, would you like to know the good news?" I ask.

"I'm hesitant."

"The good news is, when you get back, I can help you shop for better guest-room sheets!"

Marcy exits without another word, likely overcome by my generosity. Even at my lowest, I'm still thinking of her guests' comfort. And I truly am grateful to be here. I want to show my gratitude, so I should work on a project for Marcy while she's out. Perhaps I can use my discerning eye to point out a list of things she can improve in her home. Her side of the family didn't come from the same wealth as mine. Their tennis court wasn't even clay!

I find a piece of paper on her counter and grab a pencil. I settle at her breakfast bar, and I start writing.

To improve:

1. Popcorn ceiling
2. Family room sofa
3. Thread count of sheets
4. Caliber of paper goods
5. Glass end tables
6. Proper teacups
7. Forehead mobility

I survey my work, and I feel a warm glow. Isn't family just the best?

Chapter Five

GINA

One month before sorority rush

Gina's Daily Do-List

- ~~Bring trainee up to speed~~
- ~~Inquire about availability of gluten-free dinner rolls~~
- ~~Finish reading Putting the "I" in Winning~~
- ~~Less coffee/more water~~
- Breathe

The parking lot is packed when I arrive. Netflix did a series on high-end strip clubs last year, and it helped destigmatize the exotic dancing industry. We've been busier than ever.

Because we serve alcohol in the state of New Jersey, we're considered a "bikini club," which means no full nudity. Our club is more like exotic burlesque; we're essentially a thong's throw from Cirque du Soleil. Jersey blue laws are no joke. Like, Newark's not allowed to sell ice cream on

Sunday after 6:00 p.m., and no one in the state is allowed to pump their own gas since lawmakers of yore deemed it too flammable for the public to handle. Yet no laws exist about flat irons, and tonight, Becky proved they can be plenty dangerous.

I circle the lot, looking for an open space. I'm glad we're busy tonight, but I'm stuck at the far end of the property, out by the dumpsters. My ancient car chokes and shakes as I turn it off. As is, it's being held together by duct tape and positive thinking. I yank off my seat belt, and it catches on my necklace, breaking the delicate gold thread. Of course.

I spend a couple of desperate moments searching for my crucifix, which flew into the cup holder. Relieved, I give Jesus a quick rub before tucking him into my jeans pocket.

This spot in the lot reeks like a cannery when I open my door. Whoever thought tuna poke would be a wise addition to the buffet was sorely mistaken.

I say hello to Marty, our six-foot-five bouncer, a man both the size and shape of a brick retaining wall. He's taking a break in a folding chair that looks comically tiny, like a dad trying out his kindergartener's desk at a parent-teacher conference.

Marty's a former Rutgers linebacker who never made the big leagues because he tore his ACL. I love that he poured all his drive and passion into turning old quilts into jackets and selling them on Etsy. After viewers saw him featured on the Netflix series, his business grew substantially. Lil Yachty recently requested a custom jacket to wear to the Grammys, so I can't imagine Marty will be working here much longer. That's the thing about this place—it's a way station, on the way to better things. Everyone intends to be the next Lady Gaga or Cardi B or Channing Tatum. All of whom got their start stripping. No one ever plans to be at the Omega permanently, not even me.

"Hi, Marty. How are you doing?"

"Hey, Miss Gina. I am outstanding. I found a great quilt at Sally Army today. I'm thinking of doing this with it." He opens a notebook and shows me a professional-looking sketch of a barn jacket with an oversized shawl collar and wide hood. I love it!

"Oh, Marty, it's fabulous!"

He nods. "I do what I can."

The wind shifts, and we're struck with a fresh wave of fish.

"How can you vape out here?" I ask. "It smells like low tide."

He shrugs. "I like the quiet."

I pinch my nose. "I need to get away from this stench. The poke was a mistake." I make my way to the front of the club.

He calls after me, "Not as big a mistake as Becky, apparently. It was anarchy down in the dressing room. Shit was wack. Had to come out here to calm my nerves."

Ugh, I don't know how long it's going to take me to find a new Becky. Who wants to be a minimum-wage assistant housemom when the performers can double that weekly salary with one three-minute dance? Even the bartenders and waitresses—sorry, Ariel, *servers*—earn bank, especially since our clientele is so upscale. The wait staff makes as much from investing on the stock tips as they do from slinging drinks. Plus, everyone tips Marty, so he walks home with wads of cash too. I'm the only one who doesn't get a cut. I thought I was so smart, asking for a salary instead of an hourly wage. I know I need to renegotiate with Sal, and I will. Soon(ish).

I notice Mr. Cavalcante's Bentley idling under the covered entrance, likely waiting for the valet, as I approach the door. There's a line of young Masters of the Universe behind the velvet rope, all high on success. The Netflix fans are lined up, too, with merch for the dancers to sign. I think one of them is holding a quilted shirt. Marty will be thrilled!

The club smells amazing when I step inside, which is a relief from the parking lot. Sal installed an air-diffuser system like high-end hotels have, so every twenty minutes, our signature blend of spicy bergamot, frankincense, and sandalwood pipes through the HVAC. What's so weird is it smells a lot like the nave at Saint Peter's Church at Christmastime. Maybe that's why Ariel does so well when she performs in that tiny plaid kilt?

Sofia is on the main stage, whirling around to a Def Leppard song. She's not our best technical dancer, but she compensates by whipping her hair artistically. As she spins, I can see the burned chunk at the back of her damp head. That poor girl! Still, the crowd loves her retro vibe and Jane Fonda–style unitard. People are lined up to stuff wads of cash in her bandeau top when she steps off the stage. Yet another archaic blue law means patrons can't "make it rain" with stacks of cash; they are required to hold on to their money until a dancer finishes her performance. Just one of those handfuls would cover my overdue cell phone bill.

I glance around the club, surprised that it's not complete chaos. The ladies must be keeping the drama contained to their lounge downstairs. It looks like an average Thursday night. I recognize a lot of the regulars. There's a couple of rowdy bachelor parties crowded around the stage, and the finance bros are scattered between the tables and the bar. There's also a small group of American Ballet Theatre dancers who come to see Ariel perform, but they rarely stick around long after her set, and they drink only tonic water and Diet Coke. They remind me of a herd of deer—all graceful, but so skittery and high-strung. They barely tip her, but Ariel loves their attention.

Everything looks normal, but for some reason, the vibe feels off. I can't put my finger on it. Something in the air feels different. I blame Becky. I wonder if she used to ruin everyone's night at KFC too.

I notice that Mr. Cavalcante isn't in his favorite booth. His spot is filled with guys I haven't seen before, each clad in brightly colored tracksuits. Must be an intramural soccer team or something. A lot of guys come after league sports, celebrating a victory or commiserating over a defeat. The five of them are huddled in conversation, barely acknowledging the stage. Normally no one can take his—or her—eyes off Sofia. Straight women come to the club now because our dancers are just that fun to watch. People want to mimic their moves on stripper poles that they've installed in their suburban basements. *How do they explain the pole to their kids?* I wonder.

I pass Ariel on my way to the bar. "Hey, where's Carina? I want to tell her Mr. Cavalcante is here."

Ariel shrugs. "Dunno. I just came up for some pretzels." She grabs a bowl of them.

"You know those are full of gluten, right?"

"I feel like that's not true," she replies.

I start to say, "Actually—" and then realize it's not worth it. "Hey, who are those guys in Cavalcante's spot?"

"Some rando Russkies," Ariel answers.

"How do you know they're Russian?" I ask.

"I recognized some of the words they were saying. Three semesters of Russian lit. *Dasvidaniya!*" Then she gives me a peace sign and sashays off. Fall semester cannot come soon enough, I swear. Can't wait until she's driving her first-year-law professors crazy instead of me.

I spot Carina in the corner, nursing a green juice. She looks like she's had a rough shift, and it's not even 9:00 p.m.

"You okay, Carina? Are you too shaken up to talk to Mr. Cavalcante?" I ask.

"Mr. Cavalcante told me to piss off."

"*What?* He's always so polite." Granted, no one who comes in here is exactly Mr. Rogers, but Mr. Cavalcante's one of our nicest customers. I knew the vibe was off tonight. Bad energy.

"Fine, he didn't use those exact words. Instead, he said I would probably be happier going home early. Basically, he told me to piss off."

"But he really loves you."

Carina furrows her brow. "I know, right? Last week, he showed me a video of his grandson, and then we talked about the safest car seats. He gave me an extra hundo for my advice. He's normally so sweet. I don't know how I offended him, but I feel awful."

I give her a side hug, and a finance bro shouts, "No touching the dancers." Then he fist-bumps everyone at his table. Full disclosure: some days I do kind of hate my job. I really need that GED; I can't stay here forever.

I tell Carina, "I'm sure it's not you. He must be having an off night; don't take it personally."

"I hope so. I mean, I don't hope so; I just don't want him to be mad at me."

"I'm sure he isn't." I look around for a problem to solve. That always makes things better. I glance over at the Russian men again. Maybe if we make Mr. Cavalcante happy, I can turn Carina's mood around. He's so old, his hips and knees probably ache from standing. Sometimes mine do, and I'm only a quarter of his age. I've got to make this right. "Do you think we should ask those guys in his booth to move so that—" I begin.

The first crack and resulting flash happen so quickly that I assume a bachelor party guest or clueless out-of-towner set off a firecracker. My ears are already ringing.

I glance back toward the door—I'm sure Marty will barrel in any second.

There's another crack, followed by a half dozen more pops and flashes, and suddenly people start running and screaming and knocking over tables. My first thought is to protect the elderly Mr. Cavalcante. I want to get him and his fragile bones out of the chaos so he doesn't fall. I fight my way upstream through panicked patrons to get to him.

That's when I notice that the kindly, affable, safety-conscious senior citizen Mr. Cavalcante is holding a smoking Glock. He aims and fires one more time, directly into the booth of Russian men.

Chapter Six

~~GINA MARIE FERRAGAMO~~ JANELLE SMITH

Two weeks before sorority rush

~~Gina's~~ Janelle's Daily Do-~~List~~

- *Watch orientation videos*
- *Pack*
- *Memorize new identity details*

I don't know how to feel.

On the one hand, I'm excited. On the other, I could vomit at any second. I'm sure there's a big word for these conflicting emotions, and I'm sure Ariel would know it.

I wish there was a guidebook or a checklist for starting a new life, organized in neatly tabbed sections so I could refer to it when I'm lost or confused. Instead, I'm taking a leap of faith. All because I insisted on doing the right thing.

I'm the only person who offered testimony against Mr. Cavalcante. There were at least a hundred patrons and employees in the club, yet I'm the only one who said they saw him shoot. Even the surviving Russians claimed they couldn't identify the attacker.

Because I was willing to go on the record, I'm the single person who got yanked out of her life. I guess I can't blame anyone else for their sudden "memory loss" about the shooting—they have families and plans and ties to New Jersey. I didn't even have that cat I kept talking about adopting.

The deal was, I would be set up with new identification, including a passport (a passport!), and moved to another part of the country. While I won't have twenty-four-hour protection anymore—except for when I go back to testify or have a pretrial appearance—I've been assured that I won't need it. My first handler told me that no Witness Security Program participant has ever been harmed or killed under the active protection of the US Marshals Service.

But if I'm here on my own, does that qualify as *active* protection? Has anyone ever been harmed while in *passive* protection? I should have asked, but I was afraid of the answer, and it wouldn't have changed my decision anyway.

The marshals promised again and again that, provided I have no contact with anyone from my old life, I'm safe as can be. They did warn me to avoid social media, but I never liked it much anyway. Social media is for showcasing your best life, and what were my accomplishments? No diploma, perpetually broke, driving a shitty car, and living in a run-down studio apartment in a rough section of town. I could never even afford to decorate the place like I wanted, even with the DIY tricks I learned on TikTok. At some point, I abandoned posting anything about my life, save for shots of a nice sunset or a particularly appetizing bowl of pasta.

On Instagram, I usually end up comparing myself to Gina Ferrigno, and then I feel bad. Gina was my best friend for more than a decade, and the only girl I still talk to from high school. Growing up, she referred to me as her "name twin." Everyone got us confused—practically the same name, the same classes, and we lived in the same neighborhood. We even looked alike, with our dark curly hair, almond-shaped eyes, and thick lashes. To keep us straight, the nuns called us Gina One and Gina Two, even though we were both A students. I always felt bad about being Gina Two, like I was the sequel that wasn't quite as good as the original, the perpetual second choice.

I'm relieved I don't have to see Gina One's life on Instagram. After Saint Peter's, she attended Tufts on a scholarship. Now she's working as a sales manager for a big pharmaceutical company in Philly. She went to Mexico for vacation last year, as well as Miami, Los Angeles, and Hawaii. She was always nice to me, so I'm happy for her. I felt so guilty resenting what she's accomplished. But how did two people with practically the same name and circumstances end up in such different places? Gina One might be one of the few to miss me now that my Instagram account is inactive. I'm glad I can't log in and check in case she isn't.

My father probably doesn't even realize I'm no longer around. It's ironic that for once, I'm the person who just disappears for no reason. *Will he miss me when he notices?*

Sometimes, when my dad was briefly going through one of his good spells, I could see what must have attracted my mother to him. Anthony Ferragamo, better known to his associates as Little Tony— he's the kind of guy who has associates, not friends—is a natural-born charmer. My mom used to say he could talk the stripes off a zebra, and I think it's why she always let him come back. When he was on an up cycle, he was full of life and plans. He could make a trip to the grocery store seem like a party. He'd fill our cart with the items I loved but my mom could never afford, like sheet cakes covered with iced roses and colorful birthday sprinkles, and thick, marbled rib eye steaks. As we shopped, he'd explain exactly how he'd grill them out back on our little charcoal hibachi, rubbing them with olive oil, and coating them with coarse salt and ground pepper, before finishing them off in a skillet with crushed garlic, fresh rosemary, and melted butter. He'd promise to make sure mine wasn't too pink inside, because seeing the juice ooze out always made me feel like it was bleeding.

We'd roll through the store, and he'd flirt with all the elderly sample ladies, convincing them to give us extra portions of whatever they were offering, whether it was smoked cheese or small squares of pizza with each pepperoni curved into a crisp little cup. He'd quiz the butcher on his very best cuts of meat and solicit his favorite recipes. More often than not, when the cashier rang us up, he'd whip out his billfold, and there wouldn't be a penny. He'd seem shocked and tell the cashier we had to run to an ATM. But we'd never even attempt to go to the bank; we'd just get in the car and drive home, and then his mood would be dark for days. But I joined him every single time, thinking, *Today will be different.*

I haven't had a real chance to think about him until now. After the extensive processing in Chicago, a couple of marshals drove me down to this small Indiana city in the middle of the state, surrounded by what I'm told are soybean fields. They wanted to stay with me until the handoff, but I figured I may as well get started being on my own. Now I'm about to meet my case manager. He's my point of contact and my first line of defense.

I choose an outdoor table close to the front door and sit with my back to the wall to maintain a clear line of sight. Everyone's assured me of my safety, reminding me that I'll be one thousand miles away from the scene of the crime, but I'm cautious for obvious reasons. I position my suitcases to the side, so that they won't block a hasty exit. I mean, there hasn't been a single incident for most of the month, but how can I not constantly be vigilant?

While I'm waiting, I decide to watch that video again, just to familiarize myself with my new home. The YouTube video opens on a grassy quad, surrounded by old brick buildings that look like castles. A perky cheerleader back-handsprings into the shot.

"Hiiiii!" says the cute coed with the long black ponytail adorned with an enormous bow. Her deep tan contrasts with her pale blue eyes, as light as a Siberian husky's. She's so chipper and happy with all that glossy hair. For a second, she reminds me of Sofia, and I'm struck with a wave of homesickness so strong it makes my knees weak.

"I'm Addie Ashford, and I'd personally like to welcome you to Eli Whitney University!"

I still can't figure out why an East Coast transplant to the South would start a university so far north and west. I would ask someone, but I don't want to sound ignorant.

"We're the Midwest's premier provider of higher education. Founded in 1821, Whitney is a land-grant research university with some of the top-ranked engineering, computer science, and law programs in the world! Goooo, Cotton Pickers!"

Oh gosh, that can't be right. I squint at the screen and rewind a couple of seconds. *"Goooo, Cotton Pickers!"*

How did I not notice this before? That is an *incredibly problematic* team name.

"There are petitions to change it."

The sound of the barista's voice startles me, although everything startles me lately. While I was still out east, I worked on my PTSD with a therapist and victim advocate. I'm getting better, but it's still a lot, and I'm not good with sudden movements or loud noises.

"I'm sorry?" I respond.

A striking hipster girl wearing an Eli's House of Beans apron stands in front of my table, holding a small order pad, a pencil tucked neatly behind her ear. She has long blond dreadlocks and a funky nose ring, and everything about her radiates coolness, like she's been places and seen things, and all of it bores her now.

The barista gestures toward my phone. "The name. The Cotton Pickers? Are you kidding me? That's not a microaggression; it's a macroaggression, and it's mortifying. Everyone wants it gone, except a few key alums. I guess their votes count more than everyone else's. They're all *blah blah blah tradition*. The university did at least change the mascot to a mechanical cotton gin about thirty years ago. The, um, *character* they used to trot out during football games was just . . . wow. Like, jaw-dropping, call-the-Southern-Poverty-Law-Center-to-report-a-hate-crime wow. Anyway, the name is gross, and what do you want to order? My champurrado is outstanding."

What in the word salad did she just say to me?

Why do I suddenly feel like Alice when she stepped through the looking glass? I have a nervous smile at the best of times, and right now, I must look like a game show host or a weatherman. "I guess it depends on what that is."

"A champurrado is a hot drink from Mexico. There's thickened masa harina in it." She says this like I have a clue as to what that is. While she waits for my response, she deadheads some of the white floral bushes that border the patio. She aggressively snaps off every bloom that's past its prime, and I keep myself from wincing each time.

"It's probably a little too warm out for that. What else can you recommend?"

"You feeling adventurous?"

Considering I'm starting a new life under a new name after witnessing a mob hit, I lean to the affirmative. "Um, yes?"

"Ooh, how about a Tibetan yak butter tea?"

Is this a joke? Are the marshals putting me through an exercise to see if I'll break? "Does that come with . . . actual yak butter in it?" I ask.

"Of course. And salt."

Should I have taken my chances and stayed in New Jersey? At least we had real coffee there. "Do you have an iced Americano, maybe with some sugar-free vanilla syrup?" I ask.

Judging from her expression, this was the wrong request. "Well, yeah, obviously, but are you sure? Coffee's so basic. I could make you something far more interesting. How do you feel about a Calabrian chili sipping chocolate?"

"I'd say, interested sometime in the future? I'm sorry; is it okay if I just stick with the Americano?"

She shrugs, and I feel like I just failed my first test. "It's your call. Coming right up."

"Thank you so much."

I take in my surroundings—it sure is nice here. The air feels extra fresh; there's not even a trace of pollution, and nothing looks dirty. Flowers are growing everywhere, and the flat, wide lawns are dotted with towering oak trees. This downtown area has lots of little shops for browsing, and cute, casual restaurants. I'm young enough to fit in here. If this is where I'm supposed to try to blend in, I'm thrilled to try to do so.

The flight to Chicago was surreal. Once I got over being on an airplane for the first time, I just stared out the window. I didn't realize how green the rest of the country was. I guess there's a whole world outside the tristate area. I'll miss living close to the ocean, but when was the last time I went down the shore, anyway? Ten years? I definitely haven't been there since my mom got sick.

When I was little, my mom would wake me up early for surprise trips to the beach on the rare days she wasn't working one of her two jobs. The sun would just be rising, and we'd load up the rickety car because we wanted to beat the heat and the traffic. I'd put on a bathing suit while my mom packed a cooler with sandwiches, fruit, and a thermos of cold lemonade. (To this day, there's something magical about crunching on a few grains of sand mixed with a PBJ, and washing it down with a Dixie cup of Country Time Pink Lemonade.) Our toes would be in the sand by eight thirty.

We'd swim in the bracing water until our lips turned blue, body-surfing on every wave we caught. Then we'd warm up on our blanket and do it all over again once we'd thawed out.

At dusk, wave-swept and sunburned (we both had her family's Irish coloring), we'd stroll along the boardwalk and look at the souvenir shops. On the way home, I always wanted to listen to Top 40. My mom was a great singer, and she'd get so wrapped up in performing, sometimes we'd miss our exit.

My dad came once when he was on a winning streak, and he brought a pocketful of quarters. I won enough tickets at the arcade for a giant green stuffed bear that I named Lucky. A stranger on the boardwalk took our picture, Mom, Dad, Lucky, and me, and she told us what a beautiful family we were. How could she know it was the first—and last—time we were all there together?

I'm lost in nostalgia when I notice a middle-aged man with a neatly trimmed, albeit bushy, mustache approaching the coffee shop. He reminds me of that Ron Swanson character from that old sitcom. I wonder if that's my new handler? He looks like the kind of guy who'd be as adept at hunting his own dinner as cooking it. Pretty much the opposite of anyone who ever came into the Omega.

The man approaches me, and from a respectful distance, he says, "Janelle Smith, I presume?"

I feel disappointed that he isn't going to be my point of contact. "What? No, I'm sorry," I reply. "I'm G—"

He interrupts me. "Janelle. You're Janelle."

Okay, second test failed. Not only did I forget my new alias, but I almost used my real name! I am going to get myself killed if I'm not more careful. "Oh Jesus Christ," I say, and then catch myself and touch my crucifix. "Please, sit, Marshal O'Brien. Nice to meet you."

He folds his large frame into the chair across from me. "Not Marshal O'Brien. Remember, I'm Pat O'Brien, your uncle. I want calling me this to become second nature to you. When you think about me, think of me as Uncle Pat." The crinkles around his eyes radiate kindness.

I extend my hand; then I second-guess this decision too. "Should I hug you? I wouldn't shake your hand if you're my uncle, right? Am I already doing all this wrong?"

I feel myself spinning out. *Damn, Gina, I mean, Janelle.*

Fortunately, um . . . *Uncle Pat* is calm and serene. "Relax. You're safe. This is going to get easier, I promise." He's so sincere that I can't help but believe him. I unclench, just a little.

The barista returns with my iced Americano and a small bowl of sugar cubes and sweeteners, plus a white ceramic pitcher of cream shaped like a cow. "My gosh, this is so cute!" I exclaim.

"Please don't steal it," she says. I suspect customer service is not her forte.

"I won't," I promise.

She turns to Uncle Pat. "What do you want?"

"Lower cholesterol and a thirty-two-inch waist," he replies.

She rolls her eyes. "Dad jokes. Fun. What would you like to *drink*? I recommend the coconut milk macchiato."

He raises a bushy eyebrow. "Drip coffee. Black. Large. Please."

She sighs, disgruntled at our bland caffeine taste. "Fine. Lemme start a fresh pot." She goes back inside, letting the door slam shut behind her, and I jump again.

"I have great news for you, Janelle."

"I could use some good news."

"This isn't something we normally do, but we found you a job. Most of the people I deal with are low-level criminals or, forgive me, general dirtbags, so I don't go around recommending them. Your reputation and positive attitude opened a door here. So I talked to an old classmate from the academy. She helped me place you into something that's right up your alley."

"Oh my gosh, thank you so much! I was worried about the job search part. I know there's a small stipend, but I figured, if I was lucky, I could get work as a waitress or a barista." I glance inside and see our current barista slamming the pot onto the burner. She does not seem like a happy camper. Maybe her dreadlocks itch. "Probably not here, though. I figured my options would be limited because of my education, or lack thereof. So, please, tell me. What am I doing?"

I feel almost giddy. I love the idea of starting somewhere new, getting everything organized, trying to build a well-oiled machine. I've had a lot of downtime in protective custody, so I've read a ton more business books and feel ready for a new challenge.

He grins behind his mustache. "How does housemother at Gamma Kappa Gamma sound?"

I instantly deflate. "Another gentlemen's club."

He looks confused. "What? No. Gamma's a Greek house, a sorority at the university. The job is as sorority housemother. All the members live there. You'd help run the place."

"I can't! I have no idea what that is or how to do it!" I wouldn't even know where to begin! And, ugh, what if they were an entire house full of women like Ariel?

"Yes, you do, Janelle. You've done this exact job for years. And from what I understand, you were very good at it." His reassurance is like the Neosporin the girls applied to their knees when they got a little too aggressive onstage. Healing.

"You'll coordinate meals, manage the staff, and oversee the facility. You're going to manage everything and help keep the girls out of trouble, just like you did at the club. Plus, you'll have your own suite of rooms in the house, which means you're done living in hotels and studio apartments."

Hope bubbles up in my chest. "That . . . doesn't sound impossible."

"Exactly. Again, we don't normally deal with placement, but everyone who met you loves you, and we wanted to set you up for maximum success. You are a hero, and we appreciate your service to our justice system. You're helping us get a terrible man off the streets."

It sounds amazing, but what's the downside? Good things like this rarely happen to me. Nothing comes without effort, and never without a back-end penalty. Remember, I'm Gina Two, not Gina One. "Wait, is it going to matter that I didn't graduate high school?"

"Wrong. Gina didn't have a diploma. But you, Janelle Smith, the new Gamma housemom, you have a bachelor's degree."

A bachelor's degree! Me! I'm excited until I realize it's a fabrication.

"Would I be allowed to take a class or two while I'm here?" I ask. I don't want to press my luck, but I've been dying to take an actual business class. I'd imagined myself as a project manager, writing up action plans, and then coordinating with stakeholders to get the job done. With my stipend, and a salary, I could probably finally afford to invest in myself.

"I don't see why not. You'll set your own schedule at the sorority house, and you'll earn more than enough to pay for it."

The barista returns and clatters Uncle Pat's coffee in front of him. A few drops spill out, and she quickly wipes them with the terry cloth bar towel she keeps tucked in the back of her apron. "Large drip," she says, already walking away.

"Not sure if she meant me or the coffee," he says. He raises his mug in a toast. "To Janelle Smith, in her new life at Whitney."

I'm so overcome by it all, I say the first thing that comes to my head. "Goooo, Cotton Pickers!" We clink our glasses and both take sips. It's bad luck to do otherwise.

He shakes his head as he sets down his mug. "Wow, they really do need to change that name."

Chapter Seven

HAYDEN

Two weeks before sorority rush

Is there anything better than the smell of coffee?

The aroma of a fresh brew is just so full of promise and possibility. Coffee smells like progress and plans, like a step in the right direction. Everyone who walks into my shop does that quick pause in the doorway, where that first whiff hits them with an empowering blast of dopamine, a liquid security blanket to cling to as they navigate their day. I take a deep breath, inhaling the undertones of chocolate and tobacco and leather.

Granted, after a busy shift, particularly at the end of the semester when everyone flocks to Eli's House of Beans to cram for finals and we're practically serving it by the gallon, I'm eager to go home and scrub the espresso off me. Some days we work so frenetically, I find coffee grounds in my hair and underwear. Fortunately, they're a natural exfoliator. My skin has never looked better.

The downside is that with unlimited access to my favorite drug, it's stopped feeling special. My favorite part of my gap year was trying coffee all over the world. One of the strangest varietals I tasted was the kopi luwak coffee in Indonesia. Asian palm civets (they're in the cat family) eat the coffee cherries, and something in their digestive systems breaks them down. I didn't care to think of the "harvesting" system postconsumption, but I couldn't not try it. Not a fan. The monkey spit coffee (which works exactly how you'd think) I had in Taiwan was much better, with a sweet, complex finish.

The problem was, I drank so much coffee, I got burned out. I still like the smell, but the taste bores me. I'm chasing the high I used to get from a fresh French press, so I've started experimenting with alternative hot beverages. My Earl Grey misto—basically a latte made with tea—is something special. I increase the complexity by blending the leaves with a lavender-and-bergamot infusion.

Summer school is over, but the fall semester hasn't started yet, so it's extra peaceful in the shop. I love days like this where I can set everything back in order, especially after the a.m. rush. In the early-afternoon lull, I've polished the delicately veined marble countertops. They gleam under the low-slung glow of the domed lighting. I also swept the vintage black-and-white tiled floor and got those few cobwebs out of the corners of the old pressed-tin ceiling. This is one of the oldest buildings on campus. I've completely restocked the refrigerated pastry display with more product and fresh white doilies, and it looks so enticing. Our lemon squares are bright and glossy, with a perfectly buttery shortbread crust. The blueberry muffins are bursting with ripe, tangy berries and a crumbly rock-sugar-and-streusel topping. The golden-brown chive-and-bacon scones are aligned in a row, just waiting for someone seeking a savory bite. Everything a treat for the eye and the palate.

I take pride in this place. It's been a real home to me over the past year.

I've had only a couple of customers since the lunch hour, and one of them wanted drip coffee. I mean, give me a challenge. I don't do well with downtime.

Later in the month, the mornings will be pandemonium when all the PNMs—potential new sorority members—come through here, loading their gigantic Stanley tumblers full of iced coffee before heading to recruitment parties. They'll scuttle in, wearing Lilly Pulitzer in loud, lurid prints, their wrists weighted down with chunky David Yurman and sleek Cartier Love bracelets, carrying handbags that come with a comma in their price tags. Their long, center-parted hair will have subtle highlights, and they'll have fully contoured makeup, despite the summer heat. Everything about them drips with privilege. Yet they'll splay their gel-manicured hands palm up to make sure they get their quarter's worth of change back instead of putting it in my tip jar.

I can't stand them even though, not long ago, I was one of them.

The glass door opens, and a shaggy golden retriever of a frat boy ambles up to the counter. He peers up at our menu board, which I've lettered in colorful chalk. Professor Oxnard, the owner, hates the pretension of calling sizes other than what they are, so we offer Small, Medium, Large, and Bucket.

"Gimme a caramel Frappuccino," he says. "Make it a Venti, brah."

I grit my teeth; I get this all the time. "We're not a Starbucks, *brah*, and we don't have the Frappuccino or a Venti size." Then I remember the "coaching session" LaVonne gave me about trying to be more personable. Her exact words: "How about we dial down the sarcasm, bitch?"

I probably need to make more of an effort to be friendly, because I do love the shop. Yet I can't help relating to that quote from the old movie *Clerks*: "This job would be great if it wasn't for the customers."

With LaVonne in mind, I arrange my face in a smile and say, "I can make you an *affogato al caffe*, which is so much better."

He cocks his head. "Say what now?"

"The literal translation from Italian is *drowned in coffee*. We take a scoop of vanilla gelato and pour hot espresso over it," I explain. The affogato is traditionally served as a dessert; it's just the right amount of sweet and caffeinated. Italian coffee bars often pair it with a biscotto or piece of honeycomb. It was my favorite when I was in Rome.

Especially when I learned that cappuccinos are considered a breakfast drink and the Italians will scorn you if you order one after 11:00 a.m. I had affogati every day I was there. They were the perfect way to cap off a meal. The way the dense, strong espresso melted into the creamy gelato was something to write home about. If I were one to write home.

Ball Cap smirks at me. "So, coffee and ice cream. Which is a Frappuccino."

I start to argue, then I realize it's not worth it. "Sure."

"Make it a Venti."

I arrange his affogato in our largest sized paper cup, not even asking him if he wants it to stay. I hate the waste created by the disposable cups—but I'm not interested in having him hang out. He seems chatty.

He points to my small silver filigree septum ring. "That thing hurt?"

See? Chatty.

I explain, "Not unless you yank on it." I got it caught in a sweater this winter. There was screaming.

He snakes his meaty paw toward my face, and I slap his hand away. "That was not an invitation."

He shrugs, in no way chastened. "Sorry, brah." He pays, leaving me a generous seventeen-cent tip, but then lingers at the counter. "You look familiar. Is your name Callie?"

I was afraid this would happen, and I've already worked out my plan. Denial, with a side of gaslighting. "Nope," I reply, and point to my name tag.

"Hay-den," he says, like he's sounding it out. Then he sizes up my tits and gives them a nod of approval. Hooray for me.

I can't help myself; the sarcasm seeps out before I can stop it. I quote that campy old Hooked on Phonics commercial that resurfaced on TikTok. "Austin, you're a reader! You're a reader, Austin, you did it!"

Sorry, LaVonne. I swear I tried to be nice.

"Yeah!" he says, smiling, completely immune to any insult. Oh, to possess the confidence of a mediocre white man. He makes his way to the exit and then looks back over his shoulder. "Catch you later, Hayden." The bell on the door dings behind him as it shuts.

"Can't wait," I say to the closed door.

I turn around to restock the mugs and hear the bell tinkle again. "Forget something, brah?"

"Fudgie, darling, why would I have forgotten my bra?"

No. It can't be.

That distinctive, clipped accent, pitched somewhere between the Philadelphia Main Line and Katharine Hepburn's manufactured Mid-Atlantic dialect when she wanted to sound worldly; it's one of a kind. I slowly turn around, hoping with everything in my being that I'm mistaken. But no. It's the elegant, effortlessly blonde Grace Kelly clone in a tweed Chanel suit. My mother.

Here.

In my coffee shop.

Calling me by my childhood nickname *Fudgie*, which was her passive-aggressive way of pointing out how I used to be a fat kid.

Had the Dalai Lama himself walked in, I'd be less shocked, largely because my chai protein smoothie is spectacular. My long-lost stutter returns, something I thought I'd fixed after years of thrice-weekly sessions with my private grade school's speech pathologist.

"Wh . . . wh," I sputter.

Damn it, Hayden, focus; slow down; take a breath. Enunciate. I clear my throat. "Mother . . . why are you here?"

My mother leans in across the counter, and for a second, I think she's going to hug me, so I dodge her just in case. We Barclays are not touchy people. The first time one of my ex-sorority sisters wrapped me up in an unexpected squeeze, I practically shoved her off me. But I don't think my mom is trying to embrace me—she's just taking a closer look at my face.

She replies, "Oh, darling, the real question is *Why do you have a bull ring in your nose?*"

I haven't seen either of my parents since after I got back from my gap year and told them I needed space. My dad was upset. He tried to rationalize with me, tried to win me over with all my favorite things, but I wasn't having it. How could I not be mad? He hooked up with Smythe when he visited in Paris!

How gross was it for him to want to cheat and with someone *my* age? Certainly Smythe is responsible for her own actions, but there's a real imbalance of power when an older guy swoops in and does a Prince Charming all over a much younger woman, so I've long since blocked her number, but I don't wish colon cancer on her or anything.

Last year, my mother said that if I needed space, I should take space. Then I got mad at her for not even trying to find out why I *wanted* space. I probably should have reached out to her after my dad absconded, but I was waiting for her to need me.

I compose myself. "I repeat, why are you here?"

My mother shrugs. "There's a law against visiting my daughter at college?"

"Law? No. Lack of precedent? Emphatic yes. Four years of under-grad and one of grad school, two and a half hours away from your primary residence, and yet you've never come down here. Not one Homecoming, not one Parents' Weekend, not even my graduation."

I mean, she sent her handyman to help me move in as a freshman. Yes, I needed someone to build a loft bed, but still. My mother was not exactly what you'd call "engaged."

"Did you *want* me to come?" she asks, confused. "You never invited me, Fudge. In fact, you always insisted I not come."

"Okay, fair enough," I admit. That does sound like me. "But why are you here now?"

"Oh, darling, I'm here because I love you."

I can't help it; I laugh. It's not that I don't love my mother or don't believe she loves me, at least in her capacity of loving anyone other than herself. I've come to accept her limitations. It's more that we don't share any common goals or interests.

Still, what if she's changed? What if her circumstances have made her introspective for the first time in her life? I haven't reached out to her, so what if I'm at fault too? What if over the past few months, she's realized the only wealth that truly matters is the people who care about you?

My mother slides onto one of the barstools that I suddenly wish had been placed at a less welcoming angle. "Not sure why you find my love for you amusing, but that's fine. Anyway, I need a loan, lovey. I spent all my liquidity on attorneys."

So, *no* on the newfound introspection. I'm not surprised, but my disappointment is a surprise. Then I realize what she just said.

"You're saying you have no money?" I confirm.

"Just this." She opens her Chanel jumbo quilted flap bag and shows me a couple of wrapped bank stacks of bills. She's easily sitting on $30,000; that's hardly destitute.

"Wait, you hid cash from the Feds?" CeCe Bondurant Barclay may not have been the best mother, but I've never known her to be dishonest. My father, on the other hand . . .

"No, no, not intentionally. I found these in an old woven beach bag that the FBI left. They took almost all my good bags. I was devastated! This cash must have been from a trip to the Hotel du Cap, back when they wouldn't take credit cards. They were cash-only for years. What a nightmare that was when we'd go to Cannes!"

I picture her expansive walk-in accessory closet in the wing off the master bedroom, just a sea of ostrich skin and calf leather and palladium hardware, with muted lighting and shelving made from polished African blackwood. That she left stacks of bills in a bag that cost as much as a year's tuition because she was too lazy to empty it—that seems completely on brand.

"Anyhoo, the government didn't seize *your* assets, so I need a favor. A small loan. I'd like you to tap into your trust fund." She assesses my body language, my arms crossed over my chest, and adds, "Pretty please."

I feel like I need something to do with my hands, so I begin polishing the already pristine marble. I take big, aggressive swipes.

"For a minute, I almost thought you came because of how hard everything with Dad has been on me. Like you found some way to be maternal for once," I say.

Such is her delusion, she legitimately looks hurt. "Fudgie, darling, that's not fair. I've always been maternal."

I rub the marble so hard I'm afraid I might wear it clean away, or possibly dislocate a shoulder in the process. "Seriously? Do you remember that summer when I was ten and I got a cramp while I was swimming?"

"You were the cutest little meatball back then, all about those Goldfish crackers. Chomp, chomp, chomp, all day long. You were like a Pepperidge Farm mako shark." She stops to appraise me again. "Oh, but you must be so relieved that you finally grew out of your puppy fat. Really, how lovely you've become."

She doesn't have to add, *"If your hair weren't ratted and your face weren't pierced,"* because I can practically hear her thoughts. She really must be trying to pour on the charm by holding this back.

I get a fresh bar towel and head over to polish the giant espresso maker. I am not going to let her disarm me, like she always does. If I remain in motion, maybe her zings won't penetrate. Can't hit a moving target. I say, "You were out with Mr. Geary, talking about having him prune the boxwoods into the shape of swans."

She taps a finger to her lip. "No, it was owls. We were having an outdoor fundraiser, so I wanted them shaped like the short-eared owls we were trying to save. They were cute little buggers, too, with round faces and round bodies—hey, not unlike you in that old swimsuit." I scrub harder at the chrome. "Darling, I tease. The thing about those owls is they don't have those unsightly pointed ears. They're endangered, you know. Hence the boxwoods!"

She makes a ta-dah gesture, like she's just worked out a complicated problem. I can feel a flush of anger radiating out from my core.

I say, "You know what else was endangered? *Me.* I was flailing and choking, and do you remember what you said?"

My mother opens a compact and checks her lipstick, just as cool as can be. "Is that how you recall it?"

My blood pressure begins to spike. "You said—and this is a direct quote—'*Shh, Mummy is speaking.*' I was drowning too loudly for you."

She wrinkles her brow, as though deep in thought. "That was the old pool, right? Before we remodeled and put in the new saltwater infinity one closer to the lake?"

"Yes," I seethe. "The location of the pool was the point of this story."

"Was it?"

"No! I'm saying our arborist had to dive in to pull me out. Do you have anything to say about this, any reaction?"

After she blots her naturally perfect ski-slope nose, the one copied by so many women on the North Shore, she snaps her compact shut and takes my chin in her icy hand. She gives it a squeeze. "Oh, you precious girl, you were so *buoyant* back then. You'd have been fine. Anyway, back to the matter of your trust."

The front door jingles, and another frat bro enters. He pauses when he sees me. He says, "Whoa, you're Callie, the girl from the—"

I stop him before he can finish. This is the last thing I need my mother to hear. "We don't have Frappuccinos," I bark.

"Bummer," he says, and exits.

"I suspect your cotillion coach owes me a refund, Fudgie," she says. "Those etiquette lessons did not stick."

Damn it, why is she so unflappable? Feels like all I do is flap. She presses on. "Anyway, trust fund. I don't need a lot, just enough to set myself up with a little pied-à-terre."

"Why don't you go to your ski place in Aspen?"

"Seized."

"The West Palm Beach condo?"

"Seized."

"Santa Barbara? Gold Coast? Door County?"

"Seized, seized, seized."

"New York?"

"It's being renovated."

"Wait, are you seriously redecorating an apartment during all of this?"

She laughs again, flashing that infamous grin that's been on the cover of every society magazine, from *Forest & Bluff* to *Town & Country*. "No, darling. A little joke. How do you not find me funny? The Gramercy Park property's been seized too. I've been staying with my second cousin Marcy in the suburbs, but . . . you know."

"What did you do?"

Mom flits her wrists. "Oh, who can say?"

I bet Marcy could say a lot. I make a mental note to text her.

"About that trust . . . ," she says, amping up her smile. How does one person have so many visible teeth? It's like she has extra molars or something.

I explain, "I'm sorry; there's nothing I can do. Grandpa's attorneys were really clear about that." I know, because I tried to tap into it myself last year. "They told me no disbursements until I'm thirty-five, no exceptions. The rules around the trust are ironclad."

Everyone used to be afraid of my dad's father, Charles, but I was his only grandchild, and we were close, especially after Nana died. Even though he was as rich as could be, he drove a Ford F-150, and he used to take me to Costco for treats. He couldn't believe their prices and variety. "You can buy socks and snow tires in the same place!" He was one of their earliest investors.

Both of my grandfathers were admirers of the self-made (like themselves), and they were always extolling the virtues of hard work. (Not sure how that trait skipped a generation.) I don't really remember my mother's father, though. He died when I was just a toddler.

Mom's parents wanted her to use her degree and establish her own career first, and instead she married my father, so they only left her a portion of their estate. The bulk went to charity. I imagine she spent all that money on herself years ago. Because that's what spoiled, emotionally stunted people do.

"Oh . . . oh, no." My mother's giant smile fades. She begins to pick at the fringe on the cuff of her tweed jacket, something she does on the rare occasion that she's nervous, like that one time at Sotheby's when someone outbid her for a Sisley landscape. "Darling, if you don't have access to your trust, then how do you pay your bills?" She seems genuinely curious. And how would she know?

Before I asked for space, Dad handled the money, and I've barely spoken with her since then. Truthfully, becoming self-sufficient isn't as easy as I thought it would be. Like, *choices were made*. Instead, I gesture toward my apron, and she looks me up and down, confused.

"I don't follow. Is it your breasts? Do you pay your bills with your breasts?" she says, and I gasp so hard, I choke on my own spit. She flutters her hands in the vicinity of my back, as though that might help me. I have to grab a cup and take a swig of water before I can catch my breath.

I say, "No, Mother, I'm saying I have a *job*. I suggest you find one, too, if you want to, you know, live indoors." I slap my glass down on the counter, feeling the full weight of twenty-three years of my family's benign neglect. I'm surprised the glass doesn't shatter on impact. She remains unruffled, and this makes me irrationally angry. "FYI, I resent being your last resort. If you're here, then you're desperate."

My mother's eyes start to water, and that's when I notice the fine lines that have formed since I saw her last year. She's aged in twelve months. I've spent so much time resenting both my parents, especially after my father's recent antics, that it hadn't occurred to me that my mother might be hurting too.

What if she's not actually bulletproof?

My voice softens. "I know Dad screwed you over too. He screwed everyone. He's a jackass." She pulls an embroidered linen handkerchief out of her quilted bag and folds it into a triangle—a cryangle?—and blots the corners of her eyes.

"How much did you even know?" I ask.

"None of it."

"You really weren't complicit?"

"You know, your father was not a perfect man. He was never going to be perfect, and I willingly let some things slide for the sake of appearances. Everyone in our circle does. Your father and I had a nice life, all things considered."

I roll my eyes. "Everything you did was based on appearances."

"Not entirely. Hayden, please understand. My foundation did good work. I was helping needy people, and it made me feel like I had a purpose, that I was building the kind of legacy that might have made my father proud. That's why I used what my parents left me to start it."

"Wait, *what*?"

She put that money toward her charity? To help . . . someone other than herself? I always assumed she started the foundation so she'd have an excuse to write off the parties she threw. An unending opportunity to exclude whomever she wanted to shun in the moment. That she was actually serious about giving back? I don't know how to process this information. I feel like I've been acting on faulty premises for I don't know how long.

Is this how people reacted when they found out Bruce Wayne was really Batman?

"The foundation started with ten million dollars of my money, mine, free and clear. That's what's particularly awful about all this. Your dad wouldn't admit he'd failed; he never said anything to me. I could have forgiven him that. But he stole from my charity and disappeared. He left me with nothing. Not even my dignity. He decimated Homeless, Not Homely. It's simply unacceptable." She blots at her eyes again. I blink hard, trying to steel myself against the charming plague that is my mother, but I can feel myself getting sucked in.

"I'm in such a bind until we find your father or until my attorney convinces the court to unfreeze my portion of the accounts. I simply don't know what to do, and Marcy was not a long-term solution. So, yes, I guess I am desperate, but you were never my last resort, Hayden."

I notice her black S-Class Mercedes parked in front of the outdoor patio.

"Looks like they let you keep your car. Maybe you need to sell the Mercedes."

Her lip begins to tremble. Argh. No. Don't do that. Please. Yell at me. Berate me. Insult me. Treat me like a recalcitrant member of your staff. But I'm totally unprepared for her vulnerability, I can't deal with it. "Oh, Fudge, that car is the only piece of my old life I have left." She looks at me with the same kind of wounded doe eyes she used on her friends to write checks to save earless owls.

My resolve begins to evaporate, a dose of self-loathing taking its place. Dr. Beekman's going to have a field day with this. My mom's hands are bony now. Her fingers look so delicate without the armor of diamonds and her trademark Panthère ring. My resolve cracks.

"I gu- I gu-" Damn it, there's that stutter again. It's probably my subconscious trying to stop me from doing something stupid. "I guess you could stay with me for a bit." As soon as I make the offer, a slow grin spreads across my mother's tasteful, filler-enhanced lips, and her eyes light up like the sunrise over French Polynesia. She pats at my forearm in an awkward attempt at affection. I've played into her hands—again. How could I forget that my mother is an emotional chess master? I wonder if anything she said was genuine. Were those crocodile tears, just another way to manipulate me?

"Outstanding!"

We smile at each other, a tentative peace. Maybe we really will start over. Maybe I should stop overthinking everything. "So, darling, where is it that you live? Who can help me with my bags? And what are we going to do about that nose ring of yours?"

Checkmate.

I desperately need a drink, but we don't have a liquor license yet. So I pull myself a steaming hot espresso and gulp it down in one shot. It burns my mouth and throat. It's not booze, but it will have to do for now.

Because CeCe Bondurant Barclay is back in my life.

Chapter Eight

CeCe

Two weeks before sorority rush

"Well, this is grim."

"You know you just said that out loud, right?" Hayden replies. She's sweating and panting as she shoulders the final piece of my luggage inside her squalid abode. I can't apologize for being so underwhelmed at this brick box located over a Thai restaurant. (On the plus side, it does smell appetizing.)

"If you'd only allowed us to buy you that lovely condominium here years ago, we could have avoided all of this," I say. Chip had called a broker and had the property all lined up after she received her university acceptance letter. Nothing extravagant, just a three-bedroom with a private elevator. One of the many condos that developers built to cater to Whitney U's high-net-worth families. Judging from all the Maseratis (Maserati?) and Range Rovers I saw as we were driving around the campus, there are even more wealthy students now than the last time I was here.

Instead of being grateful for our largesse, our girl pitched a fit. She insisted on living in the dormitory and then a sorority house, sharing a room and bathroom stall with a bunch of random women from Podunk locales like Akron and Arkansas. I didn't get it—what's the point of being privileged if you don't enjoy all the privileges? Hayden really did become more difficult once she hit her teens. Hormones and all. When she was a little girl, she was the sweetest thing in the world. Her countenance was just so sugary and delicious that we called her Fudge.

"No, we could have avoided all this if Dad didn't steal and then disappear," she replies.

"Potato, po-tah-to."

"Besides, I like it here. I can afford it, and I'm close to everything I need," she insists. True, this loft is conveniently situated a block down from that place where she wears an apron and makes coffee for strangers. By choice. Can you imagine? Fudge suggested I keep my parking space and we just walk here, with my baggage. I insisted we could do better. Ironically, we had to park even farther away, but how could I know that would happen?

"Why didn't you put all this stuff in storage?" she quizzes me as she neatly stacks my bags by size against the wall, just like she used to with those brightly colored Playskool blocks she loved. I never saw a child who enjoyed sorting and organizing as much as she did. Even as a toddler, my Fudgie was a little adult.

"I did, darling. I stored almost everything I was allowed to keep. You'd be so dismayed if you saw how much they seized, or rather, civil forfeited. These are just my essentials."

Fudge kicks the largest trunk. "What essential items are inside this monster?"

My vintage Vuitton trunk took up most of the back seat, and I had to drive the whole way from Marcy's with the top down. I did not find the trip pleasant. So much wind on the expressway! I had to repin my chignon in the parking lot. "It's surprisingly light, isn't it? The frame is made with wood dried for four years—that's what gives it strength without adding a lot of excess weight."

"Yeah, it was a real pleasure to lug up three flights of stairs," she responds.

"See? It worked out," I say.

I peer inside the loft, which is sunnier than I'd prefer. Who wants to see every laugh line, each bit of creped skin under my neck? Certainly not me. What she needs is a fine set of custom drapes; no one looks good in this much daylight. Maybe a vibrant silk print, lined, gathered, and draped at the top, trimmed with a pom fringe, buffered with some chiffon sheers, like I had in the dressing room of the Aspen house. Or was it Door County?

"Seriously, what's in there? Is it our old photo albums? Wouldn't mind taking a look at those, actually. I'd like to see shots of my grandparents again," she says. Fudge bends over and starts monkeying with the brass locking mechanism.

I make my way around her home. Fudgie's a bit of a minimalist. I examine her few knickknacks, none of which I recognize. Most of them have an international flavor. Ethnic, or perhaps they just feel ethnic, what with the fenugreek fumes emanating from the first floor. She did seem to change after that backpacking business postgraduation. Yet is it *really* considered backpacking if you occasionally check into a Four Seasons for a warm shower and a hot stone massage?

When Fudgie declared she was done taking our money, it was only *after* we'd spent almost twelve months paying her American Express bill as she flitted from country to country. Chip explained that she was feeling a burst of independence, and it would pass if we gave her space, so we did.

The artwork she's hung is sparse and disappointingly modern. Did she learn nothing from my impressionist collection? One entire wall is taken up by computers and screens and other bits of electronics I couldn't possibly identify. I didn't realize she was so techy. Is she a nerd? I start to ask, and then stop myself. I suspect nerds don't know they're nerds, a lot like how Talitha Johnsburg, my old neighbor, didn't realize that her twenty-five-year-old face but seventy-five-year-old hands weren't fooling anyone. If you're going to invest in that much plastic surgery, it's imperative one address everything, and not just what's above the collarbone. Her face belied her body's portrait of Dorian Gray.

I explain, "Oh no. All that memorabilia nonsense is in storage. This trunk contains my tack."

Fudgie's mouth gapes. It's not her best look. "Your *tack*?"

"Yes, darling, don't you know what tack is? It's the usual—saddle, stirrups, bridle, assorted gear. All the equestrian works. I thought someone taught you to ride? No, wait," I say, snapping my fingers as the memory returns. "You did take lessons. But I recall Praetoria bit you once and that was it; no more stables for you. You had quite the set of lungs back then. Oh, the screaming! To be fair, you were the one who tried to give him a nonorganic apple, so you can hardly blame him."

Fudge blots the sweat from her face and expels her breath through pursed lips. She sounds like Praetoria, my old dressage horse, himself.

"I know what tack is, *Mother*. What I don't know is why you consider it essential when the government *took all your horses to sell at auction*."

I don't care for that tone. Shrill. She doesn't get that my sainted mother had that saddle made for me not long before she passed, and I'll not let it out of my sight. "Darling, all that coffee you drank at your little shop is making you testy."

"Yeah, it's the coffee," she huffs. I wonder if she has her menses. Best not to ask.

"Anyhoo, where's my room? Please tell me there's an ensuite." I try to open a door over by all her computers, but Fudge slams it shut before I can peek inside.

"This is a one-room loft." She points to a platform connected to a ladder. "It's open concept."

"Open to what concept? Poverty?" Oh, it feels good to laugh again.

Hayden tells me, "That's my bed." Then she gestures up at a wooden platform above her technology wall. "And there is yours." She turns toward a lumpy, unstructured something over by her kitchen table with its mismatched chairs. Is that a dog bed?

"Do you have a wolfhound?"

"That's a futon. It folds out flat."

I don't know how to digest this information, so I opt to ask a question with a simple answer. "Where may I powder my nose?"

"The bathroom is on the other side of that partition, through the closet," she says, so I go in to inspect the facilities. Surprise! The bathroom is equally depressing. One sink! Did we lose a war or something? Even the apartments we'd set up for my charity's recipients had dual vanities.

"Darling, there's no bathtub, only a stand-up shower."

"I'm aware."

I poke around a bit more. I open the medicine cabinet and find a stick of natural deodorant. Yes, that would explain all the sweating, but I feel like this is not a welcome observation. "There's no bidet either."

"Yes, you'll have to wipe your butt with Charmin, just like the rest of America."

I pop my head out of the bathroom. "Darling Fudge, I did not raise you to be so crass."

She mutters something under her breath about me not raising her at all, and it occurs to me I might be pressing my luck. Marcy took the same tone when she suggested I'd be more comfortable staying elsewhere. At least her guest bathroom had a Jacuzzi and Bliss spa products.

Perhaps this temporary lodging situation would work better if I tried to have a more upbeat attitude. I should show her that I'm flexible, that I can go with the flow. I am *of the people*. After all, I went to a rodeo once in Jackson Hole, although that was an accident because I thought it was a pop-up of Rodeo Drive stores. Oh, did Chip and I laugh when I came back to our suite in that cowperson hat.

How can I convince Hayden we're on the same team? Show my gratitude? I need to keep her from going the way of Cousin Marcy. Prove to her that together, we can get through all this and come out stronger on the other side.

I tell Fudge, "It's no problem, darling. Staying here will be like camping, only . . . indoors."

Chapter Nine

JANELLE

One week before sorority rush

Janelle's Daily Do-List

- *Meet with every member of house staff*
- *Memorize policies/procedures*
- *Create a profile on every sister so I can get to know their likes and dislikes*
- *Talk to florist about display for entry hall*
- *Pinch self—this can't be real!*

"Dean Grace, thanks so much for checking in on me! I really appreciate your taking the time to get me settled in."

If everyone on campus is as nice as Dean Grace, the faculty advisor for the Greek system, then I'm just going to love it here. She's gone out of her way to help me get my bearings, and she insists I call on her if I need anything. Even though I've only been here a week, she's been great about stopping by and monitoring what I'm doing, which feels so helpful. And today, she even brought a friend!

Dean Grace just oozes authority in her plain, no-nonsense business suit and low heels, even when she's not saying a word. I can't believe that someone like her has been so kind to me, and I'm really grateful.

"Small favor to ask, Janelle. Mr. Wu is interested in seeing what the inside of a sorority house is like. Would you mind if I gave him a little tour?" She says this more as a statement than a request. I think that's how really competent people sound.

Mr. Wu, an Asian man with impeccable posture and a fancy suit, holds out his hand, and I give it a firm shake. He smiles, so that must have been the right call.

"Of course! And you're going to be so impressed!" I say, stepping aside so they can enter. "Is your daughter considering Whitney?"

A fleeting look passes between Mr. Wu and Dean Grace, before he finally says, "Yes."

Oh, I know that kind of pause. I didn't last as long as I did at the Omega by not understanding discretion, so I don't ask any more questions. Instead, I excuse myself, saying, "Then I'll leave you to your tour. I'll be in the kitchen with Chef Montez if you need me."

As I walk away, I hear Dean Grace tell Mr. Wu about the house's architectural significance. "The home accommodates up to one hundred women, if they're sharing rooms, and there are approximately forty separate spaces if they'd prefer singles . . ."

When Uncle Pat and I pulled up last week, I couldn't believe that homes like this exist outside of that *Million Dollar Listing* show with all those guys named Josh on it. This place is like what would happen if a mansion and a five-star hotel had a baby. It's all so beautiful, with its giant gathering spaces and crazy amenities. Like, they could absolutely film *The Bachelor* here.

The alumnae remodeled this house a few years ago, and it has every luxury. The Omega girls would die if they saw the massive gym in this basement, with a whole row of Pelotons and Pilates reformers. They could take classes together! There's a beautiful teak sundeck on the roof with lounge chairs and outdoor showers so the sisters can rinse off if they get too hot while lying out. The bathroom has a bunch of mirrored makeup tables with great lighting, like the Omega's dressing room. I bet it's chaotic fun in there when all the ladies are getting ready at the same time. I guess a lot of successful businesswomen were once sisters here, over the years, and they give back by donating to make this place extra nice.

I pass through the two-story dining hall with its tall paned windows that overlook Greek Row, and through the swinging kitchen doors. Chef Montez is washing the last large roasting pan. "Let me help, Chef Montez!" I insist.

"First of all, you have to call me Joellen. And I have nothing for you to help me with," she says, wiping her hands on her apron. "I'm all done. We're so far ahead of the game already. We've got meals planned for the next month and the supply order placed. Everything has been managed. You're really very good at this, Janelle, and we're lucky to have you."

Her praise makes me feel a little light-headed.

Chef Joellen continues. "The kitchen's spotless, and I even did some deep cleaning. In the service fridge, we have a grazing board and other appetizers ready to set out when the officers begin to arrive today." She looks around and shrugs in disbelief. "We're all set. I'm going to go put my feet up. These dogs are barking."

"So what do you think I should do now?" I ask. I've finished everything on my checklist and more, but I want to be useful.

"Take a nap?" she suggests. "You've earned it."

"But I'm not tired." And for the first time in forever, I'm actually not. My little suite at the back of the house is so quiet and peaceful that each night I fall asleep minutes after I say my prayers. The nightmares have mostly stopped, thankfully, and now I'm sleeping so deeply, I don't dream at all.

Maybe that's because my life now feels like a dream.

I check in with the other department heads and find Dean Grace and Mr. Wu with Tereza, the head of housekeeping, peppering her with inquiries about how she sanitizes the bathrooms. It's a weird line of questioning, and I don't want to consider whatever of Mr. Wu's kinks this speaks to.

Behind her back, Tereza makes an obscene gesture for me to see, and I stifle a laugh. Tereza reminds me of Des; she doesn't suffer fools gladly. It's nice to feel like there's a little piece of home here with me.

As no one needs me and none of the girls have arrived yet, I find myself with nothing to do. I'm too pumped to take Chef Joellen's nap suggestion, but Jerome, our handyman, suggests I go do something fun, because it's going to get really busy really soon and I should make the most of this downtime.

So I put it on my list, and now . . . I'm off to have fun!

Even though I'm not totally sure what that looks like.

Chapter Ten

CᴇCᴇ

One week before sorority rush

I don't hate Hayden's little coffee shop. In fact, I find it charming, like a place one might visit in Gstaad. I've been spending a fair amount of time here figuring out what's next for me. I suspect Hayden welcomes my company, although I'm sure it would go against her new hipster persona to admit it. Perhaps that's why she's making me pay for my own drinks.

It's interesting to see her scurrying around with a sense of purpose, how she bustles to and fro behind the counter. And whatever it is she does with the Earl Grey, I heartily approve.

I notice the remote on the counter and flip the television over to CNN. Wolf Blitzer is talking about a grand jury in New Jersey that has indicted some Mafia kingpin. So dull. Yet what a relief that the news cycle has moved past us! Hayden takes the remote out of my hands.

"The TV is supposed to stay on soccer," she tells me, changing the channel. "That's basically the owner's only rule."

"Soccer? I see I've raised my daughter to be a communist."

"Raised? You've never raised anything but a martini glass."

In the past week, I've discovered that it's easiest to ignore or sidestep her little jabs, rather than directly counter them. "Darling, that's simply not true. I've raised plenty of glasses of champagne too."

"And Aperol spritzes," she adds. I swear I see the hint of a smile as she says this. "Have you checked your email?"

"For what?" I reply.

"For something from your attorney. Will you have an update soon? It's been a week. A very long week."

I scan the email I received earlier. "Carolyn says her investigator has a lead on your father's whereabouts, so that sounds promising. She's worried that unfreezing my assets could take a while without him here to stand trial. She told me that I should find work for now."

"Exactly what I suggested last week." Hayden sets a stack of newspapers in front of me. "Do me a favor and check out the classified job listings."

I perch my reading glasses on the end of my nose. "I guess it couldn't hurt. Do you think many places are hiring art historians?"

"You won't know until you start looking." She yanks a pencil from where it was lodged behind her ear and hands it to me. "Go nuts."

I open the paper and fold it in quarters so I don't get any newsprint on my sleeves. I don't really want to read the whole thing, so I scan for key words. Ooh, this one could be promising. "Darling, what is *Denny's*? Is it an auction house, like Christie's or Sotheby's?"

"Not even remotely." Too bad. I cross it out, and I keep reading.

"Fudgie budgie, how many words would you say I type per minute?"

"Zero." Yes, that sounds about right. So probably not this listing. I cross it out too.

The bell at the door tinkles as a customer enters. Hayden steps away to greet some young woman. They exchange words and a few bills, and then Hayden starts banging around on the giant espresso machine. It chugs and hisses and spits steam as she works it. How she mastered this so adeptly when she never could figure out all the features on the sauna in our Gold Coast townhome eludes me.

The customer takes a seat a few stools from me and gives me a big friendly grin. I nod and quickly turn back to the newspaper to avoid a conversation; I don't trust people who go around smiling for no reason. It's disquieting. A smile is your currency. That's also why one doesn't go flashing around wads of cash for no reason; it's unseemly. A chief stew on a yacht once mentioned that smiling is for lunatics and Labradors. She wasn't wrong.

Okay, *help wanted, help wanted.* Who wants my help? I scan the listings again. I wonder if maybe I'm approaching this job-search thing wrong. Perhaps I should assess my abilities first. I've never actually held a paid position, so I'm not entirely sure of my professional skills.

What are my talents? I grab a paper napkin—so much more convenient than linen!—and write *CeCe's Strengths* at the top. I underline it twice for good measure.

Let's see. Number one, I'm quite adept at buying things—my taste is exquisite. That's not an opinion; it's a documented fact, as per *Architectural Digest.*

I supervised staffs in seven (or was it eight? who can recall?) homes concurrently, making sure each domicile was up to snuff should we choose to come stay. I managed every part of the process from meals to staffing to décor. That means I can multitask. I draw a star next to this entry. I feel like this is an important strength. It makes me come across as a real *can-do* kind of gal.

Two skills don't seem like enough, though. What else can a can-do gal do? Oh, I've got it! Number three is my ability to communicate. I'm practically trilingual. I spoke French with Grand-mère growing up, and then I spent that semester in Spain in college. I never had any trouble communicating with my gardeners, which is why my apricot-colored Juliet roses on the Lake Forest property were always so lush and fragrant, redolent of fresh peaches. If I recall, Gustavo said something about *Costoso* when I asked him to plant them, and he did the fingers-rubbing-together thing to emphasize their price. But, really, if they came from that warehouse store in Mettawa that my father-in-law loved, how much could they be?

Obviously, I was a great fundraiser, so perhaps there's something there. I could talk almost anyone into anything, like that time I convinced Bono to perform at my friend's climate change gala. Lovely man, darling accent. It was all *Soonday* this and *Soonday* that. He developed a bit of an attitude once he found out it was a benefit for climate change denial, but my friends from Exxon and I had a good laugh about the misunderstanding once he stormed off.

I count the entries on my napkin. Four skills seem like plenty. I run across something that could be interesting. "Darling, how about accounting? How would you rate my accounting skills?"

She looks up from her task—dumping hot espresso shots into a small pail full of ice. "Dad stole fifty million dollars right out from under your foundation."

"So . . . not ideal, but not out of the question? Shall I circle the entry anyway in case I need to come back to it?"

The young woman next to me beams again, as though she's just waiting for me to invite her into our private conversation. I stir in my seat, uncomfortable. No one should be that happy.

Hayden glowers at me. "I'm not even going to justify that with an answer."

I scan a bit more. "Would I be right for a work-from-home position?"

Through clenched teeth, Hayden responds, "I need you to be in my apartment less often, not more often." Okay, twist my arm to not have to spend time in that brick pizza oven with its locked mystery closets and lack of an ensuite. Then I run across something that looks legitimately up my alley.

"Fudge, listen to this."

She glances over at me and shakes her head. "Let me stop you right there. No, you can't drive a long-haul eighteen-wheeler. You had trouble managing an SUV."

"Shh, Mummy is reading. Ahem. *'Sorority housemother needed ASAP. Manage operations. Oversee staff of cooks, gardeners, and housekeepers. Position includes luxury accommodations.'* Why, it sounds tailor-made for me. It's perfect."

The woman next to me shifts closer, so I shift farther away.

"It's the opposite of perfect," Hayden says. She's so negative sometimes. She gets that from her father.

"Why?"

"Because 'mother' is right in the name, and let's face it, that's not your strong suit."

"Debatable. Yet I'm outstanding at managing a household staff, so you can see my dilemma."

Hayden sets the pail on the counter with a bang. So much banging with this one! "Bucket of iced Americano with a sugar-free vanilla pump for Janelle."

The woman next to me smiles but doesn't take the oversized cup, which looks more appropriate for building sandcastles than drinking coffee. She just beams at me, blinking her anime eyes. Hayden and I exchange a glance. Besides her, we're the only women in the shop. See? What did I tell you about the smiling?

After a beat, the woman laughs sheepishly, grabbing the giant beverage. "Of course, that's me. Because I'm Janelle. Who else would I be? Anyway, I'm so sorry, I wasn't paying attention to my name because I was eavesdropping. I just started working as a housemom up on Greek Row."

Now *this* is of interest to me. "What are the odds!" I exclaim. "Would I like the job?"

She gushes, "Well, I love it so much! All the other housemoms are so nice and helpful, and my apartment in the house is just a dream. We get together every day after breakfast for a walk, and on Wednesday nights, we have a book club—with wine!"

"Do you talk about the book, or is more about the wine?"

"The first one was just about the wine."

"Do go on."

"I can't wait till the students come back so I can meet all the girls. If you're seriously interested, I can introduce you to the dean who oversees the sororities. I've been working with her all week, and she's just the best. The Alpha house is in a huge bind because their housemom had a stroke a few days ago and fall recruitment is coming up. They've got to get someone, like, today."

I hold out my hand so that we can shake. "I have no idea what any of that means, but I'm CeCe Barclay. It's a pleasure to meet you."

She gives me a nervous smile, only this time it annoys me less. "And I am . . . Janelle. Janelle Fer—Smith. Do you want to grab a table and chat a bit?"

"That would be delightful, thank you, Janelle Fersmith. I would love an introduction. And I shall bring my skills résumé." She seems sincerely interested in helping me, which is more than I can say for almost everyone else I know. I guess I'm a bit thrown off because her East Coast accent doesn't quite gel with her Midwest nice attitude. Is she from here or not? There's probably a story, but I don't really care to get into it, so I don't say anything. My policy is to not ask questions when you don't want answers. I decide to take the chance that her friendliness is sincere and not indicative of her being disassociated from reality. I scoop my napkin up off the bar and tuck it in my bag. To Hayden, I say, "I'm going to sit at a table to discuss a possible *job*. How nice is it for Janelle Fersmith here to extend her services to me!"

"Sorry, it's just Smith," she says.

"Of course, Janelle Justsmith, you're just so kind. Honestly, Fudge, I don't understand how you always say other women are the worst."

"No!" she barks. "I don't! *You* say that. *You* have problems with other women, not me."

I quickly flash to when I possibly could have complained about other women, except for that time at Neiman's when a shopper tried to buy a limited-edition bag before I saw it in her hands and decided I deserved it more, or when I took the chairman position away from Delilah Carmichael because I didn't like her shoes. But those were isolated incidents.

I shrug. "That doesn't sound like me."

As we head to a spot by the window, a young man enters and approaches the counter. He says to Hayden, "Hey, you're—"

Before he can even finish his sentence, she snaps, "No, okay? I'm not. You don't freaking know me, so stop acting like it!"

His whole face falls and he stammers, "Sorry, I just thought you were Hayden from my Applied Sociological Theory class."

Then they both glance down at her name tag; it's awkward.

As we settle into our seats, I tell Janelle, "I really feel like her cotillion coach owes me a refund."

Chapter Eleven

JANELLE

One week before sorority rush

Janelle's Daily Do-List

- *Buy a book on Greek life*
- *Tweak house budget*
- *Help CeCe get hired!*

"Hello . . ." I look at the nameplate and address the person aggressively chewing gum behind it. "Hello, *Kaylee*. Would it be possible to get a few minutes of time on Dean Grace's schedule? I'm Janelle Smith." She's been insisting I stop by if I ever needed anything, so I'm taking her at her word. "I'm hoping to introduce her to my friend here. She's another potential housemom."

CeCe gives Kaylee the kind of flat-handed, wrist-turning wave that you'd see Kate Middleton offer adoring crowds from her balcony. We headed right over after talking at Eli's, largely at her daughter's insistence.

I step back to survey my surroundings. I was so intent on getting CeCe here that I'm just now taking it all in. The interior is exactly what I imagined academia might look like, only with fewer wizards, thank you, *Harry Potter and the Sorcerer's Stone*.

The administration building is inside one of the Gothic limestone castles on campus, and the inside looks like something out of *Downton Abbey*, with high ceilings and walls decorated in polished dark wood. The massive windows are stained glass, and the light shining through them showers the old rug with glowing spots of color. A stone fireplace takes up part of one wall; it gapes, almost big enough to walk into it. There's a golden framed portrait of Eli Whitney hanging over it. (Given his comb-over in the painting, I'll bet his painter was not a fan.) Built-in bookcases span another whole wall, filled with leather bindings and old silver trophies. Federal, state, and university flags greet me from their brass stands.

This office may be one of the most beautiful places I've ever seen. I would get married in this space if I could. I feel so proud to even be here. Of course, all things being equal, I'd rather not have witnessed a shooting, but so far, WITSEC has not been the horrible existence I feared.

The assistant to the dean of student affairs—Kaylee—looks around her workspace, an area filled with empty energy drink cans. They take away from the fairy-tale feeling of the surroundings. I hope she didn't consume all of those herself—her heart will stop! One night, Ariel was tired from studying, so she downed three of them before showtime, and I practically had to defibrillate her.

Cans clatter as Kaylee digs. Somehow during the process, she does an entire 360-degree turn in her swivel chair. "Lemme just figure out where I keep the log-in to the dean's schedule." She riffles through the dozens of Post-its she has stuck to her computer monitor. While I prefer paper, even I'm not Luddite enough (Ariel taught me that one!) to know that it's a terrible idea to leave your password written on a little flag stuck to the thing it protects. She finds the password Post-it, and CeCe raises a groomed eyebrow at me. It is seriously perfect, with the arch in just the right place and not a hair out of order. I imagine she paid someone a lot of money to get them to look so good.

How cool is CeCe? I mean like a cool customer, like nothing could faze her. She's just supersophisticated and chic. That girl in the coffee shop (Fudge? Fudgie?) is so lucky to have this elegant woman as her mom. I feel like the sorority would love someone so cosmopolitan, and I hope Dean Grace agrees.

Kaylee pumps her fist. "Yes! I got it! Here we go, Password1234, baby!" She inputs the characters and pulls up the dean's schedule.

"Aren't passwords meant to be kept private, darling?" CeCe asks.

"Pfft, like anyone would want to hack into the dean's schedule," Kaylee replies. "*'Ooh, let's break in and see her meetings,'* crime of the century, right?"

CeCe responds, "I concede the point."

Kaylee slaps at the keys. "Let's see. She's in there with Mr. Wu right now. It says here he's the director of—"

"Are we supposed to know these details?" I ask. She ignores my question. I feel quietly justified; I knew he wasn't a "father" so much as a "sugar daddy."

Kaylee continues. "The Shanghai Development something or other. Anyway, after she's done with him, she's got a little break until noon when she meets with the head of the International Student Coalition. Huh, that one's scheduled for a few hours, and she'll be out of the office. I wonder what they're doing. If it's lunch and I'm not invited, I'm gonna be salty."

"Have you been an assistant long, Kaylee?" I ask. I guess competent people are in short supply everywhere.

"Ever since my aunt hired me," Kaylee replies.

"Ah, nepotism," CeCe remarks. "Been there, done that, had the T-shirt seized."

I laugh and Kaylee responds, "I don't get it."

I don't entirely either, but I don't say anything.

The heavy door to the inner office swings open, and the dean strides out behind Mr. Wu. I take another look at his navy double-breasted suit. I know very little about men's clothing, but I do know expensive when I see it. The more seasoned dancers used to instruct the new girls how to spot a high roller. Des said you never push a private dance to the guy dripping in gold jewelry or wearing a Rolex. Half the time, it's fake, and the other half, that flashy decoration is all he has. Her advice was to target the guy in the Apple watch and Patagonia vest, because he's wealthy enough to not GAF about what anyone thinks of him. She'd say, "Money talks but wealth whispers." I wish I was allowed to keep in touch with her.

The dean's telling Mr. Wu, "To reiterate, one never knows what might happen over the course of a semester."

"Anderson & Sheppard," CeCe says, making a grand sweeping gesture at the man's suit.

"No," Kaylee says in a stage whisper. "Mr. Wu."

Mr. Wu appraises CeCe. "You are a woman of discerning taste."

CeCe nods. "I would recognize that English drape cut anywhere. My husband shopped Savile Row tailors exclusively. No, scratch that. Soon to be ex-husband."

I have no idea what either of them are saying, but this may be the most glamorous conversation I've ever heard.

"Perhaps I will see you around the campus," he tells CeCe, eyeing her respectfully.

CeCe holds out her hand, and Mr. Wu shakes it. "Perhaps you will."

Dean Grace steps in front of CeCe and does an exaggerated bow toward Mr. Wu. Okay, that seems problematic. I may not have finished high school, but I'm pretty sure it's awkward to bow to someone just because they're Asian. Then the dean says, "My point is, I'm sure we can work out something mutually beneficial."

"I am confident as well," he replies, his eyes not leaving CeCe until he exits.

"Hey, Auntie Karen," Kaylee says.

The dean flushes red. "Kaylee, we've discussed this."

"Oh, right, *Auntie Dean Grace*," she responds. She points to us. "These guys, like, want something?"

"Are you asking me or telling me?" Dean Grace says, looking annoyed.

"I don't know?" Kaylee replies.

I step in. "Dean Grace, hi, you said I should—"

She gives me a tight smile. "Come to me if you're struggling? Are you over your head already, dear?"

Why would she have that impression? Everything was in great shape today! Unless I missed something? Instead of falling apart, I try to project confidence, like the author says to do in *Fake It Till You Make It.*

"No, quite the opposite! Actually, I'm hoping to help *you*," I reply. "I'd like to introduce you to my friend CeCe. I think she'd be perfect for the open housemom job at Alpha. This is CeCe Barclay. Would you maybe have a few minutes to speak with her at some point?"

The dean looks CeCe up and down, and CeCe just stands there, all confident, as though she knows the dean won't find her lacking. What would it be like to be so sure of yourself?

"Do you have a résumé, Ms. Barclay?"

"Better. I have a napkin," CeCe says, pulling the folded paper square out of her bag with a flourish.

The dean pauses for a moment, then tells me, "Thank you, Janelle." And to CeCe she says, "Step into my office, please. I have a few minutes."

I take the long way back through campus, admiring the architecture as I walk the winding path beneath old oak trees. Acorns are just beginning to drop, so the lawns are filled with squirrels stocking up for the winter. Obviously, we have squirrels in New Jersey, but my neighborhood was way more urban, with only a couple of scrubby bushes that every local mutt peed on, so I'm not used to much nature.

I am enchanted by this place. The staff was so welcoming on my first day. Chef Montez (I mean, Joellen) made me the sorority's official celebration cake, which was covered in sweet white chocolate frosting with a raspberry filling. Hector, one of the gardeners, gave me an armload of hydrangeas, and the pale green blooms were as big as dinner plates. He even showed me how to manage the water in the vase so they'd dry perfectly. Jerome built me a little shelf to keep my binders organized. And Tereza fusses over me like I'm a guest in a fancy hotel. I keep trying to tell everyone they work with me, not for me, yet they insist on treating me like a queen. It's overwhelming.

The house itself is a legit mansion, close to forty thousand square feet. Every hallway wall in the house is covered in "composites." They're giant framed pictures with the names and faces of each member, all of them in the same pose with a black drape and a string of pearls, a lot like the seniors' photos at Saint Peter's. There are composites dating back to the 1960s. It's fascinating to see how hairstyles and makeup have changed over the years and, in some cases, changed back. The hair in last year's composite is a throwback to the 1970s, long and straight with a center part, but thanks to makeup tutorials, all the girls now look like models. The women from the 1980s crack me up, with their tight perms and blue eyeshadow. They look more like middle-aged hospital administrators, like they should all be named Barbara.

I'm trying to come to terms with loving it here but hating the circumstances that made it possible. Uncle Pat says this is to be expected. I've been doing well so far, finally unclenching. I'm not looking over my shoulder nearly as much, and when a car backfired yesterday, I only screamed a little. The nightmares are far less frequent, and not nearly as graphic. Uncle Pat says that recovering from this kind of trauma isn't linear, and that it's totally normal if I have a bad day, or if I need to reach out. But so far, I'm just feeling grateful.

I stroll past the big fountain on the Whitney Memorial Mall. From what I'm told, students run through the fountain when the Cotton Pickers win a home football game. I hear something like fifty thousand alumni come to town on football weekends, and everyone throws tailgate parties on Archer Hill. They can be formal affairs. Some people bring huge grills and tents, and they even hang little chandeliers. At Homecoming, all the men dress up in blazers and bow ties, and the women wear sundresses when it's warm enough. It feels good to be hopeful and excited. I never expected a big do-over in my life, but I have one, and I should recognize it as a blessing. I give my crucifix a touch.

The other housemoms told me to enjoy the quiet over the next few days because it won't last. Move-in and recruitment are going to be as chaotic as it gets, but I'm not worried. The Omega prepared me well.

Being alone in the house with the rest of the team has given me the time to organize myself and figure out how to work with everyone. The support staff knows their jobs far better than I do, so it's more like I'll be helping coordinate all the moving parts, rather than telling them what to do. I mean, look at Joellen—she's been cooking for the sisters for twenty-seven years, longer than I've been alive. How could I possibly know how to make her work better? My task is to make sure she has the tools she needs to be successful, so the sisters can succeed too. It's funny exactly how much this place and the Omega overlap. Who knew?

The sisters are going to start trickling in today and tomorrow, with everyone arriving by Monday to prep for sorority recruitment, when a couple thousand freshman women will come through the house for a series of parties before classes start. I don't quite understand what the parties entail, whether there will be a lot of late nights or men or alcohol, but I'll find out soon enough.

Whitney has the largest Greek system outside of colleges in the South, and recruitment is a big deal. It's supposed to be like one solid week of blind dates, where everyone tries to determine if there might be a match. That must be exhausting, so I'll do my best to help keep everyone motivated and upbeat. If I can get the Omega through Fleet Week, I bet I can handle Gamma's rush.

While I haven't been here long, I'm getting the sense that I could maybe make a difference, especially if I'm able to help CeCe get that job. She didn't say much about her situation, but I read newspapers. I suspect it's been rougher than she lets on. I recognize false confidence when I see it.

I reach the base of the hill leading up to Greek Row, just north of campus and west of the football stadium. Wow, it is something! Every fraternity and sorority house is a gigantic mansion, like a governor or the president would live there. The lawns are manicured, and the houses rise three or four stories tall behind them, made of brick or stone, with wide porches and big white columns and huge double front doors. Each is beautifully lit at night, with spotlights shining on the Greek letters, so there's no mistake as to whose house it is. (Full disclosure: I'm still getting the Greek letters confused.) I wonder if this is what the neighborhoods in Beverly Hills look like.

As I approach the Gamma Kappa Gamma (or is it Kappa Gamma Kappa?) house, I see a fifty-something dad climbing the steps. He's trying to manage a stack of boxes, but he's staggering comically under the weight of them all. He's followed by a gorgeous girl with long black hair, toting a snowboard. "You know what you need, Addison? More shoes," says the dad-type guy with box after box labeled *Shoes*. She turns her head and laughs. It's the girl from the video! Whoa!

I rush over. "Let me get the door for you." I punch in the code and swing open the giant door that exposes the two-story entry. In the membership recruitment TikToks, the whole sorority crowds in the foyer to sing welcome songs to the potential new members. Some of them do hip-hop dances too. (They're cringeworthy, and Des would call it appropriation.)

Addie smiles and says, "Hi, I'm Addie. Who are you?" I already love her energy.

"Hi there. I'm Janelle Smith. I'm the new housemom and—"

Addie drops her snowboard and begins to squeal and jump up and down, and then she hugs me. Now we're both squealing and jumping up and down and *What is happening?*

Addie's enthusiasm is infectious. "Oh my God, I can't believe we finally have a young housemom! We begged and begged and begged national to not send us an old lady! I am loving this! Mom Hoogstratten was a million years old and she always smelled like ointment and she had a tiny dog that bit everyone on the ankle and I seriously thought we were going to find her dead in her suite one day and then what? No one wants to pledge the place that someone died in, right? So haunted! But you're young! Like, superyoung! We can't call you Mom Smith; you're too young and hot for that! Ahh, I'm so excited you're here! Yay!"

Her dad sets down the boxes and steps toward us. He's wearing sensible khaki shorts, sandals with socks, and a T-shirt that says *My Kid and My Money Go to Whitney.* I'm willing to wager there's a barbecue setup at this house he'd love to discuss. "Please be patient with Adds. She's shy. Her mother and I have been trying to bring her out of her shell."

"He thinks he's hilarious," Addie says, rolling her eyes and nudging him with her shoulder. He responds by nudging her back. They're perfectly in sync, and I push down a small pang of jealousy.

"Does your father embarrass you too, Janelle?" she asks.

I have a sudden flash to the last time he came to borrow money from me at the Omega. He was so drunk—or so something—and so belligerent that Marty had to pick him up and put him in a cab. My reply comes straight from my heart.

"All the time."

"You brought a crucifix? To college?" I am incredulous. "I thought I was super Catholic, but you might take the cake."

I've been wandering the third floor, getting to know the young women who arrived today. My ears hurt from all the shrieking.

Addie laughs as she hangs the cross behind the door of her room. The leadership gets their pick of the best accommodations, and she's in the sorority officers' wing. It's all one-person rooms up here, and they've got the nicest views and the most space; some of them even have (nonfunctional because of fire code) fireplaces. The newest recruits are packed on the second floor; sometimes as many as five of them share one room. Everything is based on seniority, again, sort of like the Omega. Addie says that when one of those pods of women gets their period, all hell breaks loose.

Addie points to the crucifix and says, "No, that would be my mom. She literally stood over me to make sure I packed this. She says that Jesus's watchful eye will keep me out of trouble. Like, please. This room is the only place I won't find trouble."

As we speak, she's slashing open boxes and taking out stacks of cashmere sweaters. They spill out a colorful rainbow all over her couch. No one has a bed in their space—they all sleep in a huge bunk-bed-filled room on the fourth floor called a cold-air dorm. Fire regulations require that the windows must be open at all times when there are so many people sleeping in one space, so they're never closed. In the winter, everyone cozies up under electric blankets and thick down comforters. Sleeping in the freezing cold sounds awful to me, but Addie says everybody grows to love it. I'm glad I have my own suite on the first floor, with windows that close and a big metal radiator.

I'm fascinated as she keeps pulling out sweaters in every color from baby pink to deep purple. I'm tempted to bury my face in them or pile them up like leaves and flop backward. I keep stroking them when she's not looking, and they're softer than kittens. She must have fifty in this pile alone.

"Why is that?" I ask.

"Wow, you are green. Did they not have sororities at your college?"

"They did not." In my fictional backstory, I went to a small commuter college out east, where I studied marriage and family science, which is a fancy term for home economics. I've been light on sharing details with the girls who arrived today, choosing to turn questions about me back around on them. Uncle Pat assured me that everyone would rather talk about themselves anyway, so no one's yet to call me out on being cagey.

She explains, "Our national charter says no boys upstairs and no alcohol whatsoever. Heck, we can't even bring up food from the dining room. We had a little mouse problem a few years ago. It was gross."

"Wait. You're not allowed to drink?" The movies were wrong?

"We totally drink, as long as we're not in the house. Like, we're not nuns. I'm chapter president, so I'll take it easy. It's up to me to set the standard. Plus, I have a boyfriend and he's a third-year law student, so I'm kinda over all the nonsense, you know?"

"That makes sense."

I try to play it cool and act like I've done all this before. But inside, I'm quietly relieved that my impression was wrong, especially because this place doesn't come with a Marty to escort troublemakers out the door. Sounds like we won't need a bouncer, and that is a blessing.

Addie tears open another box, this one brimming with cute little dresses from Hill House and LoveShackFancy, each with smocked bodices and ruffled sleeves in ditzy-looking floral prints and seersucker. One by one, she hangs them on narrow velvet hangers before placing them in her small closet. I have no idea how all her stuff is going to fit, especially with her snowboard taking up so much real estate.

Addie asks, "Don't you hate how Hollywood portrays sororities? It's always drunk chicks having pillow fights in lingerie and chopping up mountains of cocaine and leading live sheep into wild parties. Give me a break."

Honestly, until thirty seconds ago, that is *exactly* what I thought they were. "So no one ever has a party here, then?"

"God, no. We go to the frats for that. Fraternities don't have these standards, so shit happens there. We're so strict, we can't even contribute to the cost of the alcohol. If we did, we would lose our charter in a hot minute. I'm always like, 'Have TV writers ever even *seen* a college?'"

I'm pleasantly surprised that their national leadership cares that sorority houses are safe. After all that time at the Omega, I feel like keeping women protected is my mission in life.

She says, "I mean, it's a sisterhood, not a strip club, right?"

I don't say anything.

But for a minute, I wish I was allowed to enlighten her.

Chapter Twelve

HAYDEN

One week before sorority rush

My mother's recent arrival has me thinking about the past. Watching her flounder through life without Chip's (or her parents') purse strings feels a little too familiar. I almost failed disastrously at this living-on-my-own thing, too, so her delusion is all the more frustrating and maddeningly relatable. Bearing witness as she tries to navigate her new existence has me thinking about my own situation last year.

I was working my ass off at the coffee shop before classes started, but my credit card bills were growing, and my bank account hovered dangerously low every month. I was just waiting for the solution to appear. I knew it had to be coming. One night, I was cleaning up at the end of a hellish shift, and I was at a breaking point. "How hard is it to say 'yes' when I ask the customer, 'Do you want me to leave room for cream?'"

It was my turn to empty the café trash cans. They were so weighted down that I struggled to lift them because of all the discarded liquid. It felt like I was trying to wrestle a surly drunk into a cab at last call. As much as I loved the shop, I'd quickly discovered that the patrons and their proclivities left something to be desired.

"What does our clientele think happens to the coffee they dump in the trash can? That it magically disappears? That it's whisked away by elves and unicorns? Despite our asking if they need room for cream *precisely* so this doesn't happen?" There was even a covered drain next to the sugar station for patrons who wanted to pour a little coffee out to add milk, but apparently it was much easier just to splash in the trash.

"The quicker you accept that you're going to have to lift a heavy-ass bag full of cold coffee sludge every shift, the happier you're gonna be," LaVonne replied. She indicated toward the recalcitrant bag with her mod floral appliqué manicure. "Be careful. You don't want that to bust open."

That day, LaVonne's look paid tribute to all things Lilly Pulitzer. Sorority recruitment had started. Her eyeshadow evoked, as she described on her Instagram story, "tequila sunrise realness," starting pink at the bottom, then turning a brilliant melon at the crease, finished with a fluorescent lemony yellow on the brow bone, made dramatic with a dense black strip of lashes. Her hair was pulled up into space buns, affixed with two giant yellow silk hibiscus, and her edges were coaxed into small squiggles at her temples. She'd painted her lips Pepto Bismol pink, a shade that is unusually gorgeous with her skin tone. We'd been in the shop ten hours, and her look was still flawless. Meanwhile, I'd sweated off my mascara half an hour into our shift.

"Recovery is a process that requires understanding that then leads to acceptance."

"That's profound," I said.

"Got the idea from *Harry Potter and the Goblet of Fire*," she replied.

"Hey, tomorrow won't be as bad, right?" I asked. It had been recruitment chaos since we were the only coffee shop between the freshman dorms and Greek Row. Everyone needed to amp up on caffeine so they could show their best selves. At no point that day did we have fewer than twenty people in line, almost all PNMs (potential new members) because our regulars couldn't be bothered to wait. It was so busy, we had to call in part-timers Glen, Glenn with two *n*'s, and Cherise. LaVonne had warned me that Professor Oxnard, the owner who bought the shop specifically to fuel his own hot tea and soccer addiction, conspicuously avoided his café during recruitment week.

LaVonne also explained that during sorority rush, anyone with any sense went to the Starbucks across campus. For most of the morning, the line snaked out the door and down the street. "With all this business, we'll probably rake in a bunch of tips," I'd said.

LaVonne just laughed and replied, "You'll see."

Oh, did I see. I watched each of those clueless freshman PNMs slip every cent of their change back into bags that cost as much as my rent. I wished I could say I wasn't like that when I was on the other side of the counter, but who knows? I blanked out those memories. It's easier thinking about when I was overly generous with those who didn't deserve it than cheap with those who did.

"How many drinks would you estimate we made?" I rolled my shoulders to release some of the tension from pulling so many espresso shots, between the filling and tamping and dumping hundreds of times.

Making the perfect shot entails specific steps. Before I filled the portafilter (the handle piece with a fine mesh basket on the end), I had to properly grind the beans. LaVonne taught me that the result should look like granular sugar. If it's too fine, it will taste bitter; too coarse makes a sour, watery shot.

Next, I'd put the proper "dose" in the portafilter basket. I love how the word "dose" is used in the barista world, like it's a medical necessity (and for many in the morning, it is). This calls for precision, as the weight of the grounds will impact the shot's flavor. Ideally, the dose should weigh between fourteen and eighteen grams. LaVonne believes the machine's sweet spot is right at seventeen grams, so that's what I'd aim for. In the beginning, she made me put every dose on the scale until I was able to eyeball it correctly.

In training, each time I pulled an espresso wrong, I drank the shot myself. LaVonne had warned me about not overdoing it, but I didn't listen.

Overdoing it seems to be a pattern for me. When I was a kid, I was obsessed with Twix bars. I would dream about Twix bars, with their chewy caramel covering the shortbread cookie, wrapped in the milkiest of chocolate. Having two bars in one package was everything, because I'd gobble up the first, then take my time with the second. My mother was conscious of my weight (or "health" as she called it), so she didn't let me consume much sugar—a fact I was not so gently reminded of every time she called me Fudgie, probably because she really wanted to say "pudgy."

When I was finally old enough to walk to the convenience store, I had all the spending money I wanted. So, I was *literally* a kid in a candy store with a fistful of bills. One day, I bought and subsequently inhaled so many Twix bars that I made myself sick, seriously sick. I remember lying on the cold tile of my bathroom floor, just crying in misery because I'd screwed up my whole GI tract. I had to go to the emergency room for an IV drip to treat my dehydration. My mother had all these doctors working on me, trying to figure out the cause. I didn't want to tell anyone the truth because I thought I'd get in trouble.

I wasn't normally allowed to have food in my room, and my mother could sniff out contraband like a Belgian Malinois at a border crossing. So before I came home from the candy store, I unwrapped every bar and stacked them in my backpack like Lincoln Logs so there'd be no evidence of wrappers in my trash. The perfect crime, or so I thought. Everyone blamed my illness on food poisoning when it was really too-much-of-a-good-thing poisoning. I imagine some beleaguered lunch lady at my school got an earful. After it was all over, someone—I can't recall who—bought me a Twix for being such a brave little soldier at the hospital.

To this day, I can't eat chocolate bars. Of course, coffee suffered a similar fate.

The whole espresso-making process takes approximately twenty-seven seconds, which was enough time to ring up a customer and make their change, *which they then shoved back into their bags and*, argh.

LaVonne worked out the math, writing the numbers out on an imaginary blackboard. "How many? Lemme see. If we served an average of one person per minute times ten hours of being open, we must have served at least six hundred. Although we were hustling, so I'd say it was more like seven hundred."

"If each of them left a quarter, you and I would walk out with almost one hundred dollars each," I said, eyeing our twin tip jars, labeled *Sherlock* and *Moriarty*. Looked like neither literary figure had inspired much generosity that day, despite LaVonne's hopeful prediction that their rivalry would be fiercely debated. Our best day was when we labeled the jars *Kylie* and *Kendall*. People really wanted their votes to count, except for the adults who asked us if those were our names.

"I never knew what a difference one hundred dollars could make in my life until I had to earn it myself. My God, imagine if every person left a dollar in our jar!" I said. I bent over and grabbed my ankles, desperate to stretch out my back and hamstrings. "I'm not looking for an easy way out, but it feels like the physical labor I put in today should have produced more results. Everything hurts, from the soles of my feet to the knot of tension at the back of my neck. My hands? I swear they're already arthritic. We should be coming out of here with bags of money for the effort we put in. If it's like this for the rest of the week, it's going to kill me."

"Your first experience as the working poor is real cute," LaVonne replied, taking a peace-sign selfie that she titled *#workinggirl #morphe #longlastingcoverage* and posted to the gram before she began sorting our tips into two little piles. She pulled out one larger coin and held it up to the light. "Someone tipped us their AA coin. You got any use for a recovery chip?"

"I'm going home to dive into a bottle of red wine, so I'd say no."

She placed it in the hip patch pocket of her floral shift dress. "I'm keeping it. Someone worked hard for this, so it's good karma. Anyway, our tips are $44.76."

"Each?"

"Total."

"Ugh," I replied, continuing to wrestle the trash bag.

"It's easier if you tilt the can to an angle as you pull. Let it drop toward you. Use the side of the can for some leverage," LaVonne instructed.

I gathered up the ends of the plastic bag, holding them upright so nothing spilled out. Then I wedged it out, one inch at a time, lowering the angle of the can until it was almost horizontal as I finished the pull. The bag was basically a trash-filled water balloon.

"I got it!" I crowed, feeling victorious. "Finally, something in this terrible day has gone right. You know, I can't get over how entitled some of these girls acted. Like, I'd greet them with a 'Hi, how are you?' trying to be friendly, and they'd reply, 'Iced latte.' That is not the correct answer. *You* are not an iced latte. Also, the right response when I say, 'Thank you and come again' is not a blank stare. Is it too much to ask for a little courtesy? If you're rude to me, I'm going to have no choice but to be rude back. How do you not have a modicum of respect for the person who's about to touch your food? Is this what we have to look forward to all week?"

"Easy does it; you gotta take it one day at a time."

"Whose quote is that?" I asked.

"That AA chip."

"Okay, I'm going to haul this trash to the alley," I said, grabbing the bag so I could drag it to the dumpster in the back.

LaVonne said, "Handle it carefully. Sometimes these girls are hella lazy. They'll throw their forks away instead of putting them in the bus tub and—"

Before LaVonne could finish, something inside the bag—likely a fork—pierced the straining plastic. The whole scene happened in what felt like slow motion, with both of us screaming, "Nooooooo!" A biblical torrent of eco-friendly paper cups and wadded napkins and Splenda wrappers in a river of dark roast exploded out the punctured side and flowed over my feet, soaking my sneakers and spreading across the floor.

"I think I hate recruitment week," I said.

LaVonne grabbed the mop. "Same, girl, same."

After sopping up Lake Lavazza, LaVonne decided to join me inside my bottle of Cabernet. She posted a new selfie to Snapchat while I fished the keys from my pocket and started working the triple locks. "It's not much," I said, already embarrassed by the impression it might give. My apartment was smaller than any of my mother's closets.

I opened the door to my loft. It wasn't huge, but I liked the simplicity of it. The walls were brick, and the floor was weathered hardwood plank, original to the building. The ceilings were high, so I had extra floor space thanks to a built-in sleeping loft. The appliances were cute and retro looking in a fun powder blue.

Giant southern-facing windows filled one side, and there was glass block in the kitchen area on the east side, plus a skylight, so my plants thrived. The leasing agent said they usually got art students in here because the lighting was so perfect. There was a Thai place downstairs that created a delicious aroma. It's where I ordered most of my meals. (I was trying not to go overboard, but their Penang curry was an obsession.)

"Mind if I look around?" she asked.

"Be my guest," I said. "I'll pour the wine."

I headed to the kitchen to uncork the bottle, and LaVonne started to poke around the loft like an eager Realtor. She rapped on the brickwork with her knuckles. "Solid, not a façade. Nice. How high are these ceilings, would you say? Fifteen feet?"

"Probably?"

With a fingernail, she flicked the window that had a view of Whitney Memorial Mall and most of downtown. "Hmm. These triple-paned?"

"Maybe?"

"Do you hear any noise from the bars down the street?"

"No."

"Then yes."

She wandered over to the living room area where I had a small lounge set up.

"You have real art," she said, gesturing toward a couple of my framed pieces.

"I got those from artists in Montmartre."

"As one would."

She moved to the shelves that held other treasures from my travels, picking up a bronze samovar and touching the tap at the bottom. "What does this urn thing do? There's not a dead person in here, right?" she asked. She ran a fingertip over the engraving. "I'm guessing this did not come from World Market out by the Wabash Mall."

"That's an antique samovar. It's used to boil water and make tea. I picked it up from a souk in Turkey. Or was it Morocco? Definitely somewhere on the Med."

"Damn, those souks are popping up everywhere nowadays." She gingerly placed the samovar back on the shelf and picked up a framed photo of me on the beach in Capri. I'm sitting in a blue-and-white striped lounger, looking out at the water, and my hair is in a messy topknot. Smythe took this shot at the magic hour, and everything has a sheen of gold. My aviator shades reflect the sunset. I could practically smell the salt water looking at it. I loved this picture as it was a candid taken in simpler times. "You look good in photos. Kinda like a model. Way better than you do in real life."

"Thank you?" I'd be offended if anyone else said this, but the thing about LaVonne was that she told the truth.

"It's the hair. I think it's because you don't have that rat's nest on your head in this shot."

"It was taken before I started the dreadlocks."

"Mmm hmm. And that's why God puts erasers on pencils." She paused and looked at me. "You seem confused. What I'm saying is they were a mistake. Anyway, which way to the little girls' room?"

"Go through the walk-in closet. It's on the other side."

"I'll just go ahead and walk *in* your closet, then."

I set our glasses on the reclaimed-wood coffee table and then went back to grab the small cheese plate I put together—a mix of sheep's, goat's, and cow's milk varieties in various textures, a few dried fruits and nuts, a honeycomb, and some Carr's Table Water Crackers.

LaVonne returned from the bathroom, saying, "You have a rain showerhead with jets on the side. You ever wash your ass and your hair at the same time?"

"I go one at a time. Feels more thorough."

She did a double take when she spotted the food I laid out. She picked up her goblet, and it made a bell-like ping against the side of the platter. "These are real crystal," she said, holding the glass up to the light and reading the maker's mark. Her eyes scanned the loft again. "Hey, you mind telling me how much rent you pay each month?"

I told her, "It's two thousand dollars."

She nodded, taking it all in. "Uh-huh, and how many roommates do you have?"

"Um, none? Or just me? I live alone," I explained. "It's open concept."

"Can I ask you a personal question?"

"Since when do you ask if you can ask?" I replied. LaVonne was the most direct person I'd ever met.

"Did you take econ classes at Whitney?"

"Yeah, a few of them. I was a business major."

LaVonne began to laugh, slowly at first, and then she picked up steam. She laughed so hard that her eyes watered. She even smacked her knee at one point. I failed to see what was so funny, but maybe we were both just slap-happy after Day One of Hell Week. When she finally caught her breath, she said, "You better get your damn money back, because you didn't learn shit."

I was taken aback. "What does that mean?"

"You think you're gonna make enough money to pay for this pala- tial apartment looking like it's straight out of an old Jennifer Aniston TV show? Plus, tuition, plus books, plus this ex-damn-squisite sheep's milk Pecorino that runs eighty dollars per pound, plus all your other expenses on a part-time minimum wage job that baptizes you in coffee backwash and bonuses in AA chips?" She was choking and wheezing with laughter as she tried to get out her words.

"Well, I . . . I don't know how to answer you in a way that won't make you laugh harder." I felt the cold fingers of panic begin to con- strict my chest. To be honest, I assumed that if I leaped, a net would appear. "I thought if I worked hard and kept my spending to a mini- mum, I could figure it out."

She stopped laughing when she saw my expression. "Oh my God. You're serious. You really thought you could. You better call the Brothers Grimm, because you are writing a fairy tale, girl. Do you understand that you're going to pay twenty-four thousand dollars in rent this year alone? You got one of those apartments meant for the crazy rich Asian students who come to Whitney from crazy rich places like Singapore, not for some girl who works part-time and pays her own tuition. How much do you think I earned in the shop last year? Do you want to guess? No, don't guess, because I'll tell you. I made about twenty thou- sand dollars. That's before taxes, and I worked all the time." She does her invisible chalkboard math again. "After tax, I brought home maybe sixteen thousand. So if you don't spend one penny on food or drink or school or this fancy-ass cheese, you are already eight thousand in the hole. I mean, I'll give you all the shifts you want, but you are not going to make it on Eli's House of Beans money alone."

As distressing as this conversation was, I couldn't help but notice that LaVonne's eye makeup game was spot-on, even after her tears of laughter. "Do you realize that none of your makeup has smudged or smeared?"

"Do you realize you always change the subject when you're put on the spot?"

She was onto me. "Okay, then if that's how much you make, how do you pay for your life? I know you're on your own too." How was she doing it?

"Obviously, I work at Eli's, as well as tutoring in the language lab. I also have a shit-ton of loans. I got that Pell Grant and some other scholarships, plus I have a lousy apartment and a bunch of roommates, so it's cheap. Also, I make a little money off TikTok and my makeup reels on IG. I'd do better if I had more time to devote to it, but I'm not going to college to become an influencer. It's a fad, not a career. Anyway, I get by, but there's no money left over for *samovars*, that's for damn sure."

I rose and started to pace. I knew all of this, but I didn't allow myself to *know* all this. Was there anything worse than being confronted with an unwelcome truth? "Tell me what you would do if you were me. How would you deal with this? If I'm heading for financial disaster, how would you head it off?" I asked her earnestly.

"Easy. I'd call my rich daddy and ask for my credit card back."

"Not an option."

"Because of them or because of you?"

"Because I made a stand." I paced back and forth in front of the coffee table, clutching my wineglass.

"Then unmake your stand. What is possibly keeping you from speaking to them?"

"My dad slept with my best friend while we were in Europe."

LaVonne recoiled as though she'd been slapped and clutched her chest. "That is some *White Lotus* shit right there."

"I'm aware."

"And what did your mom do?"

"Nothing."

"Hmm. Sounds to me like she's kind of a victim too."

"Trust me; she's not," I said, yet a part of me started to wonder.

"Regardless, let me see if I've got this right: you've got a family who will not only help but also give you everything your lil heart ever wanted, and probably more, because they have the incentive to win you back."

I took a drink and held the wine in my mouth for a moment before swallowing. "That's one way of looking at it."

"Your people helped build this school, and you could probably go to the administration office and get special dispensation if you throw your dad's name around. But instead of saving your own damn life, it's more important that you're right and that you do it all yourself. You're like, *'This is the hill I plan to die on.'* And it's all because you accidentally did some poverty tourism, and now you feel bad about your privilege. Do I have your number here?"

"It's way more complicated than that," I protested, remembering the look on Smythe's face when I caught her leaving my dad's hotel room.

"But is that the gist of it?"

I shrugged. "I guess."

LaVonne picked up her glass, took a big sip, and announced, "*This is not Two Buck Chuck.*" Then she looked at me, then at the cheese, then at the loft. "Scale of one to ten, how desperate are you going to be in the next month or so? Do you have anything to live on after you finish paying tuition?"

"Are we going to be stuck with twenty-two-dollar tip outs all week?"

"I pretty much guarantee it. If we're lucky, maybe we'll get a one-year chip instead of a one-month."

I chewed my bottom lip as I considered. "My level is maybe a five or a six?"

"Let's assess: You won't ask for help from your family." She held up a finger. "It's too late for you to try for financial aid this semester, and even if you did, they'd probably laugh at you." She held up another finger.

"Maybe a six."

"You gave away most of your expensive shit, so you can't even cash out on the RealReal." Another finger.

"Okay, seven."

"You have a trust fund, but you can't go near it." Finger.

"Fine, eight."

"And you work a shitty gig that isn't gonna cover the palace you live in, but you don't want to get a real job in a city because you want to be at a school in the middle of a cornfield 'cause you saw something on your trip that gave you the feels. Spoiler alert: you don't have to go overseas to help kids without access to clean water. You can just go to Flint and stay at my grandmama's house. Now, did I get it all?" All five of her fingers were extended.

"Yes. If I'm being fully transparent, I'm closer to a nine. What do you suggest?"

She flapped her open palm at me. "Nothing, because *ya fucked.*"

I flopped back onto the cushions. "Not helpful, LaVonne."

"What you're telling me is that there is nothing more important right now than your taking care of yourself without your family's interference, for whatever bizarre penance you feel like you need to put yourself through?"

"Yes."

"Well . . . like Raskolnikov said, 'Pain and suffering are always inevitable for a large intelligence and a deep heart.'"

I considered her words, and they felt so appropriate. "Profound *and* true."

"I *know*, bitch. That's why Dostoyevsky wrote it."

LaVonne thought for a minute and then pulled out her phone. "If you're willing to do anything, I may have an idea. Let me show you something. I do have this one cousin who . . ." She tapped, then scrolled, then stopped and looked at me before shaking her head. "No, forget it. It's good money, but it's not for you. I shouldn't have suggested it."

I took in my place through LaVonne's eyes, and I began to see the full extent of my folly, from the walls of windows to the rain shower-head to the fancy appliances.

"But what if it is?" I said.

She grabbed the wine bottle and drained its entire contents into my goblet. "Then you're gonna need all of this."

Chapter Thirteen

CeCe

One week before sorority rush

"They *hired* you? Are you sure?"

Fudge scowls at me from across the counter. First she wants me to get a job, and now she's questioning the job I get. Make up your mind, darling! "Why do you seem so skeptical?" I ask.

Typical Hayden. She wants what she wants, and when she gets it, she finds she doesn't want it anymore. Take that day in the pool, for example. She trots out that story as evidence of my bad parenting whenever she can, but she insisted on swimming alone that day, and then when I finally allowed her to get in the water without her nanny—*because I was supervising her*—she pulled the drowning act. This is a fact because that first pool in the Lake Forest house was only four feet at its deepest; it was what's called a "cocktail pool." We didn't put in the new saltwater diving pool until Hayden passed her deep-water swimming test. She conveniently forgets she didn't need to be saved that day; she just needed to stand up. The water only came to her shoulder. She was never unsafe, not for a moment. The only victim was Mr. Geary's cell phone, which I immediately replaced and upgraded.

Her mistrust in me is Chip's doing. He and Hayden were thick as thieves, always two against one, either off sailing or having little adventures on the Lake Forest property with woodland creatures. They were such a self-contained unit, there was no space for me, especially as she got older and he'd try to pit her against me, buying her affection with bags and trips. It was his idea that she spend a year traveling. And he's the one who gave her the black card.

As I've come to understand more every day, Chip is largely a terrible man, but he was a wonderful father—so engaged. He called her every night when he was on business trips, and he'd arrange his schedule so that he never missed one of her water polo games. (To reiterate: she's always been a strong swimmer.) Every girl needs her daddy, so I took a back seat in the parenting realm. I think that's why their falling-out was so devastating for them both.

Hayden says, "I ask because I can't imagine who'd give you a job."

"Fudgie, darling, I've received offers of employment before."

"When?" She looks at me like I'm a madwoman.

I explain. "Before graduation, I had my choice of career paths! In fact, I had jobs lined up at the Tate, at Hauser & Wirth, and LACMA. I was so busy trying to choose between London, New York, and Los Angeles that it never occurred to me that your father would propose in the interim, making all my choices moot. Oh, was your grandfather upset! But I rationalized with him. I said, 'Daddy, marriage is the only possible scenario where you don't end up paying my rent.' I mean, can you imagine me living somewhere on a gallerist's wages? I was quite persuasive."

Hayden is still skeptical. "Okay, walk me through this. The sorority said, 'You're hired. Here is your salary; here are your benefits; here's how much vacation time you get.'"

That smiley Janelle person was right—the dean was a dream, so helpful; she just put all the wheels in motion so quickly with the sorority's leadership that I walked out of her office with the job. She didn't even check my references. (Although I doubt Katie Couric takes my calls anymore.)

"Yes, yes, the whole nine yards. They even have a thing they call a 401(k). No idea what that is, but it sounds intriguing. If I put in five dollars, they match five dollars. Look, I'm already doubling my money! Anyway, I start immediately." I hold up a janitor-sized ring of keys. "See? These are all the keys to the house and to my suite. I will be out of your hair"—I look at those hideous dreadlocks and shudder involuntarily—"your knotted, knotted hair in two shakes. You'll never have to see me again if you don't want."

"We're going to live half a mile apart."

See? She wants me gone, and then she doesn't want me gone. "Then I'll probably see you more like every day, because you do make an excellent Earl Grey misto. Best I've ever tasted."

Hayden stops frowning for a moment and stands a little taller. "It's my lavender infusion."

"Obviously, yes, because it evokes the lavender fields of Provence."

Who knows if she remembers, but we passed through there once when she was still a toddler, traveling from Cannes to Barcelona. She saw those endless fields of purple and begged us to stop the car so she could run through the rows. They were taller than she was. I tried to stop her, but she still snapped off some of the stems and stuffed the pockets of her little jacket with the flowers. When we got home, I had one of her stuffed animals filled with the dried lavender, and she slept with Monsieur LeFleur for years.

Hayden flushes, just like she always did when anyone complimented her as a child. Even her teachers noted it on her report cards. It's another reason she and I had trouble connecting; compliments are my currency. I live for them.

Hayden mumbles something that sounds like *thank you*.

I say, "Hold on. Are we having a *moment*, Fudgie?"

Hayden rolls her eyes. "Not if you keep calling me Fudgie."

She can't fool me. We absolutely were.

Hayden helps me load my car; then I make the short trip from her place to Greek Row. After double-checking the address, I pull into the circular drive at the Alpha house, parking right out front, with all my baggage stacked precariously in the back seat. I pass the dean, who is out with a group of stylish Asian students. They're clad in the latest from Supreme and Off-White, paired with Balenciaga runners, all of them taking photos of the sorority house down the block.

"I made it!" I exclaim to the dean, holding up my enormous key ring.

The dean gives me a brief wave in response.

Then I notice a strange old woman across the street at one of the fraternity houses. She's surveying the scene with binoculars, and I'm not sure what to make of her, but it seems like none of my business.

I am pleasantly surprised once I take a good look at my new digs. This is a fine old stonework building with freshly painted white shutters on every window, accented with window boxes, topped off with a gambrel roof. It reminds me of my childhood home in Chesco. The only thing missing is the stables. I loved growing up in a grand stone house, probably because of that nursery rhyme about the piglets. No big bad wolf could ever blow it down, and I always felt so secure within its walls.

There's a wide bluestone path leading to the door, bordered by landscaping on either side. As I take in the scenery, a very dirty woman approaches me from the side of the building. She's clad in odd, perforated plastic shoes, and her denim overalls are streaked with soil. I briefly mourn the loss of Homeless, Not Homely again. I'm confident we could offer this ragamuffin a shred of hope.

"Hello!" she calls to me. "You must be CeCe. The dean told me to watch for you. She said you'd be moving in this afternoon. I'm Rain. Dr. Rain Levinson, actually. I'm here to show you around and help you settle in. I'm the mom at Pi Mu next door."

She offers me her hand, but it's caked in mud. I'm not sure what to do here.

"Oh Jesus, sorry, I've been mulching," she says, wiping her palms on her dungarees.

"My goodness. Don't we have people for that?" I ask. One of the selling points was that the sorority house comes with a gardener, as well as housekeepers, a maintenance staff, and chef.

Rain grins at me, and I feel like under all the grime and hemp, there could be an attractive woman lurking. "We do, but I can't help myself. I'm a former botany professor, and the garden is just a playground for me. This is the perfect time of year to plant seedlings for leafy greens like lettuce, spinach, and kale. I've been working on a hybrid of iceberg and romaine. In theory, it should have the coloration and nutrients of romaine, but the tightly packed leaves of the iceberg variety."

I'm not sure what I'm supposed to do with this information, but maybe I'll be better off if I don't consider every woman I meet to be a rival. This approach did seem to work with Janelle, as well as the dean. It definitely shouldn't be a problem with this, umm, gardener either. I say, "Very interesting. And then what happens?"

"And then we make fresh, delicious salads from the bounty!"

"Are you familiar with Juliet roses?"

Her eyes light up. "Am I ever! The Ausjameson rose is magnificent, with notes of lilac and sweet vanilla, and that ombre coloration is just such a wow. In my opinion, it has the most spectacular petal formation given its cupped shape. Did you know it took David Austin almost fifteen years to create the hybrid?" she says. "It's sometimes called the three-million-pound rose, as that's the estimated cost for him to perfect the plant."

Finally! Someone who speaks my language. "I think I might like you."

Rain shrugs. "Good, because I'll like you back. Shall we take the tour?"

"Why not?"

She punches in a code and swings the door ajar. "After you."

My initial impression of the house fades when I enter. Oh goodness, these color choices, especially with this slate flooring? What was the decorator thinking? The open entry hall is a nice touch, as is the sparkling crystal chandelier, but the dated tchotchkes and muted shades of gold and red are totally discordant. None of this styling works with the house's architecture. All the pieces are so off-key, like an orchestra playing the wrong notes. One needs to pull inspiration from the stone and mortar—I'm thinking pale gray, soft taupe, accented with cool blues and chinoiserie accent pieces. This edifice is crying out for ginger jars.

"A ketchup-and-mustard palette? It's like Ronald McDonald's boudoir. Not lovin' it," I say.

Rain nods. "Yes, some of these houses are a bit dated on the inside, and it's a shame, because it impacts recruitment numbers. Pinterest ruined it for everyone. Now everyone wants a page ripped right from HGTV. The Alpha sorority colors are crimson and maize, so that does limit some of the—"

Already, I'm faced with a task in my wheelhouse! "No worries, we can change it. I have access to the discretionary fund, yes?" I ask.

"Um, yes, we housemoms do control some of the general maintenance budget, but the sisters would have to vote first. They're moving in within the week, and recruitment is after that. I'd say it would be better to concentrate on—"

"On calling a decorator, stat." I shoot a quick text. "Done."

The house does have good bones; I'll give it that. The original plaster and the wood herringbone floors beyond the entryway are a delightfully whimsical throwback. I approve of the ironwork on the sweeping staircase, as well as the original crown molding. It's just that the colors are so garish and former Soviet Union; I really can't get past them.

Rain shows me to my suite, and it reminds me of the space my parents set up for Grand-mère when she moved in. There's a lovely little parlor with a darling tasseled velvet settee, a small kitchen area, plus a good-sized bedroom with a walk-in closet and sloped ceiling. The bathroom has what looks like the original pedestal sink, a deep claw-foot tub, and entirely appropriate hexagonal penny tile flooring. This is the style the rest of this house is crying out for. It's a definite update from Fudge's utilitarian digs.

I step back into the bedroom and give the linens a tentative touch—and oh, do they disappoint. Then I remember the discretionary fund. I can take care of this in two shakes.

All in all, this space is a victory, especially because there's a tiny private patio, connected to the bedroom with french doors, surrounded by a boxwood hedge. This won't be a terrible place to bide my time until my accounts are unfrozen. My attorneys tell me that since I came into the marriage with so many assets, I should be able to get back at least a little something. Restoring my reputation is another matter, but that's why publicists exist.

"What do you think?" Rain asks.

"I don't hate most of it," I reply.

Rain laughs and says, "That's certainly a relief."

Then, out of nowhere, my senses are assaulted. "Wait, what is that godawful stench? Did something die in the walls?"

Rain surreptitiously sniffs herself and then shrugs. In my opinion, most natural deodorants are like tossing a cup of water at a forest fire. I sure hope Hayden passes through this phase soon.

"That smell, it's coming from this direction," I say; then I stride down the hallway to the kitchen. I swing one of the double doors open. "Aha!" I cry.

A pleasantly plump sixty-something stirs what looks to be a cauldron on an industrial stove. She's wearing an apron that reads *Never Trust a Skinny Chef* and small AirPods in her ears. She hums quietly.

Rain taps her on the shoulder, gesturing for her to remove her earbuds. "Loretta, hello! I want you to meet CeCe. She's the new mom starting today."

Loretta waves a wooden spoon at me in greeting; then she leans in to get a good look at my face. "You're that old rich lady from the news?"

Old? Me? "Definitely not," I reply. Dr. Conseco assured me that I could pass for late thirties, so she must have me confused with someone else.

"What's cookin', Loretta?" Rain asks. "It smells divine."

"I'm making the vegetable stock for my famous vegan white bean chili. Always gotta have individual servings in the deep freeze ready for my girls, plus Meatless Monday."

My olfactory nerves are under assault, so I sneak an N95 mask out of my bag and place it over my face. I hope they get the hint.

"Oh, I've heard about this! It's legendary!" Rain exclaims. "Everyone loves it. You'll have to give our cook the recipe."

Loretta beams. "You know it. I'll send a Tupperware over for y'all when it's done. Low cal, low fat, low guilt. It's the perfect lunch."

I have a great deal of difficulty believing this claim. "For whom, livestock?"

"Those girlies love the chili, and it only costs fifty cents per serving." She says this like it's a point of pride, her soft, weathered face wreathed in a smile.

"Let me ask you something," I say, trying to figure out the politest way to phrase my question.

"Go on now," she responds.

"Would it smell better if you were to spend sixty cents?"

Rain abruptly yanks me out of the kitchen by my shoulder-bag strap, saying, "Lemme introduce you to the head of housekeeping."

"Outstanding!" I say. "I have a lot of ideas to share with her."

Rain replies with a tight smile that turns into a grimace.

I imagine the scent of the chili has finally hit her.

Chapter Fourteen

JANELLE

Less than one week before sorority rush

Janelle's Daily Do-List

- *Meet the moms for our walk*
- *Introduce self to housemom at Zoo*
- *Talk to CeCe!*

"Is anyone else concerned?" Rain asks as we power up to the top of Greek Row. All of us are dressed in some variety of Lycra and holding water bottles with our respective sorority houses' insignias. Lots of the housemoms are wearing visors. Marilee, one of the few other young ones, says we look like an advertisement for that probiotic yogurt that makes you go to the bathroom.

Most of us walk together every day, save for a few of the moms, like the one everyone calls Mean Helene. She's been here forever, and the fraternity where she lives is the only one with a housemom. Apparently, they're more of a sorority thing. Everyone says she's a million years old and simply terrifying. I haven't met her yet, but I'm told she's usually out front, spying on the other houses with binoculars. The speculation is that she's some sort of ex-military operative and fought in a war, but no one knows which. The more likely explanation is that after decades at a place nicknamed the Zoo house, she's completely out of *f*s to give.

We walk after breakfast, as that tends to be the quietest time in the house. The other moms tell me the girls are generally gone for classes at this time of day (or in the case of the slackers, still asleep), and the chaos of dozens of girls anxiously pushing for their turn in ten shower stalls has worn off, so this is the best time.

Initially, I was worried about leaving to walk, but the moms forbade me to feel guilty about taking this time for myself, especially since we're on call twenty-four seven. In fact, two nights ago, Delia, the house's treasurer, woke me up at 3:00 a.m. because she'd badly skinned her knees on her way home from a party. She banged herself up pretty good, even tearing the bottom of her palms where she braced her fall. I used tweezers and peroxide to clean her skin and remove the debris, then smoothed on antibiotic cream and applied sterilized gauze and bandages. All fixed up, good as new, I assured her.

I am an expert at rudimentary first aid, as the ladies at the Omega were always twisting ankles and scraping shins from the insane platform shoes they wore to perform. Once Ariel bonked her head and refused to go to the ER, so she ended up onstage with her forehead wrapped to look like a Civil War soldier after battle. I hate to give her the credit, but she made it work.

The dancers often developed weightlifters' calluses on their hands from gripping the pole, and when those broke open, it was messy. Plus I dealt with blisters and headaches and muscle strains. And, oh, so many menstrual cramps. In the early days, I tended to the bruises on the women who stayed in bad relationships. As conditions at the club improved, so did the dancers' circumstances and their expectations, and the bruises greatly decreased. I won't be surprised if I see some of those same injuries on the sisters; I've learned that violence isn't limited to strip clubs.

Just like when I'd patch up the Omega girls, I made Delia some hot chocolate afterward, because what can't a Hug in a Mug fix? (It's my special blend of Droste cocoa powder, half-and-half, chocolate rainbow sprinkles, and tiny pinches of salt and cayenne pepper. It is decadent.) We laughed when Delia tried to grip the drink through bandages that made her hands look like she had on oven mitts. She insisted she wasn't *that* drunk. She just couldn't walk in her platform wedges because they had ribbon ankle ties. I promised her I'm the last person to judge anyone. We ended up having a nice talk about how whatever happens will stay in the vault, and that no matter what, the sisters should always come to me.

Delia must have spread the word because in the last day or so, it seems like every ten minutes, someone's knocking on my door for something, from what to do about a difficult boyfriend to how to iron a sequined blouse to how to fight the urge to purge after eating too many carbs. I truly feel like I'm back at the Omega, and I mean that in the best way. The issues women face are universal.

Marilee taps Rain on the sleeve of her tie-dyed Grateful Dead tee. "Wait, concerned about what?"

Marilee is a hoot, but I've been cautioned not to follow her example too closely because she has low-level contempt for her entire chapter. Rain gave me the whole story—she says Marilee sort of hates Beta Iota for the sole reason that they aren't Lambdas. Marilee was one of the founders of the Lambda chapter when she went to Whitney, and she likes to say she bleeds pink and green. Today, her workout pants are lime green, covered in the hot pink Greek letter for Lambda, and her fuchsia tank sports a giant green llama. The llama is Lambda's mascot, and Marilee has collected so many, she says it's why her husband divorced her.

In confidence, Rain told me, "I suspect that wasn't the only reason."

Still, I understand her fervor. Lambda is the first African American sorority to join the National Panhellenic Conference Member Organization. Until Lambda, the member sororities were only white. Lambdas are now considered the top sorority on campus. All the frats want to partner with them for events, and every freshman wants to receive a bid from them. Beta Iota is definitely third tier with an older facility, the lowest grades of all the chapters on campus, and the fewest social invitations. Marilee resents their failing because she built and comes from the best, but I don't know why that prevents her from trying to empower her Beta Iota girls.

Marilee scowls at the stately Lambda house as we pass. The elderly Mama Shirley is on the porch, reading the Good Book on a rocker and looking utterly content. Marilee says, "Concerned that Mama Shirley refuses to die? She has diabetes, high blood pressure, and glaucoma, yet there she is, rocking away, alive and kicking." Louder, in a fake, sweet voice, Marilee waves and calls, "How are you doing this fine day, Mama Shirley?"

Mama Shirley replies with a beatific smile, "I am blessed."

"Uh-huh, that is exactly the problem," Marilee whispers in response.

"Are you ever going to stop resenting your poor girls for not being Lambdas?" Rain asks.

"Not until they suck less," Marilee replies, gathering her box braids in a topknot and securing them with a llama-embossed scrunchie.

"Is there a way we can help you make them suck less?" I ask. Behind Marilee, a couple of the moms are shaking their heads and making slash-across-the-throat motions.

Marilee stops and looks me directly in the eyes. "Honey, I cannot fix stupid, and neither can you. Do you know that last semester, one of those geniuses thought she was pregnant? I had to take her all the way to Planned Parenthood in Illinois because of this backward-ass state. And do you know when we finally got there, she explained to the doctor that she thought she was with child because she rode a Divvy bike—one of those shared rentals on campus—right after a boy and the seat was still warm."

"And then . . . ," I ask, assuming there must be more to the story.

Beta Iota is a bit of an outlier in the Greek system. Most of the students at Whitney are academically gifted. Even on Greek Row, which you'd think would be more relaxed about schoolwork, there's major competition between the chapters for highest GPA, *except* at Beta Iota. Those members are largely the girls who got into Whitney less because of their ACTs and more because of the enormous checks their parents donated to the university. Marilee calls the house members "the confluence of arrogance and ignorance." There's a whole TikTok hashtag devoted to mocking the Beta Iota's OOTD (Outfit of the Day) videos. The drag queen Bianca del Rio makes videos about them that are particularly scathing—and hilarious.

Marilee sucks air in through her teeth. "Just the hot bike seat. And then she went *to her biology class*, where I have to imagine someone at some point discussed the female reproductive system. Because lil dumdum is a *science major*." She points to the giant banner hanging from the balcony of the Beta Iota house. "Just look at that sign, and you will see the cross I have to bear."

The large vinyl sign reads "Welcom Potential New Memberse." (As Addie would say, it's cringe.)

"You know why it says that? Because when I read over the printing proofs for the rush chairman last spring, I mentioned it was missing an *e*. It did not occur to me I would have to show her *where to place said* e. I wash my hands of them; I really do. Stupidity is terminal."

Rain clears her throat, in an obvious ploy to change the subject. "Anyway, as I was saying, is anyone else concerned about the new mom at Alpha?"

"Alpha has a new mom? Get the fuck out! What happened to Doris? I saw her two weeks ago at mahjong!" says Phyllis, the sassy octogenarian from the Theta house. She has purple streaks in her snow-white hair and a filthy mouth; she's a firecracker.

"She had a stroke last week," Rain replies.

"It's never the ones you hope," Marilee mutters, shooting murderous looks back at Mama Shirley.

"Wait, I was the one who introduced CeCe to the dean. Is there an issue?" I ask. I suddenly feel a pit in my stomach.

"It wouldn't be your fault if there were," Rain assures me. "The entire house staff is furious with her; in a couple days, she's managed to insult or alienate everyone. She doesn't grasp they work *with* her, not *for* her. She told Edyta to unpack for her and then steam all the clothes in her closet. Edyta, who's trying to get the house ready so it's in shape for recruitment. Like she has time for that even if CeCe asked nicely, which she did not. And poor Loretta? I had to talk her out of quitting!"

"Why?" asks Phyllis. I have a sinking feeling and don't really want to hear her answer, but I had to ask.

"Because CeCe threw out everything with carbohydrates! I'm talking hundreds of dollars' worth of supplies, a total pantry purge. Loretta told her, 'If you want to avoid carbs, then just don't eat 'em yourself, but don't make that decision for the others.' But then CeCe said she'd seen a few of the members in their swimsuits on the roof deck, and in fact she *should* make that decision for the others."

"She's had a hard time of it," I say in CeCe's defense, even though this sounds bad. "You guys follow the news; you know what she's been through."

Rain replies, "Exactly. I want her to succeed, as much for herself as for the sisters. That's why I keep going over there to offer my help, but she shuts me down. She said, 'I've supervised staff in seven, possibly eight houses; I'm sure I don't need your help managing just the one.' I mean, look at what she's doing now."

Everyone cranes their head toward the Alpha house. CeCe's out front with Bob, one of the landscapers for Greek Row. Everyone loves

Bob. He's got a bushy white beard and twinkly eyes, and he's always jolly; he's like everyone's personal Santa Claus. I hear he even wears the red suit and passes out gifts at the Wabash County Children's Hospital every December.

Poor Bob is currently elbow-deep in suds, drenched with sweat, with his pant legs rolled up and his work boots neatly placed on the steps. He's holding a sponge while a hose runs at his feet, a stream of water snaking its way down the drive and into the gutter. CeCe's making circular motions with her hands, seeming to instruct him on a better way to wash the hood of her Mercedes, which is in no way part of his job description.

I think CeCe's getting a lump of coal in her stocking next Christmas.

Chapter Fifteen

JANELLE

Less than one week before sorority rush

Janelle's Daily Do-List

- Reorganize linen closet
- Check in with Uncle Pat
- Finally learn Greek alphabet

"Are you rushing?"

I look up from my book to see a cute guy at the outdoor table next to mine. How did I miss him sitting down? He's exactly the kind of man I'd notice because my first impression is that he looks like he'd be kind, like he'd want to help old ladies across the street, or he'd recycle his glass bottles because it's the right thing to do. He comes across as sporty, gives the impression of having grown up in fresh air. I bet his mom has lots of pictures of him with ruddy cheeks when he was a kid. He has light brown Timothée Chalamet–style swoopy hair and a spray of freckles on his nose that make him seem approachable.

His sense of style completes the package—largely because he's not wearing cargo shorts or (please make it stop) joggers tucked into socks. This look is particularly popular with the college guys. It seems to me like its own form of birth control. Also, I don't know the how or the why or the physics behind it, but every guy's shirt has perpetual damp spots in front, like the condensation from their beers dripped onto their midsection. I'm only a few years older than most of the male students I've encountered here, but they seem so young to me that I barely notice them. But this man next to me has taste, like he just stepped out of the pages of *Esquire*. He's wearing fitted pants that hit above the ankle, and instead of sneakers or those stupid soccer slides, he has on actual lace-up leather shoes with hard soles. His well-cut V-neck shirt is completely (and attractively) dry.

Maybe this guy is nothing special, but the *possibility* of him is so intriguing. I haven't even looked at guys for a while now, and I appreciate that I'm finally in a place that meeting someone decent could actually happen.

"Your book—do you want to pledge a sorority?" he asks.

I'm reading the *Dummy's Guide to Going Greek*, because the more I do the job, the more I don't understand the nuances. I mean, the women, my coworkers, my tasks—that's under control, having already established the list-based protocols I need for success. In my short tenure, I've negotiated a better rate on our energy costs by allowing the power company to put a small solar grid on a hidden piece of roofing at the back of the house, and I found a less expensive, higher quality vendor for our coffee service, thanks to a tip Hayden at Eli's offered. (I think she and I might be friends now?)

That said, I'm having trouble understanding how the organization functions, like, the clubby and historical parts, and all that ritual and meaning. The jargon is so confusing! I keep hearing stuff about legacies and recs, and someone's always saying, "We'll have to vote about that in chapter"; I didn't know that meant secret meetings only initiated members can attend. Apparently, these are different from the executive council meetings with me and the rest of the staff.

"Me? No, I, um, I already graduated," I say.

"Then you're just frat-curious," he says, nodding toward my book. If I didn't know better, I'd say he's flirting with me.

I look down at my open book. "Yes, I'm getting a handle on my new job. I just became a housemom at . . ." Wait, what are those letters? I find myself flustered. "Kappa Gamma. Greek life is all new to me."

Nothing about his approach feels oily or aggressive, unlike almost everyone I've spoken to at the Omega. He's the right amount of interested. "No frats at your last school?"

I flash back to Saint Peter's, remembering the kids in uniforms milling around the entrance, smoking before morning Mass. "Not so much," I reply. I steal a glance at the thick book he's holding, trying to read the title.

"*Legal Rhetoric*," he says. I like that he's out here with a real, old-school book, rather than playing a game on his phone, or swiping right. "It's riveting. You're welcome to borrow it." He holds the thick volume out to me.

Definitely flirting. Interesting! I try to hide my smile, but it's impossible. How surreal is this? I'm enjoying a quick break from a great job on a beautiful day, in an exciting new life where a cute non-dirtbag is talking to me. This is best-case scenario, all around . . . and then I start to overthink.

Just like that, I feel guilty for enjoying this moment, as I'm only here because of those Russians. I shouldn't be enjoying the circumstances that stemmed from their demise. I touch my cross in contrition.

The counselor said to recognize there will be moments when I feel bad for feeling good; it's normal in my circumstances. This is the very definition of anxiety. My anxiety is causing me to link up two unrelated things, and it's a mindset I must recognize and fight. When I get like this, I'm supposed to remind myself that bad things won't automatically happen because I've allowed myself to feel joy, according to *Bad Day, Good Life*.

I take a deep breath and try to center myself, try to be present. "I'm okay, thanks," I say, even though he has no idea what I'm really talking about.

"You sure?" he asks, watching my expression. He waggles the book, trying to tempt me, sing-songing, "You'll learn Greco-Roman elements of forensic style."

I can't help but reply, "I think I'll wait for the movie."

He laughs, showing me two rows of straight, shiny white teeth. They are truly perfect, not too big, not too small, no weirdly pointed incisors, no distracting metallic fillings or grayish film on his tongue, and no disproportionate teeth-to-gum ratio. Someone wrote checks to buy a smile like that; no one's lucky enough to look that way without medical intervention.

What is it about good dental work that makes a person look trustworthy? I have the same bias with glasses. For whatever reason, I think if someone's wearing prescription lenses, it's impossible for them to be dishonest or mean. My first thought when I saw Mr. Cavalcante firing the gun was *But he's wearing bifocals!* No wonder Ted Bundy hid so easily in plain sight, between that smile and those big plastic frames.

The cute guy looks me right in the eyes. His are hazel with small gold flecks, rimmed by long eyelashes, just the perfect complement to his floppy hair. He says, "Whoa, she's pretty *and* funny. That's a rare combo."

I'm glad I'm sitting, because I feel weak in the knees. This is full-contact flirting, and I'm out of practice, although I was never really in practice. Fortunately, I'm saved from him seeing me blush when my text notification pings. Uncle Pat. He's constantly in touch, though the messages are brief. This time he writes: *Okay?* No word wasted in Uncle Pat's world.

I reply honestly, trying to match his brevity: *All's well!*

He replies with a thumbs-up emoji. I recall Ariel telling me that this symbol is considered passive-aggressive, but I'm sure Uncle Pat doesn't mean it that way.

Hayden comes outside carrying a cup of something I did not order. She's been doing this every day when I stop by for my afternoon iced Americano. It's the same sort of gesture as when your cat brings you a dead mouse because he believes you're too dumb to hunt for yourself. She plonks the drink down in front of me. "Try it." She's warmed up to me, likely because I'm responsible for getting her mother off her couch.

"What is it?" I ask, inspecting the contents of the glass Irish coffee mug. It's filled with a burgundy-colored liquid, and steam billows off the top, despite the fact that it's almost eighty degrees outside.

She places a hand on her hip, already getting impatient. "Something I'm trying out for the fall menu. I want to feature more international flavors. This is Canadian; it's called a Caribou. Don't be shy; drink up." I can see the law school guy watching me out of the corner of my eye, so I lift the mug and take a sip, letting the Caribou sit on my tongue while I assess the flavor.

The spices are nice. There's something like maple and, is that . . . acid burning a hole through my mouth? I choke and spew the drink everywhere. A geyser of fluid gushes out of my face.

One time, in high school, Sister Mary Margaret got the end of her habit tucked in her underwear. Everyone could see her pink floral French-cut panties. That wasn't the surprising part. Even though she was (what we thought then was) old, she had strong, defined quads and kind of a great butt. She must have done nothing but squats and deadlifts in her off time at the convent. Seeing a part of her, literally and figuratively, that was always hidden was so disconcerting that no one said anything, and she spent twenty more minutes lecturing us about past participle use while flashing her toned glutes to God and everyone. I will never forget the look on her face when she realized that not one of us little shits in her class had said a word. My point is, I'm feeling connected to her brand of humiliation right now.

"What the . . . ," I sputter, trying to catch my breath. My throat is on fire, and every time I breathe in, it burns even more. "Are you mad at me? Because you literally just served me a cup of liquid rocket fuel. What's in this?"

Hayden hands me a dry bar towel, and I begin to wipe everything within a three-foot circumference. "The Caribou is very popular in Quebec. It's got spices and maple syrup, and also vodka, brandy, Canadian sherry, and Canadian port. I thought it would be warming for when it gets cooler outside, I mean, provided we finally get our liquor license. You think it's too strong?"

"Little bit." My eyes are watering, and it's like a tap inside my sinuses has turned on a river of snot. I try to sniffle discreetly into a napkin. Law school guy has averted his eyes, probably experiencing his own secondhand shame.

"Too much booze then, or not enough syrup?" she asks. Hayden retrieves her notebook from her apron, ready to take down my critique. Mute, I give her an affirmative nod as I wipe up the table and blot the reddish spots on my shirt.

"All of the above." I dab drops of sweat at my temples with the bar towel.

Hayden chews on the end of her pen. "Okay, I have a different one inside for you to try. Are you up to taste the Swedish white glogg? It has hot vodka, ginger, and raisins. It's pretty good." She starts to walk away, then pauses. My expression must be distinct, because she says, "Wait, I feel like the look on your face is telling me no. It's drinking raisins, isn't it?"

Law school guy inserts himself into our conversation like a white knight. "I'm sorry, *drinking raisins*? Did you lose a bet or something? You ever consider serving something basic, like a pumpkin spice latte or a Frappuccino?"

Hayden's expression indicates that his suggestions offend her so deeply, she can't even find words to fight him. She goes back inside without saying another thing, the door banging behind her.

"Is she your friend?" he asks me.

"Maybe?" I reply.

I try to get back to my reading, but I still feel humiliated. It figures that the first decent guy who's talked to me in forever had to witness this. I'm ashamed; I'm embarrassed; I'm—

"I'm Trevor, by the way." He leans over to shake my hand, and his grip is firm and warm, with just the right amount of pressure.

Warmth radiates through my chest, and I'm relatively sure it's not the Caribou, although it would be best if no one lit a match around me, just in case. "I'm Janelle."

"I have an important question for you, Janelle."

"What's that?"

"Dolly or Whitney?"

Not the question I was expecting. "I'm sorry?"

He unzips his battered leather messenger bag and pulls out a pair of Ray-Ban Clubmaster eyeglasses, half tortoiseshell and half metallic gold frame, and places them on his head to keep his hair from falling into his eyes. I may or may not have to catch my breath.

"The song 'I Will Always Love You.' I'm curious which you prefer. It's my version of a personality assessment, like Coke or Pepsi, the Sox or the Cubbies, Biggie or Tupac. So which version is your favorite? Dolly Parton's or Whitney Houston's?"

"What are you talking about?" I ask. "Dolly Parton never sang 'I Will Always Love You.'"

Trevor looks horrified. "Never sang it? Are you kidding me? She wrote it!"

There's no way this can be true. Whitney Houston was the GOAT, as was that song. My mother had all her CDs, and she'd play them loudly when she was cleaning our apartment, sometimes too loudly, and Mr. Santini upstairs would bang his cane against his floor to get her to turn it down. Mom would belt out the verses, and we'd sing the chorus together, like I was her little backup singer. (To this day, it's the one song I sing well.) My mom always said, "Music makes short work of hard jobs." Before I was born, she trained as a professional singer. She even booked some small-time gigs, which is how she met my dad. He thought she had the voice of an angel. Once life got in the way, she just performed for an audience of one—me.

"Impossible," I say. "That song was made for Whitney. The legato passages? I die." I still get chills every time I hear her voice, and then I feel sad. Both Whitney and my mother had endings that came way too soon.

Trevor appraises me, like we're in a cross-examination. "Do you not believe me? I feel like you don't believe me."

"I'm sorry; it's just that I *can't* believe you. Whitney *owned* that song." Because of Whitney, my mom would make me watch *The Bodyguard* whenever it was on TV. The way that weathered guy from *Yellowstone* swept her up in his arms and whisked her away from danger? He leaped in front of a bullet for her! The romance, that level of devotion. Then, years later, Ariel pointed out the misogyny of that film, and she kind of ruined it. I really don't miss her.

"Care to put a friendly wager on it?"

I do not say what I'm thinking, which is *Sir, I'm from New Jersey. I am not agreeing to any bet until I know the stakes.* "Depends on the wager."

"Okay," he says. "I'll bet you a—"

"Iced coffee?" I suggest.

"Nah, too easy. Dinner? If I'm right, I'll take you to dinner." This conversation is cheesy and ridiculous, and I'm kind of reveling in it. *When Life Hands You Lemons* was right; I need to embrace what's good without expecting something bad to follow.

"What if you're wrong?" I reply.

"Then I'll still take you to dinner." He grins.

Hayden walks out with a handful of clean towels. "Thought you might need these." She dumps them in my lap.

"Can you please settle a bet for us?" I ask.

"Do I look like Google?" she asks. Still, I feel like she likes me, she's just not that good at . . . people.

"No, but you look like you know things," I reply.

Hayden seems to like this. "You're not wrong," she says. "No one ever gives me credit for everything that I know."

I ask, "Who wrote the song 'I Will Always Love You'?"

She looks at me like I'm an idiot, like the answer is so obvious, she can't believe she has to waste breath to share it. "Obviously, Dolly Parton. She wrote it in 1973 just before she made a break from Porter Wagoner, who was her mentor and business partner at the time. She got her start on his television show. The song was a tribute to their long-standing friendship, so it really changes the meaning when you give it that context. Did you know she wrote 'Jolene' on the same day? Imagine writing two iconic songs in a lifetime, let alone on the same day. It's like, how did she accomplish so much in twenty-four hours, and I could barely even remember to brush my hair every day, you know? The dreads really do make things so much easier." She walks away, shaking her 'locks.

I return my attention to Trevor, prepared for some flirty gloating, but he's rising from his seat. "Yeah, I should go."

I feel a stab of disappointment. I thought we'd made a connection, like this could be the beginning of the beginning. I guess I read the signs wrong. Maybe this was just him being polite to someone who looked like she could use a friend.

Trevor brushes the wrinkles from his pants and gathers his things, then turns to me and says, "I suggest you wrap it up too. We have dinner plans."

Chapter Sixteen

CeCe

Less than one week before sorority rush

"Yes, this is more like it."

I survey the atrium, adorned with scaffolding and drop cloths everywhere. Gone is every trace of that hideous condiment palette from all the public spaces on the first floor. For a fee to expedite, my designer came down and orchestrated a look that will be absolutely brilliant, relying on inspiration from the house's good bones in shades of sand and greige, with pops of Athenian blue and oil-rubbed bronze fixtures.

In a lovely surprise, Dean Grace and Mr. Wu happened to stop by when they were in the neighborhood yesterday, and they both seemed delighted by my progress. Mr. Wu just loved the ginger jars. If only the other fraternities and sororities were so concerned about aesthetics!

The best part is that I convinced Bob, that Santa Claus fellow who works on the Greek Row landscapes, to dig up those terrible flowers lining the walkway and replace them with the fabulous Juliet roses I ordered from my old vendor. He did try to dissuade me. He said, "Daisies are the Alpha's official flower. Are you sure you want me to replace all of these with your roses? You want every one of the daisies gone?"

"Who chooses a weed as an official flower?" I replied. And how does one argue with this? Bob willingly conceded and began denuding the planter beds as soon as my roses were delivered.

I appreciated Bob's attitude. It was nice to have at least someone who wanted to listen to me, as no one else on the staff affords me the same respect. Loretta's reticence to cook anything vaguely appetizing feels as though I'm pushing a rope some days. I do not know what a "tater tot tuna casserole" is, and I'll be damned if I intend to find out.

Honestly, I haven't trusted an institutional kitchen for years, ever since poor Hayden got so sick after eating a school lunch. She had to be hospitalized! And her school wouldn't do a thing about their kitchen staff, claiming that no other student had fallen ill that day. I just remember how sad and frail the poor lamb was in that railed bed, hooked up to an IV and just white as a sheet. It broke my heart! I spent the entire thirty-six hours she was there waiting by her bed in a plastic chair. I didn't want her to wake up alone.

The doctors said she was hyperglycemic and that was a tremendous concern, as my mother was a type 1 diabetic. I always monitored Hayden's sugar consumption, knowing her genetic precondition. From then on, I had our chef pack her a low-glycemic lunch every day—I wasn't taking any more chances. Fortunately, it seemed to be an isolated incident. After she was better, because life is all about balance, I gave her one of her favorite things—a Twix bar. But our conversation about diabetes must have hit home, because I never did see her eat that chocolate, or any other chocolate bar ever again for that matter.

Anyhoo, when I heard that the sorority house would serve nothing but little cakes and sweet tea during their recruitment parties, I had to put down my foot. These girls will need protein! I insisted that Loretta do a series of seafood towers—because what says party more than a seafood tower?—and she's been griping nonstop about the idea of having to shuck so many oysters and devein all those shrimp. When no one passes out on the lawn because I kept their blood sugar in check, she will thank me. Because I wasn't sure I could trust Loretta's suppliers, I ordered the seafood from my fishmonger back home. It's due to be delivered shortly.

Edyta, the head of housekeeping, has offered me nothing but grief either. She's questioned my every request, like when I suggested she polish and buff the marble floors in the library, instead of just damp-mopping them. If first impressions are so important when new girls walk into this house, then why wouldn't we want every single surface sparkling? Bring those floors to a high gloss, I say!

Don't even get me started on the other housemothers—they keep dropping by to offer me unsolicited suggestions on all the things I'm supposedly doing wrong. *"We want you to succeed,"* they say. *"We're here for you,"* they promise. They keep asking me where I need help, and offering up their services. Apparently, Janelle is handy, and Marilee is essentially the reincarnation of Martha Stewart and can fold napkins into fifteen different animal shapes. Rain says her specialty is "listening." But I see their ruse. This is just me as a new bride again in Chicago; nothing I ever did was right. I prefer not to repeat history. I've politely told Janelle, Rain, and that Marilee person that the moment I need them, I'll ask, thank you very much, and I think they finally got the hint as I haven't seen them in a few days. There's one ancient housemom who hasn't come by, but she's out there watching the house with binoculars. It's disconcerting, but at least she keeps her opinions to herself.

Besides, if there were any problems, I'm sure the dean would mention them, as she pops in every day.

The way the other moms and the members are running around here, you'd think they were preparing for the Huns to invade, not just to host a group of anxious young women for what sounds like a series of dull mixers. I guess I don't get it. If they wanted an all-girl environment, why come to a coed Big Ten school? My alma mater, Bryn Mawr, was lousy with flower crowns and rituals and occasions that required white dresses. These girls would love it. In my opinion, all that sisterhood can get old.

I did enjoy a few of the Bryn Mawr traditions, though, like Lantern Night. Every fall semester, once the weather turned crisp, the first-year students would gather in the cloisters, wearing the black robes to welcome the new Mawrters to rigorous academic life. The sophomore students would give each freshman a beautiful handcrafted lantern, lit in their class color. The ritual was meant to symbolize passing on the quest for knowledge. Then everyone would gather in front of Taylor Hall for a Step Sing, where we'd perform the songs in their original Greek lyrics. It made me feel like I was a part of something larger than myself. My senior year, winter came early and it snowed, making the whole night that much more magical. My lantern survived the asset seizure. I now have it displayed on a bookshelf in my little lounge area.

Perhaps all this rush nonsense isn't *so* out of line with my past experiences. I do see the appeal of living in this house, rather than some terrible dormitory or sad apartment like Hayden's. While my suite of rooms doesn't feel like home, per se, it is certainly coming along. I can at least ride out my banishment from society somewhat comfortably, especially since my new bedding came. I did prefer it when the sisters hadn't arrived yet, as there's far too much shrieking, and why is there so much hugging? Did girls always hug so much?

Plenty of the young women in this chapter have style and grace. A few have stopped by to see me, and we had perfectly civilized visits, especially now that Loretta understands the proper way to make a cucumber sandwich. Oh, the look on the sisters' faces when they spotted my (now abbreviated) shoe collection! They remind me of the youngest members of the North Shore Junior League, with their poise and enthusiasm. But Natalie? Natalie is not a favorite.

The squeaky mouse of a sorority treasurer has been nipping at my heels for a few days now, constantly second-guessing my vision, as though I weren't the most admired hostess in all of Chicago *and* West

Palm. Natalie is barely five feet, with grabby little hands and eyes that are too big for her face and a personality that trends toward persistent whining.

"Hi, CeCe, can we go over the budget?" She gives off the energy of a small dog, like a barky little Pomeranian, defloofed and damp from a bath.

Before she can get out another word, the call I've been expecting comes in. "CeCe Barclay speaking," I answer, holding up a "one sec" finger.

"We sort of need to discuss your spending," Natalie says, trailing me into the formal living room, currently empty of its furniture, as I'm having everything re-covered with gorgeous silk toile that I had sent from Fishman's.

"Shhh, Housemummy's on the phone with her attorney," I tell her, and I place my hand over my ear so I can better hear Carolyn.

"I have good and bad news," Carolyn says by way of greeting. For someone being paid by the hour, you'd think she'd be a bit more inclined to offer a nicety before just plunging into this unpleasant business. Ask a gal how she's doing, for goodness' sake!

"Carolyn, darling, thank you for calling. I hope you're well," I reply. I should bill *her* for etiquette lessons, ha!

Natalie, who also has no etiquette whatsoever, completely disregards my ask for a pause. She's a typical Generation Z, just wanting to talk about me, me, me. Everything is *"Why did you have the marble polished? It's all slippery and I fell and hurt myself"* this, and *"Why did you tell the cook to stock up on market-price lobster?"* that. She's a pest, if I'm being honest. It's like she's trying to make my job more difficult.

Natalie says, "Like, the colors are cool and all—"

Carolyn says, "My investigator found Chip. That's the good news. The bad news is he's in Madagascar."

I reply to Carolyn, "Darling, that is not how good news and bad news work. If Chip's in a country with no extradition treaty, that's commensurate with not finding him at all. You're not coming to me with a solution so much as you're coming to me with a new problem."

I peek out the front window to watch Bob expertly wield his shovel, planting each Juliet bush equidistant and administering the appropriate fertilizer mix to encourage the last blooms for the season. They should be spectacular! At least *that* project is progressing per plan.

Natalie maneuvers in front of me, though she's only eye level with my collarbone. She huffs and puffs in little circles around me.

"It's just that the cost of the fabric you want to put on the couch is, like, insane? Sure, the fabric is sick, but we can't pay that much per square foot. I know you have access to the discretionary funds, but you blew through—"

"Why Madagascar, anyway?" I ask, trying desperately to ignore this annoying gnat buzzing about, only I'd be the bad guy if I were to swat at her.

"You know where Madagascar is?" Carolyn asks. "Because I have no idea."

"My father was the Map King; I know where everything is. Madagascar is off the southeastern coast of Africa, and it's one of the four largest islands in the world."

"Really? Then where's French Polynesia?"

"French Polynesia is a tiny island, deep in the Pacific, somewhere between New Zealand and Chile, not too far from Bora Bora. Why, was he there?"

"No, a friend vacationed there, and I saw her pictures on Instagram. It's gorg," Carolyn replies, and I can feel my fist clench. Now she's *wasting* my precious hourly payment.

"My question, Carolyn, is why would Chip not go someplace more hospitable? The poverty rate in Madagascar is off the charts, and it's not well-developed. Why not camp someplace like the Maldives or Brunei where there are facilities commensurate with his lifestyle?"

"Well, there's that really charming set of films about Madagascar," Carolyn says. "Have you seen them?"

"No, I have *not* seen the charming films about Madagascar," I respond.

"They're animated," she tells me.

"*Madagascar* was my favorite movie when I was a kid," Natalie chimes in.

A lady does not raise her voice, but my attorney and my gnat are making it increasingly difficult to avoid doing so. "Carolyn, how is this conversation helping me get my assets unfrozen?"

Natalie sees this as her opening. "Anyway, CeCe, you spent a ton, and we don't have that much money allotted. You blew my budget, and I worked really hard on it all summer. Like, I gave up weekends, you know? I'm not an accounting student or anything, but I really feel like I could excel in this leadership position. I wanted to put it on my résumé, but along the way, I learned about debits and credits and cash flow and now I'm way more confident and—"

I turn so Natalie's not yapping directly in my face, keeping my attention on Carolyn. "Pray tell, what is your plan, Carolyn? What are we going to do? I'm paying you to think."

"Well, the thing about living in Madagascar is it's inexpensive, so he can probably last a while there on fifty million dollars, even with ample bribes," Carolyn says.

The problem with losing access to all my money and becoming a social pariah is that I can't get any of the top-tier, white-shoe law firms to work with me. Carolyn was far down my list. Quite far. While I didn't exactly find her advertised on a bus bench, it sort of feels like it on days like today.

"One can likely make a go on fifty million dollars in most places," I reply dryly. "What you're telling me is in no way a positive development. Again, what are we going to do?"

"You're going to have to hunker down and wait, I guess," Carolyn says. "If you're in a stable living situation now, hold on to it. And if you have any cash left, sit on it. Now is not the time to spend. This won't be an expedient process, so don't expect to see any of your money or return to any of your properties any time soon. We do hope this will happen in the future, but you must give the process time. We can't force him back, even though he knows he's been found."

"Wait, how does he know he's been found?" I ask.

"The private investigator accidentally introduced himself," she replies. I clamp my palm over my mouth to prevent myself from screaming.

"That would make him more of a *public* investigator, then, wouldn't it?" I ask, after a lengthy pause to compose myself.

"I even missed Lollapalooza for this," Natalie says. "Dua Lipa was there. And those old guys who had their metal song on the last season of *Stranger Things*. Plus, the weather was perfect. No rain, low humidity, not too hot."

I turn my shoulder away from Natalie again. "Also, yes, I realize we can't force him back; that is the very definition of not having an extradition treaty," I reply, my patience now worn down to a small, hard nub. "If we can't get him back to stand trial, then it's all for naught. My point, darling, is that finding him in a magical cartoon country does not constitute good news."

Natalie taps me on the shoulder and I try to shoo her, but she doesn't take the hint. "New member recruitment starts next week. I don't feel like your renovations are going to be done in that time, and even if they are, how are we paying? Like, do you even get what happens if we don't meet our recruitment numbers? We could be over. That could be Alpha's death knell. National says we must get a certain number of pledges, I mean, PNMs, if we want to keep our charter, and it's super competitive because we're not one of the top houses, and if we don't—" I duck under an elevated sawhorse to dodge her, but she keeps in lockstep with me.

"What am I supposed to do?" I ask Carolyn.

"Stay the course, I guess?" she responds.

"Carolyn, I need you not to guess," I reply.

Natalie continues to yip, a Chihuahua in an angora romper, vying for attention. "What are we supposed to do? If Alpha gets shut down, I can't live in an apartment! I don't know how to cook! I spent all my time trying to learn how to use Quicken! Am I just supposed to eat sandwiches? I can't have that many carbs!"

I can feel my blood pressure rise, and my voice with it. "If we can't get him to return to stand trial, I'm done! My assets will never be unfrozen! I'll be stuck in this purgatory forever!"

Natalie raises her voice too. "We can't have recruitment in a construction zone! Although if we made it a theme, it could be kind of adorbs with, like, little hard hats, and we could do vests and signs that say 'Caution: Women at Work' and stuff, which would be kind of empowering. Regardless, that would cost more money. We have to finish this, or we're probably screwed!"

Safe and secure in her glass office, sitting on my six-figure retainer, Carolyn probably finds it easy to tell me, "You'll have to make it work."

"Make it work? That's your advice? Seven hundred dollars an hour to quote Tim fudging Gunn?" I hang up.

Natalie's still standing right here. I tell her, "Hanging up on people was a lot more satisfying on a landline. Anyhoo, you were saying something, darling?"

Natalie squares her shoulders and stares up at me, her doll-sized jaw firmly set. "I was saying you have to fix this, or we find a new housemom."

From deep within the kitchen, I hear the normally placid Loretta shout, "What in the hell am I supposed to do with three hundred pounds of shrimp?"

Oh dear.

Chapter Seventeen

CeCe

Less than one week before sorority rush

"I had to get out of there; it was a madhouse," I say. After all the to-do, I needed to go somewhere quieter, so I've come to Eli's. "Such yelling! Who communicates that way? It was a mistake anyone could make, Fudge."

"Was it really?" Hayden asks from behind the counter where she's polishing glassware. "Pieces and pounds, those seem like two very different units of measurement."

"All I'm saying is that Izanagi should have confirmed that I meant three hundred pieces, not three hundred pounds," I reply. "He's been my fishmonger for years, but with his lack of attention to detail or a fair return policy, why, I don't see myself having him cater any of my parties again."

"Most likely not going to be an issue," Hayden says. She places my empty mug in the sink and then looks at her phone, frowning.

Her charming coworker LaVonne approaches me. "Want me to hit you up again, Mrs. Barclay?"

"Why not? I'm just drinking my problems now," I reply.

"Hayden, your mother wants another," LaVonne says over her shoulder. She leans over the counter and props her chin on her hands. I appreciate her adoring gaze; no one's looked at me like that for a while. "Tell me again about that time you ate dinner with Stephen King. Start with the wine you served."

"If I recall correctly, we had a 2010 Yvon Métras Fleurie Cuvée l'Ultime."

She sighs happily. "With the spice and licorice top notes?"

"But of course!"

"Chilled but not refrigerated?"

"Never refrigerated!"

She nods her approval. "Okay, now tell me about him again."

"You have to stop egging her on," Hayden says under her breath.

"Oh, hush up, *Fudge*. This is like being at the zoo, only I'm watching rich people in their natural habitat, and not the animals," LaVonne replies. "I feel like Jane Goodall. Lemme have this."

"Suit yourself," Hayden says with a sigh.

"My goodness, what a lovely man King was! Well, I was chairing a dinner to raise money for expanding the children's programming at the Harold Washington Library, which is in downtown Chicago, so I invited him as a special guest," I say.

Hayden begins making my Earl Grey misto, banging around louder than necessary.

"Getting kids interested in reading is the surest way to guarantee their success in the future. Did you know that in Arizona, the prisons base their future budgets on the literacy levels of fourth graders?" LaVonne tells me.

"Isn't that tragic," I say.

"Yes, it *is* tragic," Hayden interjects. "That's why I'm getting a master's degree in sociology so I can help others. *I* am. *Me*."

LaVonne says, "You know, Mrs. Barclay—"

"I really wish you'd call me CeCe, lovey."

Her slow smile gives me a rush of joy. "Okay, CeCe, I'm saying I'm here at Whitney because I benefited from a program that gave low-income kids access to books. There is a direct correlation between literacy and poverty rates, and I'm real lucky someone cared."

"I'm so glad!" I say, and I give her hand a squeeze. LaVonne exemplifies why I've always been so passionate about giving back. There's nothing more satisfying than providing a leg up. The results from Homeless, Not Homely were so powerful because we saw them almost immediately. A haircut here, a new suit there, a warm meal and a hot shower, some job training, and within weeks, the people we helped managed to get employment, which got them into transitional housing and off the street. So many of them went on to get their own places, reassembling lives that had previously fallen off the rails. My venture was an enormous success, and I will never forgive Chip for taking the opportunity from so many people.

"So, back to Mr. King," LaVonne says eagerly. She winks at Hayden, who rolls her eyes.

"Naturally, we wanted our event to do well, so we brought in as much literary firepower as we could muster. Darling, the talent we had under one roof, from Ann Patchett to James Patterson to Dave Eggers! I had the good fortune to be seated next to Stephen, and oh, what a delightful chatterbox he is!"

I was going through a particularly difficult spot with Chip at the time, and Stephen gave me such insight into what a good marriage should look like. "He spoke so lovingly of his wife, Tabitha—what a fantastic couple they are. He's a famous author because of her. She's the one who pulled his first draft of *Carrie* out of the garbage after he tossed it."

"No!"

"Oh yes! And guess where he and Tabitha met."

"Ooh, lemme think," LaVonne squeals, tapping her forefinger to her forehead. She scrunches up her eyes, which are covered in a complicated eye shadow pattern that looks a lot like leopard spots. They trail out from her lids and snake up her temples in a way that's showy, yet still appealing. "Was it a bookstore, or is that too basic?"

"Better," I say. "They met in the library at the University of Maine."

"Oh snap, the library, that is perfect!" LaVonne cries, clapping her hands together.

Hayden sighs again. "You should be a theater major, LaVonne."

LaVonne cuts her eyes over to Hayden. "Please. I'm just having some fun with your mom, *Fudge*. She's harmless."

"Thank you," I say. I'm not sure I understand the compliment, but I recognize it nonetheless.

"Now, get back to Mr. King," LaVonne insists.

Hayden's phone pings, and she glances at it, pulling yet another face.

"He told me one of the most profound experiences of his life was when his childhood friend was struck by a train. He'd gone out with that friend, and when he came home an hour later, he was completely by himself, which his mother thought was so odd. He was pale and shaking, and he wouldn't speak, so it took a while for her to get what happened out of him."

LaVonne gasps. "Oh my God, that trauma is his origin story! That's why he wrote *The Body*, isn't it?"

Before we can continue, Hayden reaches in front of LaVonne and sets my cup down with a slam, hissing, "Brownnoser" under her breath, and then stomps off to the back room.

"Is she like this with every customer, or do I bring out the worst in her?"

"Nah, it's probably you," LaVonne says.

"But why?" This feels like news to me.

LaVonne shrugs. "Moms and daughters always have a *thing*. Maybe it's because you're always calling her Fudgie."

"What's wrong with her nickname?"

"It's hella insulting—there's not an ounce of fat on her, and she doesn't even eat chocolate."

I laugh. "Goodness, no. You've got it all wrong. We call her Fudge or Fudgie because she was the sweetest little girl, just pure candy canes and gumdrops. My dear father used to say she was so sugary, she gave him a toothache, like biting into a brick of fudge. She was probably too young to remember that he came up with it. He passed a long time ago."

"Does she know this?"

"Of course she does." She does . . . doesn't she?

"Maybe you should tell her again, in case she forgot. Anyway, her people skills aren't great, but she's not usually this bad," LaVonne admits. "Something's way up her butt today. She keeps looking at her phone and sighing real loud, and then when I ask her what's wrong, she says, 'Nothing.'"

"It's never nothing when she says 'Nothing,'" I say.

"Right?" she replies.

I'm suddenly in the mood for something sweet, so I add a half a spoon of raw sugar to my misto and stir. "Anyway, LaVonne, you're a bright and creative girl. Tell me, darling, what would *you* do with three hundred pounds of frozen shrimp?"

Chapter Eighteen

Janelle

Less than one week before sorority rush

Janelle's Daily Do-List

- *Wax*
- *Like, wax everything*
- *Don't panic!*

"I wish you'd have let me pick you up."

I insisted on getting to the restaurant myself because I didn't want the girls to know my business. I didn't tell them about my plans. I have to maintain boundaries. They should come to me with their problems/hopes/dreams, but it would not be appropriate to reciprocate. Professional distance and all.

Meeting Trevor felt too good to be true, so I didn't tell any of the other moms I was going on a date tonight. If the chemistry is all in my head, I want to keep it to myself. The only person I told was Uncle Pat, because he always needs to know my whereabouts. He sent the prayer hands emoji in response—I think he thought he was giving me a high five.

Trevor jumps up from the booth at the back of Spezzano, a cozy Italian joint down the street from the coffee shop. He kisses me on both cheeks, and I try hard not to swoon when his light stubble brushes my chin. He looks particularly handsome in his dark jeans and fitted sport coat. He dresses like an Instagram model, and I don't mean that as an insult. It's such a refreshing change from the boys I see on the Row.

I'm glad I decided to dress up a little. I have on a summery spaghetti-strap maxi dress with a fitted bodice and a wide square neckline. I'm showing a little skin, but the open cardigan I added makes it not too much, right at the beginning. If I think I like him, I can always take off the little cardi. Des used to call this look "altar appropriate" because I could (and did) wear this outfit to Mass.

As I slide into the quilted red leather banquette, I tell Trevor, "What can I say? I'm cautious. I can't warn the sisters about getting into a strange man's car if I was to do it myself."

Trevor looks confused. "Wait, do you normally have to speak with them like they're children?"

"No, it's . . . just a holdover from my old job. We didn't run into a lot of nice guys."

"What'd you do before?"

This is a normal first-date question, but I'm not here under normal first-date circumstances. How do I answer him? I should have thought about this ahead of time. I don't want to be dishonest, but the whole truth is not an option.

I just say, "Troubled youth outreach."

"That sounds really noble," he says. I check out the scenery while I compose myself. This restaurant is darling. It's just like the Italian places I loved in Newark, where they cooked old family recipes. There are checkered red-and-white tablecloths, and each booth has a dripping candle stuck in an empty bottle of Chianti. The walls are covered in old black-and-white framed photos of what I assume are the owner's big Italian *famiglia*. I'm even charmed by the dusty plastic grapes and vines woven through white fencing in the corners, a detail that would have horrified my mother. We didn't have much, but every item in our home was meticulously kept, even after she got sick. She taught me to be tidy and organized.

Trevor takes the empty glass at my place setting and gestures toward the open bottle of wine. "May I?" I notice that he hasn't yet poured any for himself. He was waiting for me before serving himself. That strikes me as so gentlemanly.

"Absolutely," I reply, even though I'm not much of a drinker. Given a choice, I always pick caffeine; it's less dangerous. But tonight feels like a celebration, so, why not?

Trevor places the full glass in front of me. I notice his hands—they're well kept with neatly trimmed nails and shiny nail beds. He's got on a tasteful white gold Whitney School of Law class ring.

"It's just red wine—no vodka, no hot raisins, no surprises." Yet he holds up his napkin as a shield when I lift my glass, just to be safe.

"You're hilarious," I tell him, embarrassed again.

He raises his glass and says, "Cheers!" While maintaining the kind of eye contact that makes me feel giddy, like anything is possible, we clink and drink. "Let's recap what I know about you so far," Trevor says. "You have questionable taste in music—"

I raise my hand as though gesturing to the waiter and say, "Check, please."

"Fine, you have *different* taste in music than me, and that's okay. And you used to work with kids. Why'd you quit?"

"I needed a change of scenery." I don't want to get too much into my life, so I quickly ask, "What about you? I don't even know what you do, except you read some boring books."

"I'm a professional bartender by night, amateur investor by day, and I'm a third-year law student at Whitney."

"Wow, that's a lot. What do you do for fun? Do you even have any free time?" I ask.

"I make time for the good stuff," he says, giving me a meaningful smile. It's a supercheesy line, but still effective because I get the goose bumps. I'm not sure if it's that my standards are low, or if he's a genuinely decent man. I guess we'll find out.

"And what else are you into?" I ask, sipping my wine. It's smooth, like liquid velvet. It must be expensive, so he's either a great bartender or a savvy investor. Or a rich kid—there's a lot of them at Whitney. It's also possible he's paying for our dinner with a wallet full of stolen credit cards, which would not be the first time that has happened to me. Hopefully, this time we'll make it to dessert before he's arrested. Their Yelp reviews say they make the ricotta for their cannoli themselves.

He lowers his head and looks at me through his shaggy bangs. I wonder what he gets away with, using this move. A lot, probably. "Um . . . don't laugh, but fantasy football. Listen, I don't blame you if you want to leave."

"Please, I've heard worse." He has no idea how much worse. One first date told me about traveling to Japan. Worldly! Exciting! Until he explained—unprompted—that his reason was for their dirty-underwear vending machines. Sex tourism was his jam. I didn't even make it to appetizers that time.

Trevor tries to justify his interest and gets flustered, which is appealing. He's not trying to show me what an alpha male he is, how he must be tougher than everyone in the room. I suspect he will not punch our busser for looking at my bare shoulders before the night is over. Won't that be a pleasant change?

"I'm so analytical," he says. "I really like breaking down the stats and figuring out the odds. That's why I'm decent at investing. It's about connecting the dots and coming up with the most logical outcome, based on the data. For example, I saw what was happening in Ukraine with their wheat production, so I shorted a wheat commodity ETF and tripled my investment."

I tell him, "I had the chance to get into TSLA at twenty dollars and I blew it."

He clutches his chest. "Ouch, that hurts. If it's any consolation, I do better in fantasy football than I do in the market. I win my league every year."

The wine is loosening me up and I pat his arm, which is surprisingly firm. "I totally get it. What you're telling me is that you create pretend teams who play pretend games. Are you a big Dungeons and Dragons fan too?" I tease.

He runs a hand through his hair, pushing his bangs out of his eyes. "I see you ran across my high school yearbook."

I stifle my laugh. "No, really? I was joking—did you play?"

"You're sitting across the booth from an official Dungeon Master," he admits with equal parts embarrassment and pride.

Again, I raise my hand and pretend to call the waiter. "Check, please." The truth is, I like the idea that he was a bit of a nerd. The coolest guys from my high school did nothing relevant after graduation, although I'm not one to talk. The point is, when you don't peak at seventeen, you're far more open to change and growth because you're not perpetually looking backward, trying to recapture your glory days.

"You're funny."

No one has ever said that to me before. I'm not sure that I believe him, but it's still nice to hear. I say, "That's it, then? You're just into fantasy football? I guess I thought you'd be more outdoorsy, for some reason."

"Well, I do spend a lot of time outside stalking Dolly Parton." He says this so matter-of-factly, it takes me a second to realize he's joking, particularly since my last crush had that *incident* with Ariana Grande's security team.

Seriously, how did I not end up a nun?

"I'm kidding, I promise. Although I do believe Dolly is a national treasure. She should be given Secret Service protection. Thing is, I grew up in Colorado, so I'm a big winter sports guy. Skiing, snowboarding, hockey, snowmobiling, anything with speed and snow or ice and I'm golden."

"You have to miss that a lot, living here." The wine is going down easy, and I am entirely okay with that. If he doesn't steal my lipstick (yep, that happened too) at the end of the night, this will officially be the best date I've ever had.

"Eh, I make do. There's a man-made mountain a couple of hours from here—it's not great, but it's better than nothing. A big group of us goes down there every few weeks in the winter. Anyway, enough about me. Tell me who you are. What do you love?"

I do want to show him who I am. "Promise not to laugh?"

"No. I promise I *will* laugh when you start off that way."

"No pressure there. Okay, here goes. I make lists. I live in mortal fear that I'll miss something, so I log everything. Checking off items when I'm finished is an actual rush."

I don't explain that when I was helping my mom manage her medications, the checklist became a matter of life and death. I don't want to bring down the mood. I want to keep tonight breezy and light and maybe make out. (This wine is outstanding.)

He listens and nods. "Totally get it. Do you ever complete a task, realize it wasn't on the list, and then write it down just so you can cross it off?"

I meet his gaze and feel butterflies in my stomach. "You just looked right into my soul."

Oh, this cardigan is coming *off*.

We've been here for hours, having long since finished our dinners. I'd normally order the mussels, but I didn't want to wrestle with shells on a first date. Instead, I chose the swordfish puttanesca. A zesty sauce with lots of olives and a rich, meaty fish. Delicious. He had the roasted stuffed branzino and later admitted their chicken parmesan with a giant side of bucatini is his favorite, but he didn't want to navigate all that red sauce in a white shirt. We decided that when we do this again (when!), we'll both get what we really want.

The cannoli were the stars of the show, thanks to the ricotta—the shell was crisp, and they didn't skimp on the pistachio. I've had my fair share of cannoli growing up in New Jersey, and this was quite good, especially in a state where there aren't many Italians.

We linger at our booth while our annoyed waiter plucks red wine bottles off all the empty tables and blows out the candles. Everything about this night feels good and right and easy. I won't even care if he does steal my makeup at this point. We have so much in common. I particularly like that he has a Catholic school education, because it gives us such a similar frame of reference.

"Man, I'm still afraid of rulers. Sister Kathleen was no joke. A swing like hers, she coulda played for the Rockies." He rubs his knuckles protectively at the memory.

Trevor is somewhat slurry at this point, but so am I. The first bottle went down so fast that we ordered a bottle of Chardonnay for our dinner, which we also demolished. Then we were having so much fun, I suggest we have sambuca with our coffees. When I learn that Trevor has never heard of the superstition with the three coffee beans, the Italian side of me is appalled.

I say, "How can you be a bartender and not know this?"

He shrugs and says, "I'm a college bartender. I pour pitchers of beer and make shitty margaritas. The SigEps are not coming in for an aperitif."

I explain the proper way to serve sambuca is with the three espresso beans. These symbolize health, happiness, and prosperity. Also, the number three symbolizes the Holy Trinity, and it's bad luck to use an even number. I explained how bartenders would add an extra bean to warn Mafia members if there were undercover agents around or trouble afoot. He laughed at the notion of the mob still existing, saying I'd watched too many *Sopranos* reruns.

If only.

"What triggers you from your Catholic school days?" he asks. "Everyone has something."

"Plaid kilts. I have PTSD when I see plaid kilts," I say. I don't explain why, but I do shudder thinking about them. Ariel would always make the most money when she put her hair in pigtails, wore her tiny kilt, and danced to "She's Only Seventeen." Men are gross, but I'm glad their cash funded feminist causes.

At this point, Trevor has his arm around me, and I am here for it. "Listen; if you're trying to out-Catholic me, give it up. I'll have you know I once played Joseph in the Christmas pageant."

I lean in. "Whoa, Joseph? You win."

"I did. I got so much ass in grade school after that."

"Ew, really?" I say, pulling away from him.

He pulls me back. "I was in second grade, so no. It was a bad joke. But Sierra Mullins did give me her extra cupcake once, so . . ."

Our waiter approaches. "Can I get you anything else? Like a check, maybe?"

Trevor asks him to give us a minute, and the waiter stomps off. We've just connected on so many levels. We feel the same way about the Catholic Church—love it, but it has some big problems. Neither of us has been to a Mass since Easter. We've also read a lot of the same management books, and we feel the same way about flowcharts. We even both quietly hate Elon Musk. (Yes, I'm still mad about the Tesla stock.)

The waiter returns to snatch up our empty water glasses. "So, will that be all now?"

"Soon, soon," Trevor tells him, as anxious as I am not to break our spell.

"Do you remember school dances, where we had to leave room for the Holy Ghost?" I ask him.

He runs his thumb up and down my bare bicep, and it's electrifying.

"Tell me, Janelle. What's on your bucket list? What do you wanna do more than anything else?"

"I want to go to col—" I stop myself before I say college, because that would blow up my whole story. I just remembered why I don't often drink. Loose lips are going to sink my small ship. I try to cover. "Col—calligraphy class. I want to go to calligraphy class."

"Random, but respectable."

"Hey, how about a check, then?" the waiter asks as he sweeps every single item from our table, including the wine bottle and its burned-out stub of a candle.

"Real soon," Trevor assures him. "But not until you tell me something no one else knows about you."

Wait. *What?*

I stiffen.

Is this a trap?

If so, why does nothing feel scary or dangerous about this?

As I look into Trevor's eyes, I just don't see . . . that disconnect. That blankness. There was always something in certain Omega patrons' eyes, the ones who meant harm. Like a light that had gone out. It didn't matter how smiley and nice those patrons were, everyone instinctively knew to keep their distance.

Looking in Trevor's eyes, I see warmth. You can't fake that.

So I take a leap of faith.

"When I was a kid, my best friend and I had the same name, so the nuns called us G—." I stop and clear my throat. "Janelle One and Janelle Two. I was Janelle Two. I always felt so bad about being called Two, like I was perpetually second place, and that really did a number on my self-esteem. I mean, when is the sequel ever better than the original?"

Trevor keeps me locked in his gaze. "Are you kidding? That's not at all true. *Godfather II*. That movie was far superior to its predecessor. It was perfection, just a chef's kiss. If anyone ever calls you Janelle Two again, remember, you're DeNiro, not Brando, and it's the biggest compliment."

That's it. I'm smitten.

"I've never seen it."

"Then we're putting it on our list."

Our list. Us. *Together*.

I lean in to him, and he smells like shampoo and cedar and sambuca. I noticed he avoided everything with garlic on the menu, which isn't easy in a Southern Italian restaurant.

"What's on your bucket list?" I ask.

"Truth?" he says. "Right now, it's convincing you to come back to my place."

I feel little fireworks erupt in my chest, and I call to the waiter, "We'll take our check now, please!"

I can't wipe the smile off my face this morning. All I want is to share my joy over the best date of my life. I'll need to save it for my next walk with the other housemoms. Until then, I'll savor the thoughts of last night like a piece of rich, dark chocolate.

I channel my energy into being useful around the house. So when I see a stack of laundry tagged *Addie* by the washers and dryers, I fold everything and bring the basket up to Addie's room.

I peek in from the doorway. Addie's room is chaos, the inevitable result of having too much stuff crammed in too small a space. She still hasn't broken down her moving boxes for recycling, and she's got a couple of dresses hanging from her snowboard. There are makeup trays on every surface and lots of half-empty water glasses on the few blank surfaces. It looks like an Anthropologie bath bomb went off in here.

I knock on her open door. "Fresh towel delivery." I set the basket down on the edge of her love seat, which is covered in pairs of leather boots. Ankle boots, over-the-knee boots, scrunch, moto, riding, stiletto heel.

She looks up at me, seeming surprised. "You didn't have to do that. Thank you! I can't believe you did that! Our old housemom couldn't even climb stairs. Something about her gout? Old-people problems, ugh."

"I like to help," I say, and then I have to stifle a yawn. "Sorry, I was up late."

Addie raises an eyebrow. "Anything interesting?"

"Do you consider Jimmy Fallon interesting?" This isn't a lie; I just wasn't watching his show from my own apartment.

Addie says, "Boo," and sticks out her tongue.

I notice she's working on some project, with little electronic parts all over her desk.

"What's happening here?" I ask.

"Something's wrong with my phone. I upgraded to the newest iPhone right before I came back to school, and it's all kerflooey. I'm taking the SIM card from my new one and trying it in the old one to see if it works better."

"What's it doing?" I ask.

Her hair is falling in her face as she's hunkered over, so she winds it into a bun and secures it with a pencil.

I let out a giggle and she shrugs and says, "People always laugh when I put my hair up in a pencil, but I tell them that it's convenient. Anyway, I'm not getting my texts. My boyfriend said he kept texting me last night, but I haven't seen anything. He was actually kinda mad that I was ignoring him. I told him I'd be busy with officer meetings and recruitment stuff, so I don't even know why he was trying, but I still should have gotten them."

"I wish I could help, but that's above my skill level," I tell her. I look around her room. "Hey, why don't I take these boxes and break them down for you? Get them out of your way?" I need something that I can fix.

Addie beams up at me. "Oh my God, you know what? You are, like, amazing."

I smile to myself as I grab the boxes. Addie's now the second person in the past day to say I'm amazing.

Chapter Nineteen

HAYDEN

Three days before sorority rush

My phone pings again. Every time it does, I feel a ripple of fear trail down my spine. I check the message. It's the same as the rest of the texts I've received from this unknown number:

need 2 talk 2 u pls its oscar

The knot in my stomach expands. After the first message from Oscar, one of my regular patrons, I figured I was best off just ignoring him. I don't know how he got my number, because I've been so careful over the past year. Fake name, fake bio, fake contact info, elaborate costumes, heavy filters, anything to contribute to the subterfuge. I ignored his message because I didn't want to confirm receipt.

I didn't expect things to blow up so much on the site. I definitely didn't realize my secret side hustle as Callie would take on a life of its own. A few frat guys thought they recognized me, but I was so rude to them that I'm sure they were dissuaded. First, Callie's shtick is that she's sweet as a Georgia peach, and second, Why would Callie be in grad school at Whitney, working as a barista? Supposedly she's a nineteen-year-old cosmetology student in the Florida Panhandle perfecting her spiral perm skills.

I've kept a solid wall between my profile on JustforEnthusiasts.com and my real life, until right now. Somehow that wall has been breached, and I'm terrified.

Ping.

pls answer, important

LaVonne's off to see her family in Michigan before recruitment begins, and neither Glen nor Glenn is working, so I'm alone in the shop, and I feel superexposed with all these big glass windows, like I can't hide. Like I need to protect myself. I have mace on my key ring, but I wonder if that's enough.

When the bell on the door chimes and that nice housemom Janelle walks in, I'm so relieved that I practically kill her with kindness.

"Hi, how are you? Bucket of iced latte with sugar-free vanilla?" I ask. "How about a lemon square, on the house?"

Janelle looks concerned. "Hayden, what's wrong?"

I recoil. "What makes you think anything's wrong?"

"Number one, you're being aggressively cheerful, and number two, you're suggesting coffee and not some llama butter beverage." She then leans in and whispers, "Blink twice if there's a *guy* in the back room."

I try to laugh off her paranoia, but I'm impressed by her perception.

"I'm fine," I say. "I'm just having a weird day."

"Listen. I'm happy to sit at the counter with my coffee if you want a friendly ear or just don't want to feel alone," she says.

I begin to make her drink. "I bet you're a good housemom. You give off positive energy," I tell her.

She smiles and sits up straighter on her stool. "Thank you. I appreciate your noticing. I would like to say the same about your energy, but, um . . ."

"I don't excel at customer service?" I reply.

"Your words, not mine." She shrugs and opens a book, but not before giving me a kind smile.

I can't help thinking about how I got into this mess . . .

"I talked to my cousin. She says you've got to make yourself come across as younger than you are in real life. In the beginning, she used her real age. Then she shaved off ten years, and her audience expanded exponentially." LaVonne was seated at my kitchen table, tapping away on my laptop.

We were well into our second bottle of wine that night last year. The idea of selling access to pics of me in boudoir poses gave me the icks, but from an economic standpoint, it made sense. Being on the site was the lowest effort/highest return option available. I didn't need a million bucks, but I wanted to pay more than the minimums on my credit cards and keep a roof over my head.

The site allows for creators to choose a tier of engagement. The first tier is photos only, no interaction with viewers. I'd sent plenty of selfies like this to old boyfriends, just like everyone else. Ideally, those would be the shots I'd post. The second tier includes the ability for patrons to direct message and tip me. I liked the tip part, but the having-to-talk-to-them part made me squirm. The third tier was live video, and that felt like a giant *hell, no*, the Rubicon I would not cross.

LaVonne had recently discovered that she had a sophisticated palate when it came to wine; the only payment she'd accept for her assistance was being able to select that night's bottles from the dwindling cache I knew I couldn't afford to replenish. It would be boxes of Franzia for me going forward, and I was fine with that. I didn't need a five-star life anymore.

By that point last year, as LaVonne predicted, I had exhausted every option to increase my revenue. The financial aid department couldn't do anything for at least another semester. When I went to Chicago to meet with my trust's administrators, the attorneys explained that there's often a trust provision for education, but I was halfway toward my undergraduate degree when my grandfather passed. He had no reason to believe my education wasn't a given. I also interviewed for better-paying jobs, but none of them could accommodate my rigorous class and fieldwork schedule. It was too late to try for a teaching assistant position. I sold a couple of things on eBay to cover a month's expenses after I'd scraped together my tuition, but I only had so many samovars. The semester had already started, and I'd be hard-pressed to find a sublease and a roommate situation. And I liked my apartment; it felt like home.

The photo thing felt like a nuclear option, but when every other fail-safe, um, *failed*, joining the site was the only way forward that meant I didn't have to call my dad. LaVonne patiently listened to me talk through every eventuality, and that led us to the night we launched my profile.

"Guys seem to be into the young things on this site. Same as in real life. How about we say you're seventeen?"

"Big yikes," I replied. I could feel my insides cramp at the notion. "That's jailbait."

She took a thoughtful sip and swished the wine around for a moment before she swallowed and nodded. "Girl, everything about this site is trash. I told you it was trash. It's a trash site for trash people. *Period*. And I told you it was a bad idea and that my cousin is a capital-*S* Skank who makes bad decisions. She voted for Kanye in the last election! I regretted even mentioning this idea to you, yet here we are. Remember, my suggestion is to call your dad and ask him for help."

"Still not an option."

"Yet you're okay with asking other daddies to give you money."

"That statement literally makes me want to retch," I said. I could feel the wine roiling in my stomach, and I pushed my glass away so I could clutch my midsection.

"You not gonna drink that?" LaVonne asked, eyeing my goblet.

I gestured for her to go ahead, and she poured the contents of my glass into hers. She added, "Speaking of, you could always go the sugar baby route if you want to make the big money."

I'd read the stories on Reddit. On campuses across the country, women had been using sites that pair coeds with lonely men seeking company and, ahem, conversation. The women describe the exotic trips they take and the designer handbags they were gifted. Supposedly, these women are just companions, and they don't have sex, but please. My endgame was not a jumbo Chanel flap bag of questionable provenance and an Economy Plus trip to Portugal; my endgame was earning a degree. Ironic that Smythe went this sugar baby route for free, and all she ended up with was one fewer best friend. She didn't even get an Hermès bag charm.

The idea of enduring a dinner across the table from some lascivious old perv renting my courtesan services made my skin crawl. It wasn't my place to judge, but the in-person element of putting on a dress and being someone's sexual plaything was outside my comfort zone. I feared I lacked the charm and ability to fake it. Looking at the blank profile, I tried to harness the third-wave feminist in me. They pose that there's nothing wrong with being paid for sex-positivity—that it can be a form of empowerment—and philosophically, I agree with that.

In practice? I'm not so sure.

"I'm not asking anyone for money; I'm posting pictures and maybe, if I must, replying to messages. If patrons want to pay to see the photos of me, that's on them. I am not *actively* participating. I'm *passively* participating. A lot of what I've seen on the site isn't any racier than what I was putting on Instagram when running around topless on European beaches with Smythe."

LaVonne swirled the wine in her glass, taking a big sniff of its bouquet. "Okay. Great. Then gimme a birth date for your profile. Too bad you weren't born in 2012, because that was a very fine vintage."

LaVonne had educated herself, figuring out *what* was quality and why, instead of just believing the marketing. She started talking about heat waves and terroir, and I glazed over. I'd noticed sometime before that she'd developed a superiority complex with wine, and it all felt so familiar. I had a flash of my mother and shuddered.

"My point is, I can't be seventeen, okay? That would attract the worst of the worst."

"Girl, this is not an enterprise for good people. You're not gonna bump into a Disney prince on here. Actually, maybe you will, because most of the Disney princes are trash. Can we talk about Snow White for a minute? If you're in the woods and you happen upon a lady who's just chillin' in her glass coffin, do not put your lips all over her, no matter how welcoming she looks. That's assault, brother."

"Please," I said. "The prince has nothing on Prince Eric. First, Ariel's got to trade her voice to get legs. She literally *gives up her voice*—could that be any less feminist? Then Eric finds out about her sacrifices and doesn't say, *'No, please, don't diminish yourself for me; that's no way to create a marriage of equals.'* It's no wonder those sugar babies' services are going gangbusters. We've been conditioned to accept that the only way we'll be redeemed is if a man comes along to rescue us."

We were both quiet for a minute.

"How about we make you nineteen?"

"Done."

She typed my answer. "What are you into? Make it sexy."

I considered my passions. "I'm interested in connecting the world. I'm into opening up opportunities for the marginalized. I'm into having a social conscience. I'm into reducing our carbon footprint. I'm into every child having the same chance to succeed as their peers."

LaVonne looked like she'd just smelled spoiled milk. "That is the opposite of sexy. Remember, this is JustforEnthusiasts, not the Miss America pageant. Your wokeness is making me soft, and I don't even have a dick."

"Do you want me to cry? Is that your plan?" I asked.

"Imma say baby animals. That'll make your audience think about you all naked on a fur rug. It's real sensory."

I laid my head down on the kitchen table. "I feel woozy."

"What name are you gonna use? Ooh, I've got it. Let's call you Callie, because it's the closest name I can think of to 'call girl.'"

I began to lightly thunk my head against the table. "Why am I doing this?"

"'Cause you won't 'Callie' your dad."

I lifted my head up and met her eye. "Callie works."

My profile didn't take off in the beginning. While my pictures were garden-variety sexy, there was no differentiator. I'm conventionally attractive with symmetrical features, but not stunning. I'm healthy and fit, but not augmented. Why pay to see backlit artistic shots of my thong bikini when every variety of the full (surgically enhanced) Monty was available for free across the internet?

I didn't start to see any real revenue until low-level desperation led me to go up to the second tier. That's where I discovered that people longed for connection. They don't just want to see; they want to be seen. That's why the Greek system, archaic though it is, has thousands of freshman girls lining up, just as they will in a few days. Rushees want to be part of something bigger than just themselves. They want to belong to someone and something.

Once I started getting and responding to direct messages, the whole game changed. Interaction was key. I stopped being an image to patrons and started being a person with, in their minds, the potential to love them back. While some comments made me want to take a chemical shower—stripping off the first few layers of skin with industrial cleanser—often what I received was sweet or thoughtful. Men wanted to know about my life, my hopes, my dreams, and I'd respond in kind. LaVonne was wrong; not every fan was trash.

I've developed a few favorite patrons. Wally is a middle-aged cop in Iowa who calls himself "one of the good ones." The past few years have been hard on members of law enforcement who see themselves as saviors. The news cycle, the cell phone footage, the deaths. None of that fit his narrative. He's clearly looking for someone who doesn't automatically judge him for his chosen profession. His requests are always tame, and his messages perpetually polite. His fantasies are, shocker, hero-based.

Jonathan, another favorite, recently left the Church of Jesus Christ of Latter-Day Saints. He didn't like how the Mormon bishops treated his gay friends. He was looking to wade into the pool of his own bisexuality, and talking to me made him feel like his first steps were safe.

And then there's Oscar. His wife recently died, and now he's all alone. My heart goes out to him. He speaks to me more like the grandfather that he is, or at least he did. He's respectful and doesn't ask for anything racy. As I've gotten to know him, he's started checking in on me, seeing how I like my cosmetology classes, asking how my vintage Trans Am is running, finding out how volunteering at the animal shelter is going. (LaVonne ended up writing me an extensive bio, one that people believed.)

He's the last person I ever expected to stalk me.

My site presence has taken the financial boot off my neck. I knew I could take some shots and reply to messages and the revenue would come, and it did . . . quickly . . . until it didn't. To keep my patrons interested and engaged, I had to occasionally "go live," the dreaded third tier of the site.

The thing about decisions that are bad or inherently harmful—no one sets off to become addicted, to go all worst-case scenario. But that's how I found myself using the third tier of the site.

On my designated "Callie cam" days, I put on some weird fetish costume, go live, and start answering scrolling questions and requests. The first time was awful, but after that, it got easier. So easy, in fact, that sometimes I leave on CNN with the captions on and out of the camera's line of sight. I felt like a seasoned medical resident who had no problem eating an apple while watching the first-year students vomit on their shoes during their initial autopsy.

Oscar never participated. Instead, if he saw that I'd gone live, he'd send me an extra-large tip and suggest I stop. In a perverse way, he made me feel cared for.

That's why I'm so freaked out about him finding out who I am and texting me. He started contacting me a few weeks ago, after my mom moved in and I had to go dark. I had enough to cover that month's bills, so I wasn't too stressed. And Oscar's worrying about me was sweet. But tracking me down so he could say he was worried? That is *not fucking okay*. Now I'm afraid that he's not who he said he was. And why should he be? It's not like I put my real profile up. Millions of people are cat-fished every day; I just didn't think I'd be one of them.

I pull Janelle's shots and pour them over ice, then I add the syrup. I set down a cocktail napkin before I serve it, and I put one of our lemon squares on a plate with a fork, then set that down in front of her.

She thanks me and says, "This must be such a terrible year for you. The scrutiny, the second-guessing. Everyone thinks they know your story, but that's so rarely the case."

I nod because she's right, yet I'm not sure what to say.

She continues. "What you might not realize is, everyone is going through something. It's absolutely none of my business, but if you ever want to talk, I'm a no-judgment zone."

I knew I was right to like her. After Smythe, I stopped letting people in, save for LaVonne, whom I didn't *let* in so much as she kicked the door in and made herself at home in my life. Somehow, I feel like I can trust Janelle, that she's genuine, exactly who she seems to be. No surprises there.

"Here's the thing—I am angry at my dad for a lot of reasons. What he's done is inexcusable. I want him to be caught, and I want justice for his victims . . ."

"And you still miss him, and you feel guilty about it. As imperfect as he is, you miss him. He's your daddy," she says with a shrug. "Even a terrible father is better than none at all."

When I was a kid, no matter how busy he was with work, Dad never missed my water polo matches. He was always on his feet in the stands, cheering me on. Sometimes he'd even show up with my picture on a T-shirt. Then he'd take my whole team out for pizza, whether we won or not. Everyone loved him, and I was so proud that he was *mine*.

During the summers, we'd spend every weekend out on his fiberglass sailboat, which he christened the *Miss Appropriation*. In retrospect, what a prescient name. That boat was the first thing he bought when he started working for my grandfather. My mother loathed the *Miss Appropriation* because she supposedly got seasick on any craft smaller than thirty meters.

People always thought my father was so mannered and refined, so you'd think he'd own a yacht, instead of a thirty-five-foot sailboat with a bare-bones cabin. No one would guess that he lovingly restored that whole boat with his own two hands, or the pride he took in skippering the vessel himself. Sometimes we'd take a whole day and sail from our dock in Waukegan Harbor all the way down to the Burnham Park Yacht Club for a cup of their clam chowder.

I tell Janelle, "I'm struggling to separate the man from his mistakes."

"I get it," she says. She doesn't say much, and the next few minutes pass in companionable silence, punctuated only by the low hum of Professor Oxnard's beloved soccer game on the television. Janelle seems awfully savvy about all the ways fathers can disappoint you, so I wonder if she doesn't have her own story. Maybe at some point, she'll want to share.

I've tried to put my dad out of my head for the past year, because every time I think about him, I fume. I'm furious about Smythe, and now I hate him for what he did to his investors and the charity. I even resent him for how his shenanigans left my mother in such a precarious spot. She may be over-the-top, but she didn't deserve that.

Janelle has me thinking about the good times, and there were so many. He was funny, so fast on his feet with a quip. We had all kinds of inside jokes that my mom didn't understand. We'd just laugh when she got frustrated. And we were always going on secret adventures.

For instance, when I was in grade school, there was this enormous "trash panda" who loved to get into our garbage cans. He made our groundskeeper crazy because no matter how secure the cans were— looped shut with bungee cords—he could use his fat little paws to open them. One night, my dad and I set up a sting operation in the garage because we wanted to see how he did it.

We heard a loud thud on the roof as he dropped down from the oak tree. The groundskeeper had fenced off an area to protect the cans, but the raccoon simply landed on the roof and climbed down the trellis, just the perfect raccoon-sized ladder.

Dad and I stood watching, our hands clamped over our mouths so we wouldn't laugh and attract his attention. We'd seen how he could terrorize a couple of landscapers, and he wasn't afraid of the leaf blower.

With the skill and dexterity of a surgeon, he made short work of the bungee cord and then removed the lid, plunging his clawed fists into the bags, excavating his treasure. He flopped himself down, using a bag as a cushion, and started stuffing his face with the chicken paillard I'd left on my dinner plate that night.

"What should we name him?" I asked my dad.

"I think his name is obvious," he replied.

"Is it?" I asked. "Do we call him Bandit?"

My dad laughed. "Nope. Try again."

"Fatty?"

"Nah, that's too on the nose." He'd put his arm around me and pulled me closer as we looked out the window. The warmth he radiated enveloped me in a little cloud of love and protection. "Think about it . . . he's a *grouch* and he lives in a *garbage can.*"

Holy shit.

I think Oscar is my dad.

Chapter Twenty

CeCe

Three days before sorority rush

The screaming starts in the officers' wing on the third floor, creating a Doppler effect as the pitch grows sharper and louder the closer it gets. The sound of tiny feet pounding down the stairs accompanies all the shouting, culminating with the beating of little fists against my suite door.

I open it to find Natalie in a complete lather, fury radiating from her. Were she a full-sized person, I might be afraid, but witnessing her rage is like watching an angry basket full of kittens, harmless and ultimately kind of adorable.

Natalie waves a spreadsheet at me. "How could you be so, I mean, where do you, I mean, how did this even happen?" She is hopping mad, literally bouncing up and down in front of me.

"Darling, are you trying to communicate something?" I ask. My genuine curiosity seems to incense her more.

"First it was the marble! You can't have Edyta polish the marble and put on sealant like that, because the floor becomes a skating rink! I thought I was going to get concussed when I fell!" she screams. "I know we're supposed to wear shoes on the first floor and not just socks, but I forgot!"

I thought she was over that.

"Natalie, dear, I took care of the whole thing with the new library rug. I realize it was a bit of an investment up front, but quality of that sort will last a lifetime. It's so luxurious. Don't you just want to roll around on it?" Truly, the rug is fabulous!

"It wasn't in the budget!" Bits of spittle fly from her wee mouth.

"You must admit the rug really ties the room together."

I'm not sure if this stops her screaming because she knows that I'm right or because she's catching her breath to yell some more, like the lull between when a small child falls down and then registers their displeasure.

"Number two, it's going to be like Red Lobster's shrimp fest here for weeks. Do you understand me? Weeks!" Catching her breath, she continues. "I don't even like shrimp! I don't want to eat anything that poops in its own shell!"

Valid point. Now that she mentions it, that dorsal vein isn't really a vein at all, is it?

"Because of *you*, you've waved our magic checkbook, and shrimp is all we're going to eat! The full Forrest Gump! Shrimp kabobs, shrimp creole, shrimp gumbo, pan fried, deep fried, stir fried. Pineapple shrimp, lemon shrimp, coconut shrimp, pepper shrimp, shrimp soup, shrimp stew, shrimp salad, shrimp and potatoes, shrimp burgers, and shrimp freaking sandwiches!"

"I wonder if Loretta knows how to make shrimp de Jonghe? The dish is divine, and one can serve it as an appetizer or a main," I explain.

"Then you're all, *'What if we turned this perfectly serviceable house into a construction zone before the most important week of our lives?'* I don't have any idea if the workmen are going to finish on time. And even if they do, how the heck are we supposed to pay them, because we're so far over budget!"

Here's the thing about budgets: while it's useful to set them as a guideline, it's not a problem to go a little over, because you can always make it up with a last-minute donation; it works out. "Now wait just a minute," I say. "Rain Mother next door told me if the house needed a little extra, you could always do a special assessment on the new members."

Natalie is now vibrating. "We can special assess a few hundred dollars, not sixty-G-damn-thousand dollars over budget! We can't saddle the new people with a two-thousand-dollar bill on top of all the other initiation fees!"

Wait, what?

"Sixty thousand? No. That number doesn't make any sense," I reply. "I know I spent a few extra dollars, but Loretta was able to absorb many of those costs by cutting back on the proteins, what with our new shrimp surplus, which I got for a wholesale price. That's because we bought it in bulk."

Natalie's response is largely nonsensical. "Arrrhhhhhhhggggggaaaaaaaa!"

Oh, I bet the poor dear is allergic to shrimp.

I take my readers out of my bag and place them on the end of my nose, scanning the columns on the spreadsheet. "Let me see. Slipcovering? It's a few hundred dollars, and you should thank me that I convinced Fishman's to give us a deal after the decades' worth of business I've thrown their way. What else? Painting? The prices down here are far more reasonable than in Chicago, and you yourself told me you had some cash set aside for a refresh. The shrimp, yes, we've already discussed that. At length. Darling, I don't see what you're talking about."

Natalie repeatedly stabs the paper with her wee finger, pointing at the last line. "You spent fifty-eight thousand dollars replanting our flowers."

"That's impossible," I say. "The roses came from *Costoso*. It's a warehouse discount store. Everything is cheap as can be there. My father-in-law was wild about the place, always talking about how you could get a hot dog and a Coke for $1.50. The man was rich as Midas, but he loved a bargain and a nitrate."

Natalie's head and neck turn the color of a ripe tomato. "No. These came from a place called Campo de' Fiori in Kenilworth. I just got the invoice."

"Oh, Campo de' Fiori! Yes! They're wonderful. They were my garden supplier for the Lake Forest house for years! That must be who my old groundskeeper referred me to. I guess I'm confused. If the Juliet roses came from de' Fiori, I don't understand what Costoso is?"

"Costoso is the Spanish word for expensive; Spanish is my minor."

Suddenly, the pieces come together in my head—the landscapers weren't saying they were from Costco; they were telling me the roses were superexpensive, exactly what Rain meant when she called the Ausjameson the three-million-pound rose.

How could I have been so clueless?

Oh no. *Oh no, no, no.*

This whole situation is *my* fault. If I let these girls sink because of my mistake, I'm no better than Chip running off after bilking his investors.

Okay, think, CeCe.

The good news is, I'm a rational person, and there must be a logical solution to all of this. "Let's figure this out. Is there a way to talk to the alumnae about getting money from national leadership or tap into any sort of discretionary fund?" I ask.

Natalie drops onto the velvet settee. "Yes and no. We have excess money in the house management fund from monthly dues, but it's earmarked for our philanthropy. We worked so hard last year to cut down expenses so we could funnel all the extra into our charity, on top of our fundraising efforts. That's why we put off the remodel. We're supposed to have a presentation ceremony a couple of weeks after recruitment with all the new members. We have balloons! I even ordered the giant foam-board check, and I got big scissors, too, even though we're not doing a ribbon cutting, but you never know when you're going to need big scissors, you know?"

"I wasn't aware the house was involved with charities."

"Duh, of course we are; it's half the reason we exist. Did you even *read* the manual I made for you?" I glance over at my little secretary desk where the manual sits untouched. I've been using my time to spruce up the place. Guilty as charged.

I can't even look at Natalie right now; I feel horrible. I've been going on and on about what a victim I am for the past two months, but it seems that now I'm the perpetrator. I'm the one putting these girls in a pinch when they did nothing wrong. I didn't see it. I thought I knew better.

"Everyone in the house pitched in to help us save. Like, Loretta came up with a vegan chili that's super low-cost, and we started a whole Meatless Monday thing. The chili low-key sucks; it tastes and smells like she boiled gym socks, but we tell her we love it because we saved so much money. Literally, we saved, like, four dollars per person per serving, which doesn't sound like much until you multiply it by a hundred girls once a week for two semesters."

She buries her face in her tiny palms. "You wouldn't even believe how relentless I was last year. I was a straight-up pest." I have no trouble believing this. "Like, I put in low-flow toilets and signs like 'If it's yellow, it's mellow,' and timers on the lights. I kept the heat at sixty-six degrees, and when people got cold, I told them to put on a sweater. I turned into my dad for this! I made everyone mad at me, but I figured it would all be worth it when we signed that big novelty check over to Live Love Lit. And this year was going to be our biggest donation ever. We were going to be recognized by our national chapter and that's such an honor and it was going to be the crown jewel in my résumé and now I'm never going to get a job!"

I don't want to ask, but I must. "What is Live Love Lit?"

Natalie lets out an exasperated sound. "You'd know if you read the manual! It's our national charity. Every year, we donate enough money to purchase six new books for every grade schooler in an underprivileged school district, and we also fund extra reading tutors. When you give kids books and make sure they can read them, you change their lives."

I think of darling LaVonne. I might not oversee my fund anymore, but I would still like to help change lives.

I must find a way to fix this.

"What you're telling me is that there's no way to fix this?" I ask the dean.

When she hired me, Dean Grace insisted I come to her if I had a problem, and I believe accidentally driving the house into sixty thousand dollars' worth of debt because I didn't learn enough Spanish when I was drinking sangria in college qualifies as a problem.

"I'm sorry; my hands are tied," Dean Grace tells me. Her words are sympathetic, yet the emotions behind them are . . . lacking.

Why does she seem like she's enjoying this?

She says, "While the university supports the Greek system, if a chapter is financially insolvent, if they can't meet their obligations, there's nothing we can do to help them. In fact, per our agreement, if they're in arrears on any of their bills regarding the property, we can revoke their long-term lease."

I knit my hands together in my lap and recross my ankles. "Meaning?"

"Meaning if anything goes to collections, the Alpha house would cease to be, at least in its current iteration, because of the university bylaws. The truth is, as tight as housing is on this campus, I'm sure another organization would happily take over the building in exchange for covering their debts."

I can't let this happen, but I do have to know. "Where would the girls go?"

She says, "I imagine they'd have to find apartments somewhere across the river. There's no room in any of the residence halls. Real estate is so scarce on this campus, and we've built on every bit of available ground." She rises from her desk and walks to the windows, pulling back a curtain sheer. "If you look out here, you can see where we're erecting another residence hall on the last of . . ."

She continues talking, but something on her desk catches my eye. While her back is to me, I quickly get up to look. There's a sheet of notes where she's doodled *Provost Grace* in the margins, which would be meaningless were it not for the document next to it.

There's a letter printed on incredibly high-bond parchment. I always say I know luxury when I see it, and this sheet of paper came from an incredibly expensive ream; I never even bought paper that nice. It's the kind the president would use to sign a treaty. The letterhead reads *Beijing Student Cooperative* in English and Chinese characters. I quickly scan the contents, and a few key words pop out, such as "luxury accommodations" and "consideration for Beijing students to live together."

The dean finishes her monologue. "And that's why we rely on generous donors to help us meet our housing objectives. A shame that we can't count on Barclay checks anymore. They were put to such good use." She sits back down and offers a self-satisfied smile that seems awfully familiar.

I've seen this exact expression before, but not for a very long time. Poppy Pierce.

Poppy Pierce would flash this same grin right before she saddled me with whatever the worst task was at one of her events. Then I'd face a Sophie's choice: either comply with something meant to shame or disgust me, or seem like a selfish princess for balking. The look said that she knew she had me and there was nothing I could do about it. *"CeCe, would you be a lamb; put on an apron, and help pass the appetizers? Some of our cater waiters didn't show,"* or *"Oh no! CeCe, darling, we're in such a pinch—can you be a team player and make all these beds? We want the shelter looking fresh in the brochure photos,"* or *"CeCe, one of the*

*children vomited after too much candy. Help the Easter bunny wipe down
his costume, won't you?"*

The dean's endgame just became crystal clear.

"May I ask you a question, Dean Grace?"

"Certainly."

"If the Alpha house were to somehow go under, say they were in
financial arrears, or they didn't meet their recruitment numbers, how
quickly would you fill that house with wealthy foreign students?"

Two giant red splotches appear on the dean's cheeks. "What do
you mean?"

I rise from my seat. "I believe you're well aware of what I mean.
This was intentional. You hired me to bring down the Alpha house. You
assumed I'd fail. When I failed, your plan was to take back the Alpha
house and fill it with Mr. Wu's international students because they're a
cash cow for the university. What do they pay, three or four times what
you charge for out-of-state tuition? But you can't recruit them if they
have no place to live, and where better to house them than a freshly
rehabbed mansion?"

Dean Grace must have thought there was no way I wouldn't fail,
and I've played right into her hands. She probably assumed Janelle
would mess up, too, because she's so young, but she had no idea Janelle
was competent. Dean Grace intentionally sabotaged the sororities so she
could fill them with higher-paying students and get herself promoted
to provost.

The dean collects her thoughts and finally says, "If this were my
plan, and I'm not saying it is, but if it were, the beauty is that *I* didn't
do anything. Alpha's problems can all be traced directly to you, Ms.
Barclay. And really, where would you have us put all these high-value
students?"

I place my hands on the dean's desk and lean in, close to her face.
"Why don't you bend over, darling, and I'll show you?"

Chapter Twenty-One

JANELLE

Three days before sorority rush

Janelle's Daily Do-List

- *Laminate and post revised fire safety protocol*
- *Research low-flow showerheads*
- *Stop daydreaming!*

Status check

Uncle Pat makes me smile every time he texts me. The man does not waste words. How do I sum up how well everything's going in a couple of words? If my life was a musical, I'd burst into song while everyone around performed Broadway-style dance moves. I feel so much joy, there'd definitely be tap dancing.

Does he want the details of my job? Does he want to hear how I live in a safe place, surrounded by such nice girls? Is he interested in the friendships I'm forming with Rain, Marilee, the other housemoms, and even Hayden? That the nightmares are less frequent, and that every morning when I wake up, I touch my crucifix and give thanks when I think about how blessed I am to be here? And that I start Intro to Management Principles soon?

What if I just surprise him at our next meeting in my new-to-me silver Honda Civic with low mileage, a functioning radio, and absolutely no duct tape? Can I send the marshals a thank-you letter for giving me an identity with a 750-point credit score? (I got a 2.9 percent APR at CarMax—2.9 percent!)

I'm not sure how to put any of this into words, so I reply with the big-eyes smile emoji, since it most closely reflects my mood. He returns my text with a purple heart. Unless he's a secret BTS fan, I'm convinced he doesn't understand how emojis work.

I feel so fulfilled, which is why I stuck around at Eli's longer than I intended. Hayden was in a weird space, and I didn't want to leave her. She's having mixed feelings about her dad, and no one understands that more than I do. Her mood was all over the place, though. First, she was opening up to me, and then she was suddenly off in another world, so I just read my sorority book at the counter and quietly kept her company.

I have another date with Trevor tonight, but Hayden felt more important than a return home to change clothes, so now I'm meeting Trevor in front of the shop. He keeps saying I'm taking away his gentleman cred for never letting him pick me up. I guess he's getting his wish. When I texted him about the change of plans, he immediately replied with a car emoji, a coffee emoji, and a heart emoji.

I haven't told Uncle Pat much about Trevor, at least not directly. The nice thing is, he's a positive presence in my life, like a fairy godfather, never too far away, always paying attention to what I'm doing. I drop him a pin wherever I go, so no doubt he's seen me going to Trevor's apartment. As protective as Uncle Pat is, I don't doubt he's already pulled his transcripts and done a criminal record search. If Trevor had so much as a parking ticket, Uncle Pat would be there with a SWAT team, so he really has to be on the up-and-up, or else I'd know. This must be what it feels like to have an engaged dad. If he has daughters, they are so fortunate.

I'm slowly getting to know Trevor, and I've seen nothing but green flags. He's diligent about school. He's polite to waitstaff. His wardrobe isn't 90 percent tracksuits. (Yes, this has been a problem in New Jersey.) He recycles. He wants a wife and a family and a couple of rescue dogs. His dream is a place in the suburbs with a lawn he can mow and a garage where he can store tools that he swears he'll learn how to use. He's started a retirement account. He's always asking what I think and how I feel, and he acts as though my answers impact him. This is all new to me.

I wonder now if nice guys always existed, but I didn't hold myself in enough esteem to attract one. Maybe I didn't have high-enough expectations for myself, so no one else did either. If I attracted the worst people, it's because that's all I felt I deserved.

I'm trying to go about things differently with Trevor. I haven't done any cyber-sleuthing, and I've kept whatever this is kind of quiet. In the past, I'd tell everyone when I had a date, and Des would profile the guys in a way that would make Uncle Pat offer her a job. She could find anything on anyone! She always talked about how there were too many sickos in the world, and she couldn't understand why they were so willing to put their weird tendencies out there for her to discover.

I'm sure I wouldn't find much if I were to Insta-stalk, anyway; Trevor disabled all his social media before applying to law school. He doesn't want to lose a judicial appointment because of something dumb he did before he was legally able to buy a beer. I imagine that's why he didn't think it was odd when I said I wasn't into social media either. We're both doing this without a net, getting acquainted the old-fashioned way, face-to-face. I like it!

Trevor pulls up in his green Subaru Outback with a snowboard roof rack and Colorado plates. He hops out to open my door.

"That is so unnecessary," I tell him.

"Oh, but it isn't," he replies.

The inside of his car is clean and tidy, and he doesn't have anything stupid hanging from the rearview mirror. I went out with one guy who had a pair of his kid's baby shoes hanging, all the while trying to tell me he didn't have the family that Des easily found online. He couldn't have been more obvious if he'd had a car seat in the back.

"Where are we going?" I ask, settling into the seat and snapping my safety belt. He looks freshly shaved and smells like cedar and sandalwood. His shirt is neatly pressed, and there are comb marks in his hair. "I hope nowhere nice, because I didn't get a chance to change." I'm still wearing shorts, flip-flops, and a lightweight, embroidered peasant blouse.

He cuts his eyes away from the road. "What are you talking about? You look amazing."

"Flattery will get you everywhere."

"Good to know, as this is our fifth date, so . . ."

"Are you even hungry?" I ask.

He looks over at me again. "Not one bit."

We tumble into Trevor's apartment, our mouths and bodies pressed together the entire time. He shuts his front door and then says, "Hold on a sec. Let me set the mood. Alexa, dim the lights. Alexa, play Dolly Parton's 'I Will Always Love You.'" We both laugh.

His place is both modern and clean, like he tore a page out of an Ikea catalog. I love that despite all the blond wood and glass, he still has an old crucifix hanging on the wall by the door.

Trevor pulls my blouse over my head, and I'm glad I thought to put on one of my "good" bras today, scalloped with lace in all the right spots. I yank off his shirt and then pause to admire his bare chest. He doesn't wax, a practice I always find disturbing. I like men to look like men. He's lean and muscular from years of outdoor sports.

"You gonna look or buy?" he asks, then he pulls me to him with such force that we both fall backward onto his couch, our lips never coming apart.

I pull away. He stops and says, "Shit, did I misread your signals? We're not doing anything without consent. I thought . . ."

"We have to leave room for the Holy Ghost," I tell him, mocking a serious expression.

With that, he leaps off the couch, picks me up, and carries me to his bedroom.

Showtime.

Hours later, I'm still wrapped up in Trevor's bed. The sheets have a Labrador-and-golden-retriever print. His mom thought it would be hilarious to send him to law school with cartoon dog sheets, knowing he'd be too pragmatic to buy new ones. She sounds like a hoot, like she'd fix herself a Chardonnay with ice when she reads a book outside.

Every time I try to get out of the bed, he pulls me down.

"Stay," he says, and buries his head in my hair. I had it up in a loose topknot earlier, but I lost my hair tie around the time I lost my shorts.

I slip out of his grip, even though I don't want to. "I can't. I have to get back to the house. How's it going to look if I'm doing the walk of shame in the morning? I'm the housemother for a bunch of sorority girls."

"You won't walk. I'm driving you."

"It's the same thing," I say. "What kind of example am I going to set if it's me coming home with my underwear in my bag?"

"Sounds like a good example to me." He pouts when I pull away, and it's just too cute.

I wrap myself in a blanket and grab my purse from the living room. When I come back, Trevor hasn't made any moves to get up. I paw through my bag for an elastic. When I can't find one, I wind my hair into a bun and secure it with a pencil while I look for my phone. Trevor sits up and gives me an odd look.

"What? It's convenient," I tell him.

Slowly, he asks, "Did you just say, 'It's convenient'?"

I nod as I locate my phone and order a car. Ornaldo will be here in five minutes, so I have to hustle and get dressed. Trevor said he wanted to take me home, but it's so late that if he leaves, he'll never find a parking space again.

I look at him again, and he's gone pale. "Hey . . . ," he says. "Where is the Kappa Gamma house, anyway?"

"I don't know. Why?" I say, gathering up discarded pieces of my outfit.

There's distinct anxiety in his voice. "Um, because you live there?"

"No, I'm housemom at Gamma Kappa."

He lets out a swift exhale. "I could have sworn you said Kappa Gamma."

I turn away from him while I dress, which is weird. He's just touched every part of me, so it shouldn't be awkward at all, yet here we are. "Eh, I probably did. I had trouble with the Greek letters at first, but I've been reading up and I've figured it out. Want me to recite the alphabet now? I totally can. Alpha, beta, gamma—"

He leaps out of bed and pulls on a pair of gym shorts. "Shit."

"What is it?"

"Oh, um, nothing. I just remembered I have an exam tomorrow."

That doesn't sound right. "Before classes start?"

He snaps, "It's a law school thing."

I'm taken aback by his sudden change in attitude. What happened? We just had a fantastic night, in sync in every way. I replay everything in my head to try to figure out what I've done wrong, why it seems like he's suddenly panicking. This all started when I put the convenient pencil in my bun.

The pencil.

The crucifix.

The snowboard.

The third year of his law program.

Wait, did I just sleep with Addie's boyfriend?

Ornaldo drops me out front. Greek Row is quiet, save for the old mom everyone calls Mean Helene. She's doing something outside the Zoo house with binoculars, as per usual. I think she watches birds. Even though I'm this upset, I wave, because I don't want to seem rude.

I plug in the entry code and quietly slip through the front door. My suite isn't far from the main entry hallway, so I'm able to avoid the girls who are up late in the TV room, prepping for Monday's recruitment parties.

I grab my iPad, open Instagram, and locate Addie's profile. Her most recent post is from today. It's a nicely filtered shot of the sorority house with the caption *Fall recruitment starts Monday. Yeet!*

She doesn't post a lot on the main feed, so it doesn't take me long to confirm my worst fears—a photo of a Subaru with Colorado plates and two snowboards strapped to the roof rack. The caption reads *#blackdiamond #morelikeredhearts*.

I cannot believe this.

I am boiling with anger. I'm so tired of being a victim, of being the nice girl who says, "I'm so sorry!" and "Please excuse me!" and "How can I help?" I never ask for anything, and that's exactly what I get. I don't yell; I don't confront; I just sit and let it all happen to me.

You know what? Not today.

I immediately call Trevor, but he doesn't pick up. Coward. He's smart. He must have figured out that I know. He's probably busy burying his tracks. How did I let this guy derail my new life, the best thing that ever happened to me? I don't get a *fresh* fresh start; this is it.

I don't know why I thought I would be done having my heart broken in this new life, but here I am. How did I get so fooled so quickly? What is wrong with me? Maybe I'll never be anything but Gina/Janelle Two, everyone's second choice.

If I was Taylor Swift, I could turn all of this into a platinum album, find a way to let this pain and disappointment pay off. But I'm not, and I just have to live with it.

I can't even talk to anyone, because what if I did? My mind starts racing. What will Addie do if she finds out? None of this is my fault. And maybe this isn't the kind of thing I could get fired for, but that doesn't matter, because I violated the girl code, even though I didn't mean to. The whole house would turn against me, and that would be as good as getting fired. Maybe it would be different if he was her ex, but her current boyfriend? No way. Now I have to sit on yet another huge secret, because someone else did the wrong thing, and I have to suffer for it. Damn it!

If he's too afraid to talk to me, I'll text him. I type:

I know that you're Addie's boyfriend and I am

This is no time to edit myself.

I am fucking disgusted with you. I'm blocking your number, don't contact me again, this never happened. She deserves better than you.

He immediately texts back.

J, please, you don't understand—am not with Addie—went out
briefly and she got obsessive and

I stop reading. No. No way. I am not allowing him to pull the "she's
crazy!" card on me. He can't attribute his slimy behavior to her crazy.
It's always the women who are "crazy" when they won't put up with a
man's bullshit anymore. My mom was as sober and sane as a judge, but
when my parents fought about my dad's behavior, he would always pin
it on her. He'd take me aside and say, "Mom isn't being rational. Maybe
things would be different if she was just a little more understanding."

I pull up my privacy settings and block Trevor's number. If I'm
lucky, Addie will soon realize what a jerk she's dating and move on.

The feelings are coming in waves, alternating between rage and
grief. We only went out a handful of times. It's not like finding out a
spouse was lying. Still, it's the first time I've let myself feel vulnerable in
years. Maybe he didn't know my real past, but I felt like he knew who
I was, and what I was about.

I'm hit with a wave of shame and regret. I'm so stupid. I blame
myself for trying to believe in something obviously too good to be true.
This makes me doubt everything about myself, like maybe I'm not really
competent to handle anything.

Maybe I really am my father's daughter, just destined to fail at
everything.

Where do I even go from here?

I look back and forth between my tablet and phone, wondering
what to do next. That's when I realize I have Instagram open. As in, I
was in such a rush to figure out if Trevor was a cheater that I *logged on
to Instagram under my old Gina Marie Ferragamo profile.*

Oh no. This is a nightmare.

I start to text Uncle Pat, but this seems like too big a deal, so I
call him instead and pray that he's still awake. He answers on the first

ring, and I immediately start talking. "I'm so sorry it's so late, but I just screwed up!" I'm on the verge of hysterics.

He's all business. "Janelle, are you safe? Do I need to send a squad car?"

"I'm safe, but I messed up—"

"Stop. Take a breath. Then take another breath. Now, tell me what happened."

I explain my error, leaving out the most personal details and bracing myself for the worst. Is he going to yell at me? Or make me move? Or tell me how disappointed in me he is? I'm not sure I can bear that. How could I have been so reckless? So stupid?

He says, "Let me understand what happened—all you did was log on to get some answers? Confirm that you didn't post a photo. Because even if you don't tag the photo, there are embedded geolocators that can help people find you. You didn't do that, right?"

I pace the length of the narrow hallway connecting the living area with the bedroom. I catch sight of myself in the bathroom mirror. I look god-awful. I quickly touch my cross. Ugh. Even my thoughts are betraying me. "Definitely not. Am I in trouble? Did I ruin everything? Do I need to run? Do I have to leave? Oh, I hate to leave the sisters without a housemom right before—"

Patiently, he tries to talk me down. "Janelle, take another breath. It's okay. Cavalcante's crew is more about brute force and racketeering than technical know-how. You didn't do anything traceable, at least outside the auspices of the Instagram offices, and not without a high court judge's ruling. Now, if you'd tangled with the Russian hackers, I might have cause for concern, but this is not on that level."

I can't stay still. I go to the windows and pull every drape shut, double-checking each sash lock. "What do I do?"

"Delete the account. That should take care of everything."

That sounds too easy. Nothing is that easy. We must be missing something. "Are you sure?"

"Kiddo, you sound like you've had a rough night. I suggest you delete the account, drink a warm glass of milk, and get some sleep. I'll check in with you in the morning. I'll come down there if you need me to. It's okay. You're okay. All is well." Uncle Pat speaks to me in a way that is direct, but also calm and kind.

My heart doesn't feel like it's about to explode out of my chest now, so he must be helping. I take another couple of breaths, and I do feel slightly better.

"Good air in, bad air out," he tells me. I work on my breathing with him for a minute.

"Uncle Pat, can I ask you something?"

"Shoot."

"Do you have kids? The warm-milk thing feels like something you've said before. If you do have children, are you even allowed to tell me?"

He laughs. "Yes, and yes. I have two little girls; one's eight and one's eleven. Stella and Nora. And I always give them warm milk if they can't sleep, which is frequently. Two little monkeys are what they are, always climbing on something. Stella got herself onto the roof last weekend. My ex-wife turned around for one minute, and there was Stella, with her feet hanging off the side of the garage."

Those little girls are so lucky. "Oh. Do you get to see them much?"

"Officially, they're with their mother three weeks out of the month, and every other weekend, but I live down the street from them. My ex and I are amicable, so we do whatever's most expedient for the girls. For example, I pick them up from school every day. They're still young enough that I don't embarrass them, but I'm sure that will happen soon enough."

I can picture his daughters clinging to him, like he's the greatest dad in the world. "They have to feel very safe with you."

"Well, that's my job. Listen, Janelle. Why don't you get some rest now?"

"I'll do that. Thanks, Uncle Pat."

"All in a day's work. Also, Janelle? This part isn't any of my business, but it's my opinion that if this guy made you feel this way, you're too good for him. You deserve someone who treats you like the queen you are. Good night."

He hangs up before I can thank him again.

What fortunate kids Nora and Stella are, to have a man like Uncle Pat in their life. Uncle Pat reminds me of Addie's dad. She's lucky, too, despite the jerk law student. Her father was so lovely when I met him, just reveling in the role of being a helpful dad. He's probably never let Addie down, never stolen money out of Addie's purse, never thrown up in the living room after overserving himself at her tenth birthday party, making her a virtual pariah for the next few years. I imagine he never got into so much gambling debt that Addie had to quit high school and work full-time so they wouldn't be homeless after her mom was too sick to keep her job.

My father must be why I'm so anxious about meeting someone nice, decent. I keep self-sabotaging because of him. As much as I want children, I never want any kid to experience what I did growing up.

When I finally stop pacing and sit down, I realize Addie's Instagram page is still open. I decide to look at a few more of her pictures before I delete my account. Her life looks charmed, with the big house in the Chicago suburbs and huge family that wears matching pajamas at the holidays. Even their fluffy white dog got in on the act in his little Santa hat. Is it weird to be jealous of a dog? In the summers, it looks like she spends time waterskiing on some clear blue lake, and then she snowboards in the winter. And there are tons of pictures with sorority sisters, some girls I've met and some I don't recognize.

There are a few older shots with someone who looks super familiar. I realize it's Hayden from before she went boho. Wow, she looks different, much more like a younger CeCe. I don't know why I'm surprised that Hayden and Addie know each other. Everyone says this is a big school, but it's in a small town. These pictures are from a few years ago, and Addie and Hayden don't look like they're interacting with each other, so maybe they weren't close. I can't see them having much in common.

Since Uncle Pat promised it's not a life-and-death matter, I go to Des's page. I've been dying to know what's happening with her. In her most recent photo, she's standing in an empty dance studio with a huge grin on her face. The caption reads *#comingsoon*. Oh, she did it—she's opening her studio! She really did it! I wish I could tell her how proud I am. Uncle Pat already warned me about making a Finsta (a fake page) because he didn't want anything to connect me to my old life, so I've been completely in the dark since that last night at the club.

Curiosity is getting the better of me, so I check in on Carina too. My heart swells when I see a shot of her son Henry's first day at Abernathy Day School, wearing a blazer and knee socks with shorts. He's too cute. There's a photo of her with Marty and . . . wait, I think they might be a couple? What? I bet there's a story there! He always had a crush on her. The night of the shooting is a blur, but maybe he did something heroic to finally capture her attention.

Per Marty's profile, he appears to be working on his quilted clothing full time. He now has his own website. Aw, every one of his designs has sold out. And yes, they are definitely a couple. Oh my gosh, there's a picture of the three of them in matching quilted jackets; it's making my heart smile.

I quickly look at Gina One, who seems happy after a couple of weeks at Rehoboth Beach with college friends and her fiancé. I love that she caught the biggest fish the day they went out on a boat. She looks so delighted in her floppy hat, posing with the blue fish in one hand and a can of White Claw in the other.

Maybe it's petty, but I don't search for Ariel, because I just don't care what's going on with her.

Not wanting to tempt fate, I decide it's time to delete my profile. I know I dodged a bullet (maybe literally?) with this huge oversight, and that's helping me keep this Trevor business in proportion. I'm glad I found out who he is now, rather than three months from now. Even though it still hurts, he's not a quality person, so I must move on. Uncle Pat is right; I can do better. I think.

I click around to find the delete button. Because I'm apparently Luddite according to Ariel (shut *up*, Ariel), I get frustrated with electronics more easily than most, and I end up just stabbing at my phone until I accidentally open my direct messages.

Wait.

There's a direct message from my father. Since when is he on Instagram?

I shouldn't even read this. I need to delete this app right now and get rid of the last trace of the old me. There's nothing I can do for him, and nothing good will come of reading whatever it is he has to say. It's probably just a lie meant to manipulate me anyway.

Yet that small voice nags at me, *What if it's different today?*

Hating myself for how weak I am, I click to the message that came in two days ago.

Gina, I can't find you anywhere. There's some new person in your apartment and you're not at your job anymore. I know something bad happened and I am sorry. Something worse will happen if I don't talk to you. I'm in big trouble. I can't get into it here. I would not ask if it weren't life and death. Can you meet me at the diner we always used to go to out on Route 9? I'll be there on Sunday at noon. Please. Your mother would want you to. Love from your pop.

Why does he always do this? I'm flooded with emotions and feel a physical ache in my chest. My mouth is dry, and I feel light-headed. Shit. Why did I read this?

Obviously, I can't meet him. That would be insane and potentially dangerous. I shouldn't be anywhere near New Jersey until after the Cavalcante trial, and even then, it's iffy.

Still, I wonder what kind of trouble he's in this time. And why did he have to drag my mother's memory into this? I'm sure her advice would be to run away from him like she never could.

I need to delete this app right now, then go to bed and get up again in this better, new life. One small stumble with Trevor doesn't have to mess everything up. All is well. All is better than well. The worst decision in the world would be for me to reply.

I type I'll see what I can do.

I never said I made great decisions when it comes to my dad.

Chapter Twenty-Two

HAYDEN

Three days before sorority rush

I did the math.

Over the course of last year, and in small increments, my client "Oscar" gave me enough money to cover my tuition. So he did it. He fucking did it. My father found a way to absolve his sins by paying for my schooling, against my wishes. I thought I was so empowered, taking control of my financial destiny, yet I still had "the patriarch" calling the shots for me.

I'm ninety-nine percent furious. He disrespected my choice to remove myself from his influence. Yet, there's that one percent that's pleased at how he fought for me. I wish I didn't feel so conflicted, that doing the right thing was entirely cut-and-dried.

Being around my father is like having someone shine a golden light on you—he reflects so much radiance that it's dazzling. You feel like you're the only person in his orbit, which renders most people powerless against his charms. I can think of hundreds of times that everyone around him just melted, from restaurant servers to heads of state. He has the *it factor* like an A-list Hollywood celebrity. I've seen him cause a fender bender and after two minutes in his presence, the afflicted driver begging his forgiveness.

In retrospect, when he pulled out Smythe's chair at our dinner in Paris, she didn't stand a chance; I should have seen it coming.

My father never worked hard for anything—he didn't have to. Between his family's wealth and status and his own allure, he seemed less like a man than a superhero; ergo he wasn't bound by the same rules. At eighteen, he was a junior member of the regatta crew that won the Chicago Yacht Club Race to Mackinac. While he was a minor cog, the photo of him at the bow, windswept and sun-kissed in a flipped collar and white chinos rolled above the ankle, landed him on a *Time* magazine cover article on 1980s youth culture. From then on, he was a heartthrob. Teen magazines included him in their pages; he even received fan mail. He was a living, breathing Ken doll.

The problem is that when the entire universe thinks you can do no wrong, eventually, you begin to believe your own press. His hubris led to the bad decisions that brought on his downfall, and he took a lot of innocent people with him, including my mother.

The tragedy is that he could have coasted for the rest of his life. He could have left everything at the firm in place after my grandfather's death and floated indefinitely on his golden life raft. But he wasn't satisfied being loved and adored. He had to chase the high of more, making high-risk investments in hopes of high rewards.

I don't know why my mother didn't leave him years ago. She must have seen behind his façade. Only after the scandal broke did I find out the extent of his infidelities, but she's canny—she must have had her suspicions, or even known. Smythe was one in a long line. In retrospect, this explains why none of my nannies or ballet instructors ever stuck around. But despite his proclivities, I idolized him. He was the best father.

Could that be why she stayed?

I think about my discussion with Janelle earlier. She made me feel better about my conflicted feelings about Dad. And if I hadn't been so focused on myself, I'd have been more attuned to what she said about her own experiences. Maybe I'm more of my dad than I care to admit. Everything is always about me. But I do miss him, despite everything. He was exactly what a little girl would want in a daddy. He just wasn't a very good human.

But my nostalgia can't supersede what's right.

That's why I called one of the federal agents and told her everything I knew.

I imagine the Feds are preparing to come for him. In the interim, I blocked his profile on the Enthusiasts page, as well as the IP address he's using. The site makes it easy to deny access to patrons who make you feel uncomfortable. I booked a couple of sessions with Dr. Beekman after recruitment next week. There's a lot I need to unpack about all this. Dad must have hated what I was doing. And while some part of me appreciates that he was making sure I was okay, it's still really fucking twisted.

I tried to get hold of my mother all afternoon because Dad making contact seems like important news. (I don't know where she is or what's more important than taking a call from me, but who knows with her.) Not sure how I can explain this to her without exposing the JustforEnthusiasts part, but I'll figure it out. For now, I'm going to have to put in extra time on live chats because Oscar was a major chunk of my revenue.

I'm not thrilled about having to log on after a full day at the shop and the emotional time bomb of finding out Dad's identity, but it's imperative to build my Enthusiast base if I'm going to replace that revenue.

I'm trying LaVonne's suggestion for my hair. I'm wearing a blunt-cut golden wig with heavy bangs and two high pigtails, paired with a Sailor Moon outfit. Like the cartoon, it's got the pleated navy short skirt and the big red bow at the neckline. Enthusiasts on the Japanese anime channel are particularly active. No one sees my feet—although there's a market for it—so I'm wearing fuzzy Ugg slides.

Dual ring lights illuminate me from either side of my monitor. Whenever I read a comment out loud, the cash register chimes go off to indicate someone's given me a tip. I try to respond to everyone; people want to be seen.

"Hey, Marcus696969, thanks, I like this look on me too. Wait, what's that?"

I lean in to read his suggestion and . . . yuck. The anime crowd is straight-up freaky. "If you want to see me suck my thumb, we'll have to upgrade to a private screen so it's just us. Sound good?" I say to the camera.

Someone starts knocking on my door, but I ignore it. My flighty neighbor is perpetually locking herself out. I have her spare key, but I can't always be here to bail her out, especially when I'm in the middle of filming. She'll have to wait.

The banging continues, loudly enough that my viewers notice. They begin to comment, and the little cash registers stop chiming. Argh.

"No, it's fine," I say. "I don't have to answer the door," I tell the screen.

Bang! Bang, bang!

"Heh, yeah. It probably is my landlord. You're right, I bet I *will* have to convince him to let me pay my rent late," I say, trying to continue smiling. The anime crowd wants to see me happy; I'd have to go to the emo channel if I want to be negative.

Bang! And then, "Hayden! Mummy is here. Open up. It's urgent."

I rip the power strip out of the wall, ending the broadcast. Everything goes dark, lights, camera, monitors. I stomp to the door, so furious that she ignored me all day and then shows up unannounced that I don't even think about what I'm wearing.

"What!" I exclaim as I swing the door open.

"That's how you greet your mother?" she asks. She takes a beat to scan my outfit, then reaches into her handbag and hands me a small cream-colored card.

"What's this?" I ask.

"Direct line to my personal stylist at Neiman's. Your taste is a cry for help."

Mortified, I pull on a cardigan. "I've been trying to call you all day! I heard from Dad!"

"I assume he's still in Madagascar?" she replies, tucking a stray strand behind her ear.

My mind is blown. "Hold up. You know where he is?"

She breezes past me and heads into my kitchen. "I'm going to help myself to a glass of water, if you don't mind." She peeks into my fridge. "Really, nothing bottled?" She busies herself in my cabinets and then pours a glass from the tap. "Anyway, yes, didn't I tell you? Our investigator found him there. Unfortunately, there's nothing the FBI can do, which is the crux of the problem. No extradition treaty. You're sure I didn't tell you?"

"I've seen you every day this week, and all you've talked about is shrimp!" I shout.

"Darling, shh, neighbors. I probably forgot because I've been in a dilly of a pickle. I've had some issues at the Alpha house." She smooths her skirt and adjusts the collar of her blouse.

"Does it have anything to do with you bulldozing the staff, treating them like they work for you, not with you? Maybe you've looked at the whole thing as a giant piggy bank instead of a responsibility?"

My mother nods. "Yes, darling. Mistakes were made," she says. I'm gobsmacked. This is the closest she's ever come to admitting her guilt.

My mother continues. "Here's the situation. It occurs to me, rather after the fact, that I went from my parents' house to the dorm to your father's home. I've never been on my own. I've never really had to be responsible or a problem solver. I never needed to make my own living, and someone was always there to pick up the pieces I dropped. I've suddenly found myself in a position where I must be the grown-up, where it's incumbent on me to make the tough choices. You've done that before, and while I might question your choices, Fudge"—she looks directly at my septum ring—"they're yours, and you've made them."

What is happening? Did I electrocute myself when I yanked the cord? Am I hallucinating? On what planet does my mother admit she's anything shy of perfect?

"So, I'm hoping you can help me. I've screwed everything up, and I need to fix it. I thought, *Hayden is competent, she'll know what to do.*"

"You want my help? Because you think I'm competent? Is that what you're saying?" Am I dead? I must be dead. This is the only logical explanation.

"Darling, is your interesting new hairstyle impairing your hearing? Yes, yes. Please. I require your assistance." She bats her eyes comedically. Why did I never realize she could be kind of funny?

I need some sort of closure, and I'm never going to get it from Dad, so I have to try the next best thing. "Before I help you, tell me: Why did you stay with Dad? You had to have known what he was doing behind your back. He wasn't subtle. He must have humiliated you. Weren't you furious? You had your own money; you had your own life. You didn't need him. So why? Why would you stick around?"

"Wasn't it obvious, Hayden? I stayed because girls need their daddies."

"That's it?" I say. That's the answer I've been looking for my whole adult life?

"That's not enough?" she replies, just so matter-of-fact.

Wait. *Is* it enough?

Is it possible that I'm truly the reason she didn't leave?

What would my life have been like if they'd split up? Regardless of custody arrangements, I'd have seen him far less often. We wouldn't have had all that father-daughter time we both loved so much and that did so much to shape me. In fact, he likely would have remarried, obviously to someone younger, and started an entire new family. I could have become an afterthought, a point of contention with his new wife and new family, eventually just shuttled out of the picture because it was easier to start over.

My mother takes a small sip and then says, "I had the best father in the world. I loved you so much that I was not going to rob you of having the same experience. Sacrifices were made." Satisfied that she's sufficiently answered what turned out to be a surprisingly simple question, she begins to root around in her bag.

I have to sit with this knowledge for a minute. It changes my perspective on pretty much everything. I feel like all the air that had been sucked out of the room comes rushing back in, and I can breathe again.

Finally, I say, "Um. Okay. I guess that's it. What do you need me to do?"

She hands me her phone. "Here. Please put the Uber on this."

I'm so confused. "What? Why?"

"Because I sold my car, and I need a ride back to the Alpha house."

Chapter Twenty-Three

CeCe

Three/two days before sorority rush

"Explain this to me again," Hayden says. We're in the back of a zippy Nissan, expertly piloted by a polite gentleman named Ornaldo, on the way to the Alpha house. "You accidentally planted sixty thousand dollars' worth of ridiculous roses, and you sold your car to make up for the overrun? How does that happen?"

"It was fifty-eight thousand dollars, and I went to an all-girls' school, darling. Sometimes we went whole days without seeing boys. One can't blame me for having a little fling with my Spanish tutor while I was in Spain. He was very handsome. Swarthy," I explain. I mean, I don't know how to make it any clearer in English that my Spanish was not up to snuff.

"Sure, that explains it," she replies. So snarky, this one!

I insisted that Hayden change her clothing if she was going to join me at the sorority house. She said she'd wear anything I liked if it meant witnessing me apologize. She has such a flair for the dramatic; it's fun to see the traits she gets from me.

Hayden points out a Tudor-style building toward the bottom of the hill on Greek Row, saying, "That's where I lived."

"I completely forgot you were part of the Greek system," I say. "That's where the foul-mouthed housemother lives?"

"That's Mom Phyllis. She's a riot; you should get to know her."

"Perhaps I will."

If I'm to be here for a while, and it sounds like I am, my best bet is to go the way of the (Tim) Gunn and make it work.

Ornaldo drops us in the circular drive, and we walk in the front door, which is wide open. The house is a complete disaster. There's scaffolding everywhere. The stripped woodwork and walls have been primed but not painted. The reupholstered pieces of furniture are only half-complete.

Natalie charges toward me, shrieking, "They left! All the workers left! What are we going to do?"

"This was all supposed to be done today," I say. "The head contractor assured me this morning. I told him it was a rush job and cost was no object. Why did they leave?"

"I have no idea! All I said was that we didn't have the money to pay them!" Natalie wails.

"I'm sorry, you told the contractors that?" Hayden asks, incredulous.

Natalie glowers at Hayden. "Who is this mean person?"

"She's my daughter," I say, feeling a swell of pride.

"Well, *that* tracks," Natalie replies. "I mentioned it to one guy because we were chatting. He's in school at Miami of Ohio, but he doesn't go back to campus until next week. He was really cute. But he had a big stupid mouth, and the word spread. Then just like that, they packed up and left. Stupid Ohio."

"The good news is, I've figured it all out. Our problems are over." I pull the cashier's check from CarMax out of my bag. Thank goodness Janelle wouldn't stop raving about that place, or I wouldn't have known what to do with my car. "This is more than enough money to cover all our arrears."

"You mean *your* mistakes," Hayden says.

"Okay, I hate her less now," Natalie admits. She takes the check and sticks it in her pocket. "And thank you so much. I don't know how you got this, and I don't care. Just thank you."

I feel something in my chest, like the flap of a bird's wings. If this is what it's like to come through for someone without praise or fanfare or media coverage, I can understand why people do it.

"We can fix this," I say, gesturing to all the incomplete work. "Let's call someone else."

"I tried everyone! I made calls all afternoon. No one can get here until next week," Natalie says.

"When does the house need to be ready for your parties?" I ask.

"Two days! If we all pitch in, we could probably finish the painting, but we can't fix the hard stuff like the woodwork and upholstery. Plus, we have so much recruitment party prep to get through."

"Can the parties be postponed?" I ask.

At the same time, both Hayden and Natalie say, "No. This is recruitment."

"What happens if the house isn't ready and you have a bad party?" I ask.

Hayden winces, and Natalie begins to cry. It's an ugly cry. It's a baby-with-a-bowlful-of-spaghetti-on-his-head kind of cry. "Then the girls won't pick us! Our numbers are already down. If we don't meet our quota, the national directors will pull our charter!" Natalie wails.

"Is that terrible?" I ask Hayden.

"It's thermonuclear destruction," Hayden says. "End of times."

If they don't meet their numbers, then selling my car will be for naught. Alpha will be over. Dean Grace will win, and I find that notion offensive. I am not losing to a woman who dresses in Ann Taylor Loft. She'll get this house, and I'm sure she won't stop there. I imagine if she can, she'll see to it that all of Greek Row goes under, and that seems like a shame.

I'm not sure what else to do, so I hug Natalie, and she sobs into my chest.

"Are you aware that you're embracing another human being? Voluntarily?" Hayden asks in sotto voce.

"Shh," I say over Natalie's head. "Mummy is hugging."

I let Natalie cry until she's done. She feels like a delicate bird in my arms, and her sobs are breaking my heart.

"Were you ever in a sorority, CeCe?" she asks, her words muffled as she delivers them against my chest.

"No," I reply. "But I went to an all-girls college, and I've been in plenty of clubs with women."

She pulls away and looks up at me. "But not a sorority. Not a real sisterhood. You don't get it."

"What's to get?" I ask. "You live together and you go to parties together and if someone gets sick, another one of you holds her hair. I've done all that."

"No," Natalie says. "I mean yes, every weekend, but no. We're so much more than that."

"How so?"

"Being in Alpha teaches us how to resolve conflict, how to compromise, how to lead, how to live with difficult people. How to make sacrifices for the good of the whole. How to give back. Membership helps us learn how to be adults, how to make our own way in the world, without dads or husbands. We learn how to empower ourselves."

I look over at Hayden, who shrugs. "She's not wrong. There's a lot about sororities I don't like now, but she's not wrong about all that."

I say, "It sounds like what's standing between us and what we need is some elbow grease. Our solution is to roll up our sleeves and get to work."

Natalie sniffles. "You think we can fix all this?"

I reply, "We'll never know if we don't try."

Natalie wipes her nose on her sleeve and says, "I'll go get everyone." She scampers off.

Hayden's looking at me with something akin to respect. "You're going to try to pull this off?"

"What choice do I have, darling?"

"Okay . . . then I'll be right back," she says.

"Where are you going?" I ask.

"I'm running back to my place. You're probably going to need something to wear that wasn't handmade in France."

We work most of the night, knocking off around 4:30 a.m. This is, dare I say, sort of fun? Between the singing and all the laughing and teasing, the sisters remind me of when my college friends and I would prepare for a big event, staying up till all hours to prepare for the campus-wide May Day fair. Bitsy and I were the chief instigators, pulling pranks and keeping up everyone's spirits while we wove our flower crowns.

I wonder what Bitsy thinks about how it's turned out with Chip and me. She must be so grateful to have married into Microsoft instead of scandal. I hated how things ended between her and me; we'd been so close. I believed in the concept of "girl code," which is why I ignored Chip's overtures for months after they broke up, even after she'd given me her blessing. The way he tried to win me over should have been a thousand waving red flags, how he relentlessly pursued me, even showed up at my hotel in Cancún on spring break that year.

In retrospect, our ten-year age gap should have been cause for concern, too, but outside of Bitsy, who'd had the good sense to dump him, almost everyone thought he was so fine a catch that it didn't matter. How I wish I'd listened to my father. People told me I'd won the lottery with Chip, yet no one ever said the same to him, as if I weren't the great prize he'd tried so hard to win. Many times, I've wondered about our beginnings—if we would have ended up together had I not been so reticent at our start, had I made it easier on him.

I guess I'll never know, and it wouldn't matter if I did.

Hayden is still asleep in my suite. Her face is relaxed, and for once, she doesn't look angry. She looks like the child I used to watch sleeping, after the book she insisted "only Daddy" read to her. I used to watch them together, so jealous of that bond. I realize now it was not Hayden's fault that Chip never made room for me.

I put my painting clothing back on—a pair of cargo shorts and a shirt that reads *Feminist AF*. I don't think she selected these items at random. I quietly close the door to my suite and head down to the kitchen for a cup of Loretta's coffee, which tastes just like what they served in my dorm's dining hall. I need to remember to tell her that I like it. In fact, I need to remember to tell everyone what a fine job they're doing, even if I didn't realize it at first.

While I stir a spoon of powdered cream into my mug, Natalie comes over.

"I don't think we're going to make it," she says, consulting a checklist on her phone.

"Why not?" I ask. "We accomplished so much last night." We knocked out all the painting and restaged a couple of the main rooms.

"We still have so much to do! No one knows how to fix the woodwork, plus the upholstery isn't done. We still have to work on our songs, on the flowers, the decorations—ugh, it's too much! We're out of time, and we don't have enough bodies to help."

She starts to sniffle; the tears are inevitable. I take in the dark circles under Natalie's eyes, her unwashed hair, and all the paint splotches up and down her arms. She looks like a lost child, and I feel my maternal instincts kick in.

I tell her, "Shh, I will handle this."

I exit the side door and go around to the front of the Pi Mu house. I knock on the door, and a girl wearing Lululemon answers. "Hi," I say. "Is Rain here?"

Lululemon replies, "Um, probably? She was out working in the garden when I left for my run. I imagine she's still there. It's fresh lettuce season!"

"Thank you so much. Which way do I go?"

She points to the back of the house, and I hurry down the pavers. The backyard on the side of the parking area is a true Garden of Eden, with vibrant plants and a profusion of flowers everywhere. I work my way through the rows until I locate Rain kneeling in front of a supercharged tomato bush, just covered in juicy, red round orbs. She's quietly singing a Peter, Paul & Mary song to the plant as she picks the ripest ones.

"The singing helps them grow," Rain says. "They respond to sound waves."

"Does it have to be folk music?" I ask.

"No, that's just what I like," she replies. "Botanists did a study at Osmania University in India where they tested music on thirty rose-bushes. Scientists played different types of music for different groups of roses. Some got classical music, some Vedic chants, rock, what have you. Surprisingly, the genre didn't make a difference. After two months, the roses that were played music did far better than the control group that was left in silence." She gives me a beatific smile and returns to her harvest.

She's not going to make this easy on me. I say, "Rain, I know we got off on the wrong foot, and I am so sorry for that. I'm not great with other women, and that's my fault; I own that."

Rain nods, saying nothing. I press on. "But my girls are in trouble, and they need help. I'm not asking for me; I'm asking for them. Please, please, if you can find it in your heart to—"

Rain holds up a dirty hand. "Let me stop you right there."

Damn it. I knew this was coming.

I say, "I deserve that. I get it. I have no right to ask for favors since you've been nothing but kind, and I've been so awful, dismissive, not listening to any of your warnings. It's just that one of these girls has gotten to me. She made me reflect on my life and wish that I'd done things differently and—"

Rain rises from her cross-legged position without her hands. She must have the core strength of a yogi master. I'm sorry that Alpha won't last here because of me, and I won't be able to ask her about her practice.

"CeCe, I was stopping you because it sounds like we don't have a lot of time to waste. Let me round up the other moms, and we can get to work."

"Just like that?" I ask. "I say I need help, and you're ready to dive in, just like that?" I'm astounded.

Rain scoops up her basket and sets it by the back door, before briskly setting off toward the front yard. "CeCe, I don't know what your life was like before, but around here, our girls aren't the only ones who have sisters."

As we cross between the properties, I see the grizzled old housemom at the Zoo house watching us with binoculars. Rain waves, and the woman gives each of us a brief nod. It's the first time she's acknowledged me.

For some reason, this pleases me immensely.

Chapter Twenty-Four

JANELLE

Two days/one day before sorority rush

Janelle's Daily Do-List

- *Print out directions, just in case*
- *Pack an overnight bag*
- *Pray*

I plot out my trip on the paper map I've printed out. This is the first car I've driven with a GPS system, but I want to have a fail-safe in case it goes down. I can't decide if I should take my phone or leave it. I don't want Uncle Pat to know what I'm doing. I normally drop pins for him throughout the day, but who knows if he has tracking software on my phone. If he had any idea, he'd absolutely forbid this trip, and for good reason. I decide to leave the phone.

Okay, I should get to Cincinnati by 10:00 a.m. I'll buy gas and breakfast there. Then I can take another break in Columbus. I'll do the Columbus-to-Pittsburgh stretch, and I'm halfway there. Then it's the long stretch through Pennsylvania, and Newark's only an hour past Easton. I'll stay at one of the hotels by the airport. I checked, and there's plenty of vacancy, so I shouldn't have a problem. I'll meet my dad tomorrow, get back in the car, do the eleven-hour drive back, and I'll be ready to help with recruitment on Monday morning.

Is this a good plan? No.

Is this a terrible plan? Yes.

I had a small nest egg in the bank as part of my relocation package, so I took that out to give to my father. Whatever trouble he's in, this money should help. Then I'll say my goodbyes, and no one will be the wiser. The best news? I'll have my punishing guilt to keep me company for the ride.

I wish I'd never seen that stupid direct message. I know he's counting on me. Good old reliable Janelle, or Gina. Good old Gina Two, willing to do anything to please others.

I run into Addie as I'm taking my overnight bag out to the car. "You going somewhere?" she asks.

"I'm heading over to see a friend. I'll be back tomorrow," I reply. I can barely look her in the eye, I feel so terrible about Trevor.

"Have fun!" she calls, heading down to the dining room for her daily cheesy baked eggs and six pieces of bacon. I don't know the science behind keto, but inhaling that much fat in one sitting can't be healthy.

I open my car door and then pause.

I don't want to do this.

I don't want to do this for so many reasons, starting with how dangerous it is for me to go to Newark. When I left, I understood that I might never go back. I walked away from that life, so returning to it, even for a day, is almost unthinkable. And this part is silly, but while I like driving my new car, I don't want to put fourteen hundred miles on it in twenty-four hours. I like its newness. At least its new-to-me-ness.

Mostly, I don't want to see my dad. Whatever his sad story is this time, it will never be his fault, and he'll try to convince me that he's the victim. Like he's some tragic hero and not the kind of guy who swiped pain meds from his cancer-ridden wife because he refused to acknowledge he was out of control. I'm only now getting past the chaos he brought to my life.

I read that when people are about to perpetrate a heinous crime or self-harm, they tell others. They know that they can't stop themselves, so they drop bread crumbs about their intentions, hoping that someone intervenes. But I can't tell anyone what I'm doing, so I have no one to stop me.

I'm putting my bag in the car when Rain approaches. "There you are! Janelle, if you have any time, the Alphas are in a real pinch. Their contractor flaked, and they're scrambling to get ready for recruitment. If you have a minute, I know they'd be grateful."

I look at the bag and then back at Rain. I can feel the vise around my heart loosen. "I'm so glad you stopped me. I'm happy to help."

"Is that the proper way to do the crown molding?" CeCe asks.

"Have you done a lot of finish carpentry in your life?" Uncle Pat responds through lips clenching a nail.

CeCe's hovering over Uncle Pat as he fixes the damaged woodwork by the staircase. When CeCe said there were projects no one in the house could handle, I knew just the man to call. The added bonus is there's no way I could sneak off to my car and drive to New Jersey while he's around.

She ignores his challenge, instead asking, "Also, how come you don't look like Janelle's uncle?"

I brace myself for Uncle Pat to stammer, but he's a pro. "She's my niece by marriage. My ex and I are divorced, but family is forever."

"Divorced . . . hmm." CeCe mulls that over. Wait, is she *flirting* with Uncle Pat? "But I just feel like this is the wrong way to go with the wood and all."

"That's your feeling?" he replies, his eyebrows raised. "You have a feeling on how I, someone who's had a woodshop for more than thirty-five years, should repair a rounded bullnose corner?"

"Yes," she replies, albeit less confidently this time.

"Noted. Would you like to discuss the thirty-two varieties of hammers and their related usage?"

"Obviously, not right now. I'm very busy," she replies. "I'm in the throes of planning a fundraising event. You see, I've come into three hundred pounds of shrimp. Would you care to discuss these hammer varieties at our Shrimportance of Literacy event in two weeks?"

"Maybe I would."

"Well, perhaps I would too."

I turn to Hayden, who's weaving flower crowns out of the roses we cut from out front. "Is it just me, or do you notice a weird sort of chemistry between them?"

Hayden makes a face. "Oh God, I thought it was just me. Seeing my mother try to flirt is going to give me nightmares. I'm adding this to the list of things I need to discuss with my therapist."

We've been at it since yesterday, and the house is nearly ready. All the moms have pitched in and made short work of what looked insurmountable. Marilee sewed the upholstery for the couches, and they look professional grade. Rain's been supervising the cleaning and décor, and Mom Phyllis is in the library, teaching some of the sisters one of the filthiest songs I've ever heard. Like, I'm embarrassed at the graphic language, and I worked in a strip club for eight years.

Hayden says, "Hey, I've been meaning to ask—does Addie still live in the house?"

I reply, "Yes, do you know her?" I know they've met, but explaining how I know requires too much explanation. "Sweet girl."

Hayden snorts. "That's what she wants you to think. Do me a favor—keep your guard up with her."

"Why is that?" I ask.

"You cannot trust her. She's a straight-up sociopath, and everyone knows it. A few years ago, she went a little out of her mind over a genuinely good guy I knew at the Pike house, a stand-up bro, which are few and far between around here. He went out with her on a barn dance fix-up, and she just became obsessed. She would not leave him alone. She texted him all hours of the day, and she even started following him. She'd plaster all kinds of fabrications about their nonexistent relationship on social media, and the worst part was, I think she started to believe them herself. When he refused to engage with her, she started rumors about him. Ugly stuff. Unfounded accusations. He had to appear before the Honor Board, and he almost got kicked out of school."

"How do you know it wasn't true?" I ask, not daring to hope.

"She admitted it all to one of my best friends."

So . . . could Trevor have been telling me the truth?

Before Hayden can say more, one of the sisters comes flying into the entry hall, in full panic mode. I think her name is Natalie? She's small and excitable, like a howler monkey.

"CeCe! There's something wrong with the toilet in the first-floor powder room, and I can't get a plumber here until tomorrow!"

CeCe asks, "Natalie, what's wrong with it?"

Sheepishly, Natalie replies, "Vegan chili."

CeCe rolls up her sleeves with a look of grim determination. "Step aside; I've got this."

"You've got this?" Uncle Pat asks, laughing. "Do you have the first clue how to fix a clogged toilet?"

"Oh God, she's trying to impress him," Hayden mutters, clutching her face in her hands. "Make it stop."

"Naturally," CeCe replies. "You flush until it goes away."

Uncle Pat looks to me. "Janelle, you want to field this?"

"On it," I say. CeCe follows behind me.

CeCe lasts for a good fifteen seconds before she runs from the room screaming. That's about fourteen seconds longer than I would have guessed, so I give her credit.

"Thank you so much for coming, Uncle Pat. It means a lot to me that you gave up a weekend with your girls for this," I tell him as I walk him to his car.

"My ex wanted to take them out shopping for school clothes, so you saved me two days of sitting in uncomfortable chairs, saying, 'That looks very nice.'"

"What did you think of CeCe?" I ask in a teasing voice.

He replies, "That woman is infuriating."

"Good infuriating or bad infuriating?" I wheedle.

"*Infuriating* infuriating."

"You're not going to tell me anything, are you?" I ask.

"Exactly," he replies, but I sense a smile behind his mustache. He pulls his keys from a deep pocket on his carpenter pants.

"I need to tell you something."

I don't like the serious look he's giving me.

"Well, I need to tell you something too. I'm very sorry, but I heard from a counterpart in New Jersey, and I have some bad news. Your father is in jail."

"Wait, what?" I stop in my tracks.

"Don't worry; he's okay, but he caught a DWI charge. He wasn't hurt, although I can't say the same for the bus shelter he hit. It's not his first offense, so he's being held."

"When did this happen?" I ask.

"About a week ago."

I can feel my blood freeze in my veins.

If this happened a week ago . . . how did I get that message two days ago? He wouldn't have Instagram in jail, right? Is it possible my dad didn't send me that direct message? If so, who did it?

Was someone impersonating him, trying to draw me out of hiding? Or, and this thought truly makes me sick, did he help someone else figure out how to get me to that diner?

Would he betray me?

That I even have to ask myself if my father would betray me tells me everything I've always tried to overlook about his character.

My hand flies to my crucifix, and I thank God for what had to be divine intervention. If Rain had shown up three seconds later, or if I hadn't stopped to talk to Addie, I would already have been in my car, headed for an ambush.

"Why do you ask?" Uncle Pat says. "Anything I need to concern myself with?"

Even if it affects my placement here, I have to come clean and tell him what I did.

When I return to the Gamma house, there's a fraternity boy in a Zoo sweatshirt waiting on the front steps. "You're Mom Janelle, right?" he asks.

I nod.

"Mean Helene wanted me to give this to you." He hands me an envelope and spots one of the sisters returning home and immediately zooms in on her. "Hey, Brynn, how *you* doin'?"

I tear open the envelope: *Something stinks on Greek Row. Meet me at Eli's House of Beans one week from Monday at 1400 hours. Helene.*

"One minute!" I shout over the chaos of a house full of girls. Between all the hair products and scented body lotion and perfume, it smells like Sephora in here.

I peek out the window and see at least a hundred potential new members squealing and laughing, each one giddy with excitement. There's a similar crowd in front of every sorority on the street. It's possible they're all hopped up on caffeine. So many of them are clutching buckets of iced coffee from Eli's. Poor Hayden.

The Gamma sisters are each clad in white denim miniskirts, powder-blue tees, and Golden Goose sneakers. They can't contain their excitement either, so we should get this started.

I can't believe how blessed I am to be here. Coming clean to Uncle Pat made all the difference. He placed a couple of calls and was able to confirm it actually *was* my father who sent that message. He'd initially gotten the timeline wrong. Then he gave me a decidedly fatherly chat about not trying to manage everything myself, because I'm not alone.

And I know that, and I believe it now. As improbable as it is, I have found my home here.

I unlatch the front door and turn to my girls. "Ladies? Showtime."

Chapter Twenty-Five

CeCe

One week after sorority rush

"Quite a change from last week, eh?" I say.

"Recruitment week didn't kill me, but it for sure didn't make me stronger. Glad this was my last year having to work it," LaVonne replies. "Seniors, yeet!" She holds out her arms and gives double peace signs, like Richard Nixon on the campaign trail. Today she has natural hair and fully contoured makeup in cocoas and creams; it's fabulous.

"If it's any consolation, I feel the same way. Also, your cheekbones are to die for," I reply.

LaVonne smiles at me. "I did the full Kardashian today."

Hayden hands me a cup. "Earl Grey misto, on the house."

"I thought you said I had to learn to pay my own way," I reply.

"That was before you put all that cash from your beach bag into our tip jars," Hayden says.

"I have no idea what you're talking about," I reply, spooning some raw sugar into my drink.

LaVonne adds, "Like we wouldn't know it was you. You're alone in the shop; we have twenty bucks in our jar. You leave the shop, and suddenly we've got thirty stacks. You're not slick."

I shrug noncommittally. I'm allowed to have my secrets. I thought I needed to hold on to that cash no matter what, but the past week has taught me that I already have everything I need. Plus, I receive a salary, and my room and board are covered for the immediate future, so I thought I would give to the less fortunate who are a little closer to home.

LaVonne continues. "I'm just glad you couldn't decide between Bridget Jones or Becky Bloomwood. I've got enough money to pay for next semester now without working a second job because your mama here kicks ass!"

I cough lightly into my hand and look directly at Hayden. "No one should have to work a second job."

Hayden's eyes widen in surprise. Please. She wasn't fooling me with that cam-girl stuff. Mummy knows everything. (Fine, I'm not clairvoyant. Let's just say that LaVonne gets chatty after a third glass of Bordeaux.)

"Have you talked to the attorneys?" Hayden asks me.

I've been so busy with my new life that I haven't even thought to pester my lawyer in a week. I'm fine with waiting for her to call me with news, instead of hectoring her day and night.

I feel different here, more connected. I don't know if it's the girls in the house or the other moms or my improved relationship with Hayden, but whatever's happening, I feel at peace. Like I can let down my guard. I'm starting to believe that I might need this place and these people as much as they need me. For the first time since that disastrous gala when the Feds trampled over my life like so many jasmine floral sprays, I don't miss how things used to be. I like where I am. I enjoy what I'm doing; it feels *real*.

"Nothing new to report. Your father has decamped to Madagascar. There's nothing we can do except to get on with our lives, darling," I say.

"Or . . . Fudge," Hayden says.

"Am I allowed to call you that?" I ask. "I thought you didn't like it."

"Maybe some traditions are worth keeping," Hayden says.

I nod and smile. "Maybe they are, darling. Maybe they are."

Hayden and LaVonne don heavy plastic gloves, tying on the kind of thick aprons a butcher would wear. LaVonne motions toward the tweed-clad owner in the corner, surrounded by stacks of newspapers and a teacup, planted in front of the soccer game. "Yo, Professor O., we're taking out the trash. Watch the counter."

He waves them off and they go, struggling under the weight of giant trash bags.

Janelle enters the shop and sits down next to me. "Hi, CeCe. How's it going?"

"Shrimply fantastic," I reply. Using my superior gala-planning skills, I've been working with Natalie on how to best incorporate our bounty of crustaceans with our literary philanthropy event. The puns have been coming hard and fast, like how nothing is shrimpossible through reading, and how literacy raises children's shellfish-steam. It's been ridiculous, in the most delightful way. Janelle's uncle Pat has been most useful in helping to build some booths for the event. I suspect I'll need to find other projects in which to involve him.

"And how about you?" I ask.

"Well . . . ," Janelle begins. "Can I ask you something?"

"Always."

"What do you think about second chances?" she says. "You know, do-overs."

I think about this for a moment. "Traf-O-Data," I finally reply.

"I have no idea what that means."

I explain. "A few years ago, I found myself seated next to Bill Gates at an event in Davos. Nice man. Love what he's doing with malaria. Anyhoo, over the course of our conversation, he mentioned Traf-O-Data. The company used computer data to study traffic patterns, with an eye to improving roads. That was his first company, and the short of it is, it failed. The technology wasn't yet there. But he and Paul Allen took what they learned from the Traf-O-Data failure and used it when they were designing their first Microsoft product."

"Okay . . . ," she replies, confused.

"My point is, darling, sometimes you don't get it right the first time, regardless of how hard you try. But you learn from the experience. Sometimes a do-over makes all the sense in the world. And I'm coming to realize that is okay. It's never too late to start over and try again. If you believe something—or someone—deserves a second chance, why not give it a whirl? Maybe you won't create Microsoft . . . but what if you do?"

"That's exactly what I was thinking," Janelle replies, smiling so hard that I spot dimples. She pulls out her phone. "Can you guys give me a sec? I'll join you after I unblock someone's number real quick."

I nod and head over to the housemothers' table where Rain, Phyllis, Marilee, and Helene, the ancient binoculars lady, are already seated at a table by the television and the professor. Phyllis watches intently. "Fuck everyone but Manchester United," she says. The professor nods and raises his cup in agreement.

I greet the ladies, saying, "I almost didn't make it on time. I had no idea what time fourteen o'clock was."

Helene scowls and says, "Fourteen hundred hours. And I was just starting to think nice things about you, girlie. Don't blow it."

Rain gets right to the point. "What's going on, Helene? You never want to get together with us. Seriously, never."

Janelle sits down in the last empty seat at the table, hanging her bag from the back of her chair. Marilee says, "Is this about taking out Mama Shirley at Lambda? I could be down."

Janelle's phone chimes. Then it chimes again. "That your boy-friend?" Helene barks.

"I definitely don't have one of those . . . at the moment," Janelle replies. "Although I'm really excited that someone might be trying."

"How was your first day of class, Janelle?" Rain asks.

Janelle's whole face lights up. "It was amazing! We talked about Peter Drucker and covered his management by objectives. Then we broke into small groups, and they named me the group leader!"

Helene interrupts. "Ahem. Anyway, the reason I asked you all to join me is—"

Janelle's phone chimes again. She says, "Sorry! It's really on mute this time. I promise." She looks at the number and smiles, switching her phone to silent. She tries to hide her goofy grin as she places her phone back in her bag.

Helene looks over both shoulders and leans in. "Something's going on with Dean Grace. She's angling for a promotion, at our expense. She's trying to clear out Greek Row."

Rain sighs, rubbing at her eyes, then running her hands through her hair. I feel like this is not her first conspiracy-theory rodeo with Helene. Mama Shirley mentioned to me that she's so over Helene's antics that she didn't even plan to come today. "Helene, have you been spying again?"

Helene replies, "It's called reconnaissance. I learned it during the war."

Marilee says, "It's called stalking, and it's a class four felony. Remember when you were convinced that Mom Hoogstratten had once been Eva Braun?"

"I stand behind that. She *guten Morgen*'d me one time too many." Helene crosses her arms over her chest. "Besides, you won't call it stalking when we're all out of a job."

Rain is not convinced. Given her attitude, I'm sensing that Helene embraces conspiracy theories of all kinds. However, she's actually right this time, and thanks to my efforts, I can confirm this.

Rain says, "This doesn't make sense. Why now? Dean Grace hasn't been the Greek system's biggest fan, but she's never gotten in our way before."

Helene protests, "She's never needed to before. She's so blinded by her own ambition that she'll screw over anyone in her path."

Marilee rolls her eyes. "Is this gonna be a repeat of when you thought the Pi Phis were running a dog-fighting ring?"

"They fit the profile," Helene harrumphs.

"It was a children's petting zoo for their philanthropy," Marilee replies. "They weren't even dogs; they were minigoats. Get some bifocals for your binoculars."

"Okay, small error in judgment. But like my friend Henry used to say, 'Even the paranoid can have enemies.'"

"Does she mean *Henry Kissinger*?" Marilee whispers to me. I shrug.

"And think about it, how many times have we all seen her on the Row in the last few weeks?" Helene says.

"More than usual," Rain admits.

"I went from never seeing her to running into her daily, so you might have a point," Marilee concedes.

Between trying to keep Alpha above water last week and planning the crustacean-based literacy event, I haven't had a chance until now to confer with the other women on anything other than asking favors and cleaning up my mess. I come to Helene's defense. "She's actually right. I confronted the dean about this last week. She wants to bring down the Greek system and use our houses as apartments for wealthy international students. Apparently, they're a cash cow. Their tuition is something like four times what US students pay."

"Seriously? Do you have proof?" Rain asks. I appreciate how Rain is always striving for equanimity, never just accepting rumor for truth.

"Would showing you her schedule be proof enough?" I ask. I pull out the printed list of all her appointments, and they heavily feature meetings with student organizations from places like Singapore, Hong Kong, and Taiwan. I'm not exactly a hacker; the list was easy enough to get. I just told her receptionist they were giving out free energy drinks on the quad, and she practically left a vapor trail as she ran away from her computer.

"How in the fuck would you have access to her schedule?" Phyllis asks, thumbing through all the pages.

Janelle and I look at each other and laugh, and I say, "Password1234."

I say, "It wasn't so difficult to figure out—I just put all the pieces together. It's amazing what one notices when one lifts her gaze from her own navel. Anyhoo, between Mr. Wu and the house tours with Balenciaga-clad international students, it became perfectly clear what she was up to. I mean, I was also the first person to realize that the husband of my old neighbor Babe van Osterman was cheating. A man does not go from twenty years of nothing but pleated khakis and Greg Norman shirts to Italian couture without a reason. So, my question to all of you is, What's our plan?"

"You want to be in on a plan with us?" Rain asks. She appears to be fighting an urge to smile.

"Didn't I say that whatever this is"—I make a sweeping gesture at the group—"that I want in? I'm almost certain I mentioned it at the Winesday Book Club, or when we were out walking."

"We need a preemptive strike," Helene says. "Like my friend Dougie Mac used to say, 'Preparedness is the key to success and victory.'"

Janelle's bag buzzes again, and a frustrated Helene reaches into it and pulls out Janelle's phone for her. Sheepishly, Janelle takes the phone from her. "Fix it," Helene barks.

"A preemptive strike? I feel like that's a little extreme, Helene," Rain says.

"Hold up, *Dougie Mac*? Do you mean *Douglas MacArthur*? What the hell war were you in, Helene?" Marilee demands.

"What are we going to do about Dean Grace?" Helene asks. "You can work with me or against me, but I suggest you work with me."

"What work? All we have to do is make sure we follow the rules on Greek Row, and everything will be fine. Basically, we do what we do every day. Rush was great! We all exceeded our numbers. Our nationals are happy. She can't have charters pulled if no one does anything wrong," Rain reasons. "This is not a crisis."

"If Lambda gets kicked off campus before I get to be mom there, we *are* going to have ourselves a crisis; count on that," Marilee vows.

Phyllis says, "Ha! Mama Shirley's gonna live forever. Count on *that*."

"You take that back," Marilee says, balling her hands into fists.

"Make me," Phyllis replies, squaring her narrow shoulders.

It takes us a few minutes to break up the squabble between Marilee and Phyllis. When we finally get them to calm down, I look around and realize one of the seats at the table is now empty.

"Hey, wait a second," I say. "What happened to Janelle?"

Rain shrugs and says, "She said she had to run and that she'll catch up to us tomorrow morning when we walk or at our Winesday meeting."

"Where did she go?" I ask. I wonder if her sudden departure has anything to do with the second chance she mentioned.

Rain shrugs and squeezes some lemon into her chamomile tea. "I'm not sure. But she said the strangest thing."

"What?" I ask.

"She said sometimes the sequel is even better than the original, so she was rushing off to watch *Godfather II*."

ACKNOWLEDGMENTS

Writing my thanks at the end of the book is always bittersweet. That's because I save the acknowledgments until the edits are final and every change has been made. My characters and their adventures are now typeset, frozen in time and space, despite the fact that I don't feel ready to let them go. (I mean, they haven't even made it to second semester yet!)

This story has been particularly special to me because I started working on it in 2016 when I wrote it as a pilot and got it into development with a big Hollywood production company. I spent a year building the Eli Whitney University universe because I felt like it had so much promise, with so many stories to tell. But because of one executive's bad day (that had nothing to do with *Housemoms*), the script was shelved and all those months of work were lost. That was rough.

Like Janelle, I didn't give up. Instead, I vowed to improve. I started taking classes at Chicago's Second City Training Center, thinking that if I developed my screen-writing skills, maybe *Housemoms* would finally reach an audience. So, my first thanks go to my talented instructor, Dale Chapman, and to my gifted and hilarious classmates, not only for this project but for what's to come next. Brandon, Nick, Mak, Kerri, and Jil, how lucky I am to have had your feedback, support, and rigorous honesty. I'm so excited to see what you guys continue to create.

After *Housemoms* as a script was off the table, I shifted my professional focus to ghostwriting and discovered how much I love it. I'm obsessed with the idea of telling a story, and I'm so proud of the projects I've had the privilege to help shape. Still, the *Housemoms* characters never left me, long after I traded the final draft for Zoom calls and transcription services. CeCe and Janelle didn't stop mentally tugging at my sleeve, looking for closure. My job as a ghostwriter is to dig into my clients' lives, really figuring out who they are and then facilitating their capture on the page. The more I worked with my clients, the more I realized that I wanted to do the same for *Housemoms*. I longed to find a way to give CeCe, Janelle, and Hayden their own rich internal monologues instead of just making them fodder for punchlines in a script, which would be open to interpretation by actors and directors. (And LaVonne wasn't letting me go anywhere without her, despite not even being in the original pilot.)

I loved everyone I'd created back in 2016; that's why I am so grateful that Little A saw fit to give me the platform to finally bring them to life. I could not be more grateful to my editor Laura Van der Veer and associate publisher, Carmen Johnson. Thank you so much for the opportunity to finally give these gals some daylight! You both are *shrimply* the best. And many thanks to Laura Chasen, my developmental editor—your suggestions were critical and right on target. I so appreciate your hard work and insight. I'd also like to thank Tamara Arellano and Emma Reh in production. To my copyeditors, please forgive me for making you want to launch me into the sun. (Imagine how rough the process was for my original copyeditors twenty books ago.) Please know that your thoughtfulness and attention to detail make all the difference. Those little catches, like asking "Would Janelle say 'I wish I *were*' or 'I wish I *was*'?" were so critical. Of course, I want to recognize everyone who brings a book to life, so I'm extending a supersized thank-you to the production, sales, marketing, and art departments. You guys rock, and I owe everyone many exotic coffee drinks, yak butter optional.

I have a phenomenal team behind me at Folio Literary Management, so I want to extend my warmest thanks to Steve Troha and Erin Niumata as well as to the rest of the team. You guys keep me working and on track, and I am profoundly grateful for your diligence, dedication, and good cheer.

Liz Elting and Josh Flagg, you are my favorites by a mile. I never knew what it was like to truly collaborate before you both, and I couldn't be happier with what we created. I'm better for having known you. Liz, you changed how I approach, like, *everything*, and you have a work ethic like no one's ever seen. Your book is going to change how people do business, and I am so proud of my small part in it. And, Josh, you are pure joy to know, and I've loved seeing you evolve. Also, we are going to bring Edith to the world; mark my words. (And ten points to me for name-checking you in the manuscript.)

For my new friends at the Alpine Club—this book was largely on time because of each of you who grilled me on how my deadline was coming every time you saw me with a margarita and not a notebook. Thank you for making what should have been a quiet summer extraordinary. (I'm keeping my promise not to write about you all.) And for my girl gang, including Joanna, Gina, Karyn, Lisa, and Alyson, I could not ask for a better cheering section. Ours is the kind of friendship people write books about, except it would be boring because of the lack of conflict and drama. I do hesitate to say too many nice things about you, because I know that will result in a mailbox full of, um, bachelorette party favors. Again.

As always, thanks to Fletch for being Fletch. Thank you for always giving me brilliant lines that I steal and make my own. I couldn't do anything without you. And, given your inability to look in the fridge and find what's staring back at you at eye level, you couldn't do anything without me. Ha!

Finally, many, many thanks to my loyal readers—from those who've been there since the early days of Jennsylvania to the newest patrons on the *It's Always Something* substack. There's nothing more satisfying than knowing that someone out there is receiving what I'm transmitting. The acts of being seen and heard are so powerful. My biggest love goes to everyone who read the script that I tacked onto the end of *Stories I'd Tell in Bars*. For those who sent words of encouragement, asking me to please, please share what happened next, this book is especially for you.

If *Housemoms* ever does become a show, I think we all agree LaVonne should be played by Lizzo.

Let's make it so.

ABOUT THE AUTHOR

Photo © 2016 Jolene Siana

Jen Lancaster is the *New York Times* bestselling author of the novels *Here I Go Again* and *The Gatekeepers* and the nonfiction works *Welcome to the United States of Anxiety*; *Bitter Is the New Black*; *The Tao of Martha*; *Such a Pretty Fat*; *Bright Lights, Big Ass*; *Stories I'd Tell in Bars*; *Jeneration X*; *My Fair Lazy*; *Pretty in Plaid*; and *I Regret Nothing*, which was named an Amazon Best Book of the Year. Regularly a finalist in the Goodreads Choice Awards, Jen has sold well over a million books documenting her attempts to shape up, grow up, and have it all—sometimes with disastrous results. She's also appeared on the *Today* show, *Oprah, CBS This Morning*, Fox News, NPR's *All Things Considered*, and *The Joy Behar Show*, among others. She lives in the Chicago suburbs with her husband and many ill-behaved pets. Visit her website at www.jenlancaster.com.